THE
GARDEN
OF
LOST
MEMORIES

BOOKS BY RUBY HUMMINGBIRD

The Wish List

RUBY HUMMINGBIRD

THE
GARDEN
OF
LOST
MEMORIES

bookouture

Published by Bookouture in 2020

An imprint of Storyfire Ltd.
Carmelite House
50 Victoria Embankment
London EC4Y 0DZ

www.bookouture.com

ISBN: 978-1-83888-181-8
eBook ISBN: 978-1-83888-180-1

To Lizi and Sel – both gorgeous human beings – thank you for being such wonderful friends

Prologue

The hole wasn't deep, the mud sticking to her hands as she fumbled in the soil. The damp smell of rotting leaves cloyed her nostrils. A fox shrieked and her chest leapt in response. It had started to rain, a light sheen on her skin as she worked, fine droplets mingling with the sweat beading at her hairline. She looked down at the hole, the outline barely visible in the dark.

She filled in the space, worked quickly, goosebumps breaking out on her skin as she knelt on the wet grass. Empty, square glass windows overlooked the spot and she couldn't stop craning her neck up at them, frightened that someone might hear something, turn a light on, appear in one of them. What would they see as they looked down? She felt her heart race, her breath loud in her ears. Surely she would wake up the neighbourhood?

Work faster.

Her fingers brushed against it, and she snatched her hand back in response, gritted her teeth. *Don't think about it.* Then she remembered: she had meant to keep one bit of it. Closing her eyes, she searched with her fingers, located it, drew it out slowly before secreting it in the waistband of her trousers. She felt it close to her flesh, lying on her skin, and her muscles recoiled in disgust.

She was soaked through now, rain dripping from the ends of her short brown hair onto her collar, trailing down her neck like a chilly fingertip. She shivered, teeth chattering. She hadn't thought to bring a coat; she'd had only one thing on her mind. Now, she knew she had to do it in that moment, didn't want to wait, to be discovered.

A rustle nearby; she looked over her shoulder. An animal? A person? Familiar shapes no more at night, now indistinct, threatening. She returned to the soil, faster and faster, filling in the gaps, finishing the job, patting down the soil, smoothing it over.

Mud on her palms, under her nails. She would scrub at them with a stiff nailbrush for days, long after it had gone.

Another noise: she must leave. She stood, backed away, eyes not leaving the spot. It was done.

It was buried.

It was over.

Chapter 1

ELSIE

Today was one of the days that hurt most. Even though so many years had passed, it didn't take much: a glance at a familiar object, a crossword clue she was stuck on, the shrill shriek of the kettle on the hob. Memories would flood back and she would be winded all over again. She had never got used to the silence. She missed her soft voice, the slight lisp that always made her shy in public. She missed her gentle laugh, a low chuckle when she read something that tickled her or in response to something Elsie had done. There were other feelings too that rose, unbidden, making her blink, but she swallowed them down.

On these days, she knew she wouldn't be able to manage anything more than her minimal, set routine, the small rituals that linked to make up her day.

The day had begun, too early, a confusing clash of dreams, of people she'd once known and people she would never meet. The quilt had slipped, pooling on the floor, and Elsie had knocked her water glass over reaching for her spectacles. She had made her porridge in her nightdress and slippers, jumping at the clank of the recycling truck on the road outside her house. She had scooped the peppermint tea leaves into the cream polka-dot teapot, noticing with alarm the hairline crack in the ceramic lid. Perhaps that was the moment the day had taken this turn?

Barely noticing her breakfast, she forced herself to change into her clothes, a sort of uniform now: black three-quarter length linen trousers, a light blue shirt and navy cardigan, one of the buttons coming loose. It was time for her to leave the house and head to the local shop to pick up the newspaper and a cucumber for her lunchtime sandwich. She was a little early so she tidied the porch. No need for her thick woollen coat and fleece-lined wellington boots over the coming months, she thought, as she placed them in the old trunk. After checking her watch she lifted her basket onto her shoulder., knotted the pale blue silk scarf around her neck, stepped outside her door and turned the key in the lock.

Next door the curtains in the downstairs window were still closed. She was careful to shut her gate slowly, cringing at the squeak of the metal that needed oiling. Everything needed oiling, she thought, as she gingerly descended the one stone step onto the pavement.

Normally no one was around at this time. The traffic of commuters out of the village was reduced to a lone car passing in the direction of the high street. The school run had finished, weary women pushing prams and tugging on the hands of resisting toddlers back in their homes or at the park. Elsie could walk along the road, past the now-redundant police station, the bus stop, the pub that seemed to permanently have scaffolding up, the library and head straight to the shop.

The door was in sight, but, too late, Elsie had been spotted. A woman hurrying across the road, barely pausing on the small concrete island – did she want to end up in traffic? – was waving at her. Scarlet, the librarian, seemed to bounce across the rest of the road, not letting Elsie sidle past. What did a woman have to do for some peace?

'Are you coming in or is it not your day?' she asked Elsie, rattling a bunch of keys in her hand. Her hair was twisted into a strange bun right on the top of her head. Elsie thought she looked like an exclamation mark.

'Not today,' Elsie said, almost adding that it was none of Scarlet's business when she visited or not. What was she, the Book Police? Elsie had barely started the last novel she had rented out. Two chapters in and she could not understand any of the rave reviews splattered across the cover. The author must have a lot of nice author friends because Elsie certainly wasn't gripped.

'Well, I'll see you soon then,' Scarlet replied, her wide smile not faltering despite Elsie's blank gaze.

She coughed and opened the library door, a quick wave back at Elsie. Elsie ignored it and headed straight for the door of the shop next door.

When she was safely inside she moved quickly across to the magazines and reached down for her newspaper. The stack was running low already, another drama on the front cover, but then there always seemed to be one and she only ever bought it for the cryptic crossword. Heading to the narrow range of fruit and vegetables, she selected one cucumber and retraced her steps before moving to the counter.

The young female sitting on the stool behind the till looked desperately bored, a mobile propped in front of her against a pot of bright red lollipops. She barely looked up as Elsie placed her basket on the counter.

Handing her a two-pound coin, Elsie waited for the change, muttering a thank you, momentarily tempted to say something about the girl's mobile phone. When had customer service become such an out-of-date concept? She didn't like the musty corner shop with its narrow aisles, items still in cellophane stacked on the floor, lights missing bulbs and a broken coffee machine near the entrance, but there wasn't much choice unless she wanted to get the bus into town and she didn't have the time for all of that.

She left, pausing for a moment on the pavement outside. It wasn't Friday but she had an overwhelming urge to walk in the opposite direction to home: to go to the graveyard. Then she scolded herself for lingering as a man skirted her, throwing her a brief 'good morning' that she didn't return. She set off for home.

When she returned, the curtains of the house next door were finally open and she averted her gaze, not wanting to be seen to pry, or invite more conversation.

She fumbled for her key, noting that she needed to replace the small sign next to the doorbell, disconnected years ago, that read 'No Junk Mail'. As she pushed inside she noticed the postman had been, circular junk mail lying on the mat. Always junk mail and nothing else. Could he not read? She placed the two leaflets next to the door without studying them.

It was almost time for her to watch some television and in the spare five minutes she decided to play an LP.

'This wasn't a favourite, was it?' she commented as the black disc started to whir, the dusty crackle before the opening bars of Ella Fitzgerald's 'Smooth Sailing' began.

The listings told her that a movie she had watched years ago with her mother was partway through. She would watch that, unable to shake the familiar ripples of grief that seemed to be chasing her this morning.

Distracting herself, she headed to the kitchen, refilling the teapot, and placing two custard creams on the small white plate edged with roses.

'There's a movie we watched once, do you remember? With Shelley Winters in it. You said you liked her hairstyle.'

There was no answer of course, there never was, but that didn't stop Elsie waiting a moment longer, as if her voice might come in reply. She sighed, loading up the pot, plate, cup and saucer on the small wooden tray and walking back through to the living room. Settling herself, she reached for the remote control and nibbled and sipped in front of the screen, the clock above reminding her when she needed to stop watching.

The movie helped to alleviate her dreary mood and she felt comforted that soon she would be moving to the next part of her day: the favourite part of her day.

She could hear something now through the shared wall of their houses, the boy Billy next door raising his voice. She tutted at the wall as if he could see her through it. He shouldn't speak to his mother like that. Only ten years old and a temper on him. Elsie was sure he should be in school. Perhaps he was ill but she doubted it. He would be round here tomorrow while she babysat him, she thought, sulking and dragging his feet, his eyes hidden under a mop of dark brown hair that needed a cut, answering her in monosyllables.

Draining the last of the peppermint tea, she glanced at the clock, the hands almost meeting. Billy forgotten, she switched off the movie a few moments before it was about to end and went to fetch the things she needed. As she pulled them on, the comforting scent of the task ahead made her heart flutter, the joy in her day. It was time to while away some hours in her favourite place and then after that, she had an important job to do. It was Wednesday, after all.

Chapter 2

BILLY

I didn't want to go. I hated it.

When Mum came in this morning, I whispered in a croaky voice how ill I felt and she reached a hand across and placed it on my forehead.

'You do feel warm,' she said, her voice filled with worry.

I'd got hot pulling the duvet right over me and breathing into the darkness. Luckily, it looked like that had worked and she left. I heard her take her shower and I lay there feeling well pleased with how it had gone. A whole day without having to face them, I thought, staring up at the peeling glow stars on the ceiling from the last boy who'd had this room.

When she came back in her dressing gown, her hair wet and tied back in a ponytail, I pretended to look as sick as I could. She gave me a little white pill, a glass of water and the plastic thermometer.

I tried to keep my face straight when I took the thermometer. 'Thanks,' I croaked, 'Don't catch a cold.' But something about what I said was funny because she reached over and ruffled my hair.

'Ten years old and already such a grown-up, I'll be back in a minute.'

When I heard the hairdryer I relaxed and pushed the little white pill down the back of the mattress and sipped some of the water to pretend.

What would I do with the day? Lie on the sofa staring at the cobweb in the corner? Bounce that tennis ball against the skirting board in the kitchen? I didn't exactly have loads of choices. Was I too ill to play football in the park later?

The hairdryer went quiet and I quickly reached across to my bedside lamp. I held the thermometer against the lightbulb and waited for the beep. That was where I messed up. When Mum came in, looking concerned, I held it out triumphantly. She took it, then her face changed and she went mental: I had a fever of 106.3.

'You look remarkably bloody well for it,' she roared, and she hardly ever swore so I knew this was bad.

I coughed, trying to look as sick as the thermometer said I was.

'Stop that.'

I stopped.

'Are you really ill, Billy?'

'I am,' I said, trying to croak again. 'I really a—'

Then, I wasn't sure how it happened, but I found that I was crying, big snotty drops down my face.

'I don't want to… please, Mum… I can't…'

My whole chest was going up and down as I struggled to sit up in bed. The panic squeezed my heart.

'You can't just bunk off,' Mum said, those two pink spots there on her cheek she always got when she was cross. 'I can't believe you lied to me.'

I felt sick now, knew this was her worst thing. She hated if I ever told lies, even tiny ones. I think maybe Dad had lied to her and that was why he didn't live with us here.

I was still crying and the thought of Dad made it worse. He wasn't perfect and sometimes I didn't want to think about that side of him, but we had to live here now because we'd left him and that thought made the tears even bigger dripping off my chin onto my navy blue duvet. I'd chosen it for the new house a few weeks ago, but I missed my *Lightning McQueen* duvet cover from London even though I'd had it since I was about five. I wished I was back there. I just wanted to be on the estate, back with Dad, kicking used cans with Liam on our way to school. Does Dad wish we were back there too?

Now I was here in this house in the middle of the countryside not even close to the estate, not even near London. It had taken us an hour and a bit on that coach.

'You need to get up, you'll be late, but you won't miss the whole of the first lesson,' Mum said, pulling back the covers.

'Please, Mum,' I blubbered, 'Don't make me.'

My tummy felt tight when I thought of making the short walk down the road to the school, past the garage with the broken car wash, the bit of pavement with loads of bird poo underneath the big tree, the wooden shed where the little children went for playgroup.

'You're going, Billy.'

I knew she was serious: her fists were curled tight and her mouth was set in a thin line. The tears hadn't changed anything.

I roared up out of bed. 'I. Don't. Want. To!' I shouted.

Mum stepped back. I never really shouted at her, but recently I just couldn't stop it. The words came out loud and fast and I felt this whooshing heat in my whole body. It was so unfair. Yesterday, I'd shouted because she'd given me a haircut with kitchen scissors and the fringe was too short.

'I hate the stupid school and this place and this house and I hate… I hate you!' I finished, panting now.

Mum's face didn't crumple like I thought it might and I waited, shoulders up round my ears. She lifted her chin, her eyes dark, and then spoke in her scary, quiet voice as she turned away, 'Be ready in five minutes.'

She left the room and I picked up the water glass and almost threw it against the wall, gripped it tightly in my fist and then flung it on the duvet instead, where it bounced once and stopped still.

I did hate her. Why had she brought us here? We didn't know anyone and the whole place smelt funny – apparently there were pigs in a field at the end of the village and sometimes farmers sprayed the fields. That's what Mrs Maple said. Oh God, Mrs Maple! I had to go round to hers while Mum was at work and pretend to like custard creams and sit in her creepy house with all the old china things everywhere and the black-and-white photos like the olden days. I hated everything about this stupid place.

Why did I have to go to the stupid school in this stupid village? I wanted to go back to London and my friends and my school and my old house and my dad.

And I would find a way, I thought, as I picked up the school top I'd thrown on the floor the day before. *I would.*

Chapter 3

ELSIE

She hadn't been able to manage it today – was that part of her life over? The thought made a hand fly to her chest, a heavy weight in her heart. Would she have to give it up? The realisation forced her to finish earlier than she always did. She'd never stopped that early, never, but she'd needed to get away from there and the worries that crowded in on her. Was she too old now? Her hand shook as she placed the kettle on the hob, water sploshing out of the spout and making her curse into the small space.

'I do mean it!' she replied to the voice that wasn't there. 'I do bloody mean it!'

Tears pricked at her eyes as she rubbed at her hip. She wouldn't return to the GP with her sympathetic tilt of the head and her irritating soft voice, her office plastered with photos of smiling grown-up children.

The shriek of the kettle reflected the noise she wanted to make sometimes: a loud, long, jarring wail.

She didn't want to do anything else; everything was ruined. And yet the thought of abandoning her daily rituals overwhelmed her and she found herself swilling out the polka-dot teapot, nibbling half-heartedly at a cheese and cucumber sandwich and locating her purse for the second walk of the day into the village. The boy would need something for tea tomorrow – she had promised his mother. She felt a churning nervousness at the thought but a promise was a promise.

The high street was a little busier this time, a cornflower-blue sky dotted with wispy white clouds overhead, the wind still containing a surprising chill. She pulled her coat tighter and muttered as she passed a dog on a lead relieving himself against a lamppost, his bald owner chatting obliviously on a mobile phone. Everyone always yabbering on a phone.

The small café bustled with life, two women sat at one of the tables outside, one of them familiar but Elsie wasn't sure how, nodded as she passed them. The bakery on the corner had a small queue to get inside, the chemist next door was practically empty. Elsie pushed open the door of the butchers and headed straight to the bell on the counter. A man in a three-quarter length white coat and a peaked white hat caught her eye just as she pressed down on the bell. He was young, a smooth chin and a glimpse of blond hair under his hat.

'How can I help you today?'

'Six sausages, please.' She jabbed a finger at the pork and leek sausages piled up on a tray behind the glass and waited as he snipped the ends, weighed them and rolled them up into paper, sealing them with the price label.

She had her purse out by the time he asked, 'Is that everything?'

Nodding briskly, she held out a hand for the sausages. 'Everything.'

'There you are.' His smile wavered as she accepted them and held out the correct money. 'Oh, let me get these gloves off.' The young butcher fumbled as an older man peered round the doorway behind him.

'Elsie!' he said, moving inside to stand next to the younger man. 'I thought I heard your voice. How can we help you today? Oh, I see

Darren here has sorted you out,' he added, his voice booming as ever as he looked at the sausages she had now placed in her basket.

'Mr Porter,' Elsie greeted him formally.

'I've told you a hundred times: it's Stanley. You must have bought three hundred Scotch eggs from me now and that certainly earns you the right. To your mother I was Stan, remember?'

Elsie pressed her lips together, the reply lost somewhere inside her.

Mr Porter didn't appear to notice. 'Excellent woman, Rosa. Excellent,' he said, always a soft spot for her mother. He had told Elsie once before that every year her mother had made them jam for Christmas. 'Everyone, Elsie, even the boys in the back, she'd think of everyone.' Other times she would bring him cough medicine if he'd had a tickly throat the day before. 'Always thinking of others in her gentle way.'

For a second Elsie wanted to halt everything and ask him to tell her another story, another longed-for memory of her mother. But grief made her slower in her response and the moment passed. 'Well, lookie now, Elsie, Darren here just got engaged, did he tell you? Asked her to marry him on a hill in Wales!' He laughed, Darren's smooth skin turning pink as he slapped him on the back.

'How nice,' Elsie said, knowing engagements were a cause for celebration, knowing why she couldn't feel the same joy. She glanced at her watch in an effort to show she needed to get on. She wouldn't normally bother with that courtesy but Mr Porter was a little different.

'The ring doesn't fit though, Elsie. She's had to wear it on the wrong finger, hasn't she, Darren?'

'That's right.'

'Oh, oh well,' Elsie said, her hand squeezing the handle of her basket.

'I told him, Elsie, I said, you should have checked her other rings, made sure. But did he listen? Did he, Elsie? No, of course he didn't.

The young never do – am I right? It's up to us to see them right, isn't it?' He smiled, displaying the gap between his two front teeth as he waited for her to respond.

'Well, I must get on.'

'Always somewhere to be, haven't you? Well, I like busy women, ask a busy person – am I right, Elsie?'

A busy person. Yes, yes, she was busy. She always had things to do.

She had moved across to the door by the time he had finished the sentence. 'Well, goodbye then,' she said over her shoulder.

'You take care, Elsie, you come and see us again soon,' Mr Porter called as she left, a new customer waiting outside the door to come in.

She could hear Mr Porter say something to Darren, his big laugh following her as she pushed back out onto the high street.

Walking home she was reminded to pop into the chemist and before she had checked through the glass, she had opened the door, a bell tinkling her arrival. Her shoulders drooped as she saw who was stood behind the counter, dressed in a plum tunic that clashed with the shade of her cropped hair, a name badge tilted above her left breast: 'JUNE'.

It was too late for Elsie to back out now – she had seen her. Elsie felt her insides squeeze as she moved down the first aisle searching for what she needed, the empty shop smelling of antiseptic, her footsteps loud as she felt the other woman watching.

She approached the counter, the small pack clutched in one hand.

'You haven't been in in a while. Lozenges last time, wasn't it?' June said, leaning over the counter to glance directly into Elsie's basket. 'Been to the butcher,' she carried on, seeing the sausages wrapped in paper. She lowered her voice, 'How is Stan? Did he look well?'

'Fine,' Elsie replied.

June took a step back, mouth puckering, 'No stomach problem?' She gave a quick glance to the back, where her younger male colleague was scanning shelves of different coloured pills. 'Obviously, we are always confidential about our customers, but I can't help caring. It's a real weakness, my friends say to me. '*June*, they say,' she placed a hand on her chest, brushing the name badge, '*You're just all heart.*'

Elsie gave her a thin smile and handed over the packet of plasters – her fingers often needed plasters, and the thought reminded her of earlier that day. She felt the gloom descend once more.

June took the rectangular packet, her mouth pressed together, eyes smaller as she swiped it through the till and handed them back. Plasters are not really juicy enough to gossip about perhaps, Elsie thought, or was it because she didn't agree that June was all heart? Elsie still lamented the time, years ago but still fresh in her mind, when she had asked the other chemist for some cream for something delicate and the next time Elsie had appeared, June had pointed out the ring cushions. The cheek!

Elsie paid, placing the pack in her basket next to the sausages. June took the change out of the till and then held the coins hostage in her palm as she looked at Elsie.

'I'm off on a girls' weekend,' she said, one side of her mouth lifting. 'Celebrating my birthday. Not a special one, mind,' she added, clearly not wanting Elsie to escape just yet, the shop empty. 'Funny, isn't it,' she mused, 'to think we're the same age?' She patted her short, cropped hair, tinged with a deep red dye. 'I remember we both had our bowel cancer screening at the same time.'

Elsie felt her cheeks grow hot as she stood there, unable to respond. Was June really talking about bowels? Was she suggesting they couldn't possibly be close in age? She bit her lip, just wanting her change and wondering whether she could simply turn around and leave. Was this exchange worth sixty pence?

'Women of our age,' June began, 'we need to live a little. You haven't really left the village, have you?' She didn't pause, within the same breath adding, 'Later this year, I'm going on a cruise. The ship has a nude sunbathing section.'

'I—' Elsie wanted a hole to appear in the pharmacy floor.

'I'm thinking I might try it, but then you never know who goes on these things, bu—'

'Could I have my change, please?' Elsie interrupted.

June's mouth pressed together again. 'Someone's got no time to chat,' she said sniffily.

Elsie didn't bother to reply, simply dropping the coins into her wallet and placing it back in her basket, turning and leaving as quickly as she could. She set off for home, wishing she had bought the plasters on her supermarket shop.

Normally the conversation might have been enough for her to brood on for the rest of the day but today was Wednesday and that was always a little bit different.

It was the first thought that cheered her since all the upset.

When she got home she didn't wait to boil the kettle; the clock told her she was a little behind her usual schedule already and her mind itched with all the things she wanted to say. Placing the sausages in the fridge and her basket on the dresser, she hurried through to the living room.

The room looked as it always did, the figurines all wiped down yesterday – a job that took a while, not because there were so many but because Elsie often paused to recall the memories of her mother that they conjured. 'He is quite, quite ugly!' Elsie had said, cleaning a goose clutching a daisy that her mother had been given by her father after he'd won it in a raffle. 'But I'm keeping him clean for you.'

The room smelt of the furniture polish she had used on the bookshelves and she felt satisfied everything was ready as she moved across the room to the desk. It hadn't been touched at all since last Wednesday. She never did. She pulled out the chair now, the fabric of the seat so faded it was hard to tell the original pattern, but she would never have it upholstered. Elsie sat down gingerly, her body sighing with relief. Everything ached these days.

The whole useless day melted away as she focused on the task in hand, the one ritual that she enjoyed.

The purple fountain pen rested on top of the smooth cream pile of paper to her right and she moved it, licking one finger and peeling the top sheet of paper away. Sitting up straight, she looked at the small framed picture in front of her, where her mother's and her own head poked out of the holes in a seaside peep board. The picture always made her smile. What would she write today? Which memory would she choose?

Bending her head over the page, she removed the lid from the pen and wrote the date at the top of the crisp sheet of paper. Then, rolling her shoulders, she began in earnest:

We…

Writing plunged her into another world, a world of memories. How she loved to relive some of those days, watching the purple ink spell out those happy times. Her writing was naturally tidy but at times her mind raced ahead, the letters spilling from the pen before she would straighten up and slow it down.

Today was no exception. Everything else faded around her as she formed the words, feeling her heart fill with love. The sounds of the carriage clock on the mantelpiece, the occasional car passing outside, the far-off bang or clatter through her walls from next door: it all disappeared. For an hour on a Wednesday it was simply her and her purple fountain pen, a clear cream sheet of thick paper and her cherished memories.

The last few sentences were crammed together towards the bottom today, the neat, large 'x' squeezed into the corner as she signed off. Then she sat back, the letter finished, staring at the two full pages, a small, sad smile on her face.

She would seal the envelope, get up, put her coat back on and make the third visit out of her house that day, this time to the postbox in the lane around the corner. Buried into the wall, the red façade almost obscured by ivy, she would push the letter through that gaping hole, imagining it already in the hands of the special person named on the envelope.

*

You always made me feel I could do anything. Hands clamped either side of my face: 'You're so special, Elsie.' Your hands were warm, your grip assured, transferring that strength to me.

The expression as you looked into my eyes: serious, believing. And although I had always felt so ordinary, I realised I was extraordinary to someone else.

It felt wonderful to have someone in my corner, with such faith in me. In those moments I felt as if I could scale mountains, fight enemies, discover a path to happiness: leave our house, our little village. Even after the start I'd had, it made me feel as if anything was possible.

Chapter 4

BILLY

Mum hadn't spoken to me the whole way to the school and I scuffed and dragged the toe of my new black leather shoes along the ground – which I knew she hated because it ruined them and we couldn't afford new ones – but even when I did that, she didn't say anything. It's so unfair. *I* was the one who should be in a sulk, but she was still cross that I lied to her about being ill. When we left the house, she told me if I'd had a fever of 106, I'd be dead. I'd bitten back that I wished I was and after that, she didn't speak to me the whole way there.

It's not the teachers or the work or anything and I suppose the school is a bit nicer than my London one – you could fit about eight of my old playgrounds into this one and they have a field too, with football goals and everything, but that's like the only good thing. It's the other children. Well, not all of them – it's Daniel. Daniel and his little group. I pushed my fringe down, wishing it was longer and, well, less crap. Bet Daniel will comment. My chest felt all squeezed as I thought of him and when we got to the school gates, I stopped, feeling the tears in my throat again.

Why didn't Mum say something at least?

She just buzzed, once, on the box next to the reception and then marched through the glass sliding doors with me behind her.

'I'm sorry we're late, Mrs Holmes,' she said, her voice a bit posher – she did that a bit in this village. Everyone I knew in London talked like us but they spoke differently here, as Daniel liked to constantly tell me. He'd do this stupid impression of my voice, it didn't sound like me, but when he did it, everyone would laugh. 'It won't happen again.'

Mum didn't tell Mrs Holmes the reason we were late. She hated lying and she wouldn't want me to get in more trouble, even if she was cross with me.

Mrs Holmes didn't say much, just waved me through. 'You know the way, Billy, break time soon,' she said, her eyes crinkling behind the glasses sitting on her nose. She was like all grandmas in the picture books Mum read me when I was little. She always kept biscuits in a tin on her desk next to the big box of tissues and she knew everyone in the school – apparently, she had worked on reception for, like, a hundred years.

I didn't wave at Mum or tell her 'bye' or that I loved her.

Stopping outside the classroom doors I could see a lot of heads bent over the tables and I knew I couldn't stay outside the door for ever. Knocking quietly, I stepped inside and Mrs Carter looked up from her desk and gave me a wonky smile, her blond hair in a plait.

'Alright, Billy, I had you down as absent.'

Some of the heads looked up and stared at me and I wished I hadn't pretended to be ill that morning and had just come in with everyone else. This was so much worse.

'IthoughtIwasillbutIwasn't,' I mumbled, shuffling across to the table in front of her desk. I'd sat there for the first few weeks, probably because I was the only new one in the school and Mrs Carter had wanted to check on me.

I could see Daniel in the second row, smirking at me with his stupid mouth. He would love me being in trouble. I buried my head in my rucksack and put my pencil case on the table. Mrs Carter came and crouched next to my desk, sliding the worksheet across the surface.

'Here,' she whispered, 'we're working in silence until break. You missed a lot of the explanation but see how you get on, it's some questions on the poems we've been reading.'

I bit my lip and nodded, wanting to just get my head down, feeling eyes burning into the back of my head from every direction.

When the bell went, I stayed hunched over the sheet, digging my pencil into the page as someone nudged the table behind me, scraping sounds on the floor as people pushed back their chairs, low conversations mumbled, the quiet ping of a banned mobile phone. Daniel and his groupies all had them. I wished I did then I could message Liam and maybe Dad, just to check that he does miss us. I bet he'd be nicer if he knew we might leave again. I bet things would be different.

As everyone filed out, some muttering thanks, Mrs Carter called out, telling us to put our names on the top of the worksheet. 'I don't always know your handwriting.'

Maybe I would stay in the classroom, say I needed to finish the worksheet. It was funny, at this new school I kind of wanted to do all the work – it was one way of not being with the other children. I was getting better grades – Liam would call me a right swot. I pictured him now, circling on his bike, trying to lift the front wheel off the ground – which he so couldn't do – laughing at me. Thinking about his face made me suddenly want to cry right there at the desk.

'You can finish there, Billy,' Mrs Carter said, straightening the worksheets into a pile on her desk. 'Get out to break.'

I swallowed the strange feeling that had come over me. 'I…' Mrs Carter's eyes darted to the clock. Maybe she wanted her break too. We saw them all in the big window over the corner of the playground. The staffroom had armchairs and biscuits on a table. Even with all the teachers, I'd choose to go there over the playground. 'OK…'

Swinging my legs over the side of the chair, I slipped off and handed over my sheet.

'Looks like you made good progress,' she smiled. 'Well done.'

'Thanks,' I mumbled, feeling my face get hot. Mrs Carter could be nice. She was probably one of the younger teachers in the school, still old like Mum but not ancient like Mrs Holmes. She wore big gold hoops in her ears and pale lipstick.

'You enjoying things?' she asked as I packed away my pencil case. 'Must be hard starting in the summer term, but you've fitted in really well.'

Had I?

She was definitely just being nice. There was no way I fitted in, with my crap clothes and weird accent, and now my hair was so short, I suddenly really noticed my big dark brown eyebrows. In London I'd never really cared about stuff like haircuts but in the last few weeks I had felt so… different. In London everyone else sort of seemed like me but here I stuck right out.

'S'alright,' I said, lifting up my rucksack and just wanting to get out of there. All I needed now was to be seen talking to Mrs Carter by Daniel or one of his mates and be called a teacher's pet. They'd made sucking noises like kissing when she'd waved me off once.

Outside the playground was big, but somehow Daniel always seemed to be in the bit I was in.

'Alright, me mate, me china plate. Nice hair.'

There was a laugh. I tried not to touch my head.

'I googled some words so you'd understand us, cockney rhyming slang,' Daniel said, smugly turning to Javid and Max, who always seemed to be right there. 'Why were you late this morning? Up late robbing?'

Looking over their shoulder for a distraction, I couldn't see anything. Huddles of kids stood around mobile phones, the occasional glance for a teacher; some kicked a football, others shrieked playing tag, some girls were sat on a bench, deep in conversation. Becky who sat next to me in English looked up and gave me a smile. It would take more than Becky and her mates to help me now.

The teacher on duty, Mr Williams, was in a maroon tracksuit and was lecturing two boys near the bin about something. Daniel didn't care and it didn't look unusual anyway – he would just sling an arm over my shoulder like he did the week before and force me to walk inside with him. Mrs Carter thought he was my *friend*. Ha!

'Mum said another person was stabbed in London last night. Was that you, Billy? Or your dad?'

At that word I looked up sharply and Daniel noticed, his eyes gleaming with the victory.

The bell went before he could say anything else and I pushed past them inside, tripping as Javid or Max stuck a foot out. I wished I wasn't skinny. I wished I had muscles and was taller and scarier so they wouldn't think I was such an easy target. More laughter as I headed inside, feeling anger burning through me. I bit the inside of my cheek hard to make sure no tears would come.

Where was Liam to have my back, to call them dickheads, to punch me in the arm and make me feel better? Where were my old friends? Why did I have to be stuck here?

It had only been a few weeks since Mum had woken me in the middle of the night with an urgent shake. I'd been fast asleep in my bed and suddenly there she was, fully dressed, her coat on. 'We're going *now*,' she'd hissed.

I'd been scared 'cos she'd turned the light on and I saw that she had carrier bags filled with things in the corridor.

'Change into this,' she'd pointed to the chair, clothes draped over. 'And your coat, it'll be colder than it looks.'

'But where are we going?' I rubbed at my eyes.

She shushed me. 'I don't have time to explain it all now. Just get dressed, OK? I've got you a banana and some biscuits too. We can eat properly when we get there.' She was talking quickly, as if I wasn't here and she was running through a list out loud.

'Where's there?'

'Just…' She waved the banana at me and I took it.

It was too early and strange and I set the banana down to pull on my clothes. She was moving through the small rooms of our flat and her voice was quiet. 'Keys to the house, money, phone, passports, bags, right… Billy, you ready?'

'Coming.'

'Bring that bag by your door.'

I looked at it and saw she'd stuffed my pyjamas in the top already. ''kay.'

Passports? Maybe we were going on a holiday that she hadn't told me about? I thought palm trees and a beach and sandcastles. But then I remembered school and there was no way she'd let me miss that.

She'd once complained about Zach's mum taking him out to go to Disneyland and that she should be fined.

'Billy, come on.'

Leaving my bedroom, the bag so heavy it bashed into my leg, I frowned. There was so much stuff and Mum was wearing her thick coat and a bobble hat, her fringe pushed down into her eyes. 'We have to go now.' She winced as she lifted up the bags, dropping one of them and clutching her side.

I stepped forward, 'Are you alright?'

'Fine,' she said, snatching her hand away from the side, 'I just… just pulled a muscle.'

Mum often did things like that.

'Come on then, Bean!' she said, her nickname for me. Apparently, I looked like one when I was in her tummy and the name sort of stuck. I hated it when she called me that in front of Liam – so embarrassing.

I followed her, pausing in the doorway. 'Where's Dad?'

'Dad'll meet us there. Quick, come on!' She didn't look at me, just flapped me out of our flat, down the first flight of stairs.

'But what about school? I've got a science project…' I didn't care about my science project, in fact I hadn't even finished it. But this felt strange and wrong and I wasn't sure I wanted to go anywhere with Mum like this.

'Mum…' I whined.

'Shush!' She spun around on the landing of the first floor, the bags clashing. 'No more questions, OK. I promise I'll explain, I promise.' Her voice was a whisper.

I blinked as we left the stairwell and went into the courtyard outside. The sun hadn't even come up, the light all grey, the orange lamps still on. There was no one out on the estate, all the curtains were closed in the apartments on the ground floor. I could make out Liam's window opposite – he wouldn't be up for hours. We were going to take our bikes out later that day and he'd told me he'd nicked one of his stepdad's fags and lighter so we could try smoking.

'Bloody broken lift I won't miss,' Mum said, putting the bags down and rubbing at her neck. She was carrying an enormous rucksack.

'Mum, where are we going?'

She was biting her lip, looking at her phone. 'He's two minutes away.' She was back to talking to herself, eyes darting up to the windows too.

'Who? Is Dad coming?'

She ignored my question. 'We're getting an Uber to the station.'

'What station?'

'Eat your banana. Oh, thank God!' she exhaled and bent down to collect up all the bags. She had brought loads. This wasn't a holiday. Not that we really went on holidays but this definitely didn't feel like one.

'Get in,' she said quickly as the silver car drew up, its engine humming as the driver stepped out and opened the boot for the bags.

'Thanks,' Mum said in a bright voice as if this wasn't the weirdest thing ever.

I stayed confused, standing by the door watching her pack the bags in tight, serious as she glanced back up towards our apartment. Something about her face made me feel even more worried. Why did she have tears in her eyes?

'Mum?'

'Get in, get in.' She dabbed at her face and came round to where I was standing.

'He can't eat that in the car,' the driver said, pointing to the banana in my hand.

'He won't,' Mum replied, bundling me into the car.

'Hey!'

'I'll strap you in,' she said and I let her. 'Remember what the man said about the banana.'

I didn't want the stupid banana. I didn't want to be in an Uber, the clock in the front telling me it was 05.04. I didn't want to be with Mum in this mood, with all the bags and the tears along the bottom of her eyes.

'Mum, you're freaking me out.'

She didn't say anything, just rested her head back on the seat, closed her eyes.

'Coach is just after six so save the banana for then.'

Why was she so obsessed with the banana?

'Mum?'

The man turned up the radio and Mum was scrolling on her phone. I never really went in cars in London because we mostly walked or took the bus and this car smelt of leather.

The sun was low in the sky as we stepped out of the Uber. Victoria Coach Station was busy even though it was so early in the morning, pigeons eating old bits of croissant and sandwich crusts as we waited in a queue to get on a coach to Calcot, Reading. I didn't know where Calcot, Reading was and I couldn't remember it from the bus or tube map. Mum was barely talking to me and I was bored, even eating the stupid banana. I wished I had a croissant but I wasn't about to ask Mum when she was in this mood.

We were quite near the front of the queue and a woman ahead of us had a baby strapped to her, her husband holding the hand of a toddler who kept peering round at me. I started making faces and that made the little girl hide behind his legs before peeking out and staring at me all over again.

I couldn't help a bit of a smile. At least someone was in a good mood. I'd always wondered what it would have been like to have a little brother or sister. Liam had one of each and even though he said they were annoying, I think he quite liked them too.

There was an announcement and the dad moved away and then suddenly the toddler was standing in front of me.

'Hello,' I said, feeling a bit awkward, like a big giant next to her. She was tiny. She was holding up her rabbit toy, which was grey and droopy.

'Thanks,' I said, accepting it. She grinned as I took it. 'Are you going to Calcot, Reading too?' I asked. She looked back at me blankly.

'Meghan? Meg?' The woman in the front of the queue with the baby was looking about her, eyes widening as her daughter hid behind my legs.

Mum was staring at the board, waiting for it to turn green or something as I bent down. 'I think your mum is looking for you,' I said, handing the girl her rabbit. The toddler screwed up her face. 'Don't want to go on the coach either, eh?' I knew that feeling. She nodded.

'Meg?' The voice sounded frightened.

'You'll be alright,' I said, feeling the opposite. 'Coaches are good fun!' She shook her head stubbornly. 'I'll be there too. Shall we go back to your mummy?'

The little girl thought for a moment and then held up her hand. I took it, walking her back past the rest of the queue to the lady with the baby strapped to her. 'Oh, thank you, thank you so much,' she gushed at me before speaking to the little girl. 'Meghan, never run off like that, never! Thank you so much,' she repeated.

'Billy?' Mum was looking at me, her eyes drawn together.

'Coming.'

Chapter 5

ELSIE

Billy was going to walk to hers straight after school and Elsie had calculated that he would arrive just before she was due to start cleaning the oven. She did it every two weeks – it was extraordinary how the dirt built up. She could delay it perhaps, if it hadn't become too bad. She had made a promise to his mother after all and she would honour it. The thought made her stomach swirl, unused to prolonged human interaction, but it was the right thing to do.

She tidied the desk in the front room, carefully polishing the wood of the desk and chair, plumping the worn cushions and straightening the blotter pad and paper. She glanced at the fountain pen, recalling the joy of holding it in her hand, knowing it was an opportunity to spill out more of her memories in purple ink, a chance to share her innermost thoughts.

Moving back through to the kitchen, she ticked her chalkboard: 'Clean and Tidy Desk'. She had prepared for Billy's visit, buying an extra pack of custard creams and, along with the sausages, she had purchased some potatoes and broccoli. His mother, Samantha, had warned her that the boy wasn't a huge fan of vegetables but there would be no custard for pudding if he didn't eat his portion. That was what it had been like for her – her mother had been a stickler, loathing any kind of food waste, a hangover from the rationing years she'd lived through.

The day felt different and she was distracted because of it. He had been there a few times now, since his mother had got the job at the local restaurant and struggled to find a babysitter for the erratic hours. When the boy came everything was thrown up in the air: her careful rituals, the order of her day either rushed or ignored completely. It made her pick at the skin round the edges of her nails, tap her feet as she glanced at the clock.

The last time he had been there it had been Saturday morning and every Saturday morning, she worked on her jigsaw. He had joined her, staring at the green felt of the table.

'Woah, it's massive!'

'One thousand pieces,' she had explained, worried that he would want to sit on her writing chair, saved only for Wednesdays, rather than stand. Her eyes glanced across to the desk.

Fortunately, he stayed put and so they began. Then after a while he flopped down onto the sofa, making a comment about one of the cushions. 'It's not a lizard,' she had said. 'It's a newt.' She was still doing the edges of this puzzle, a railway station scene, one thousand pieces and trickier than the last. A lot of sky in shifting shades of blue. She suspected Billy didn't like her system, piling the similar shades together before selecting which ones worked. He had wanted to dive in with any old part of the picture.

He'd wandered back to the table again: 'There's the chimney part... there's the passenger with the hat...' He didn't want to search for the edges, wanted to race ahead. Youth. He had started to get fidgety, asking her questions about some of her figurines, the print above her desk. She didn't really know what to do with him, felt like she should. Then he had almost spilt his pear squash all over the pieces and it had made her rather short with him and he had fallen silent after that.

That time she had only needed to watch him until two o'clock. His mother had been called in to the lunch shift at the small restaurant in the village unexpectedly as there was a special party in. Her manager didn't sound very understanding. Elsie had often walked past the place but had never gone inside. She didn't want to dine alone – people thought it was odd and anyway, she didn't have time to lounge around all day eating three-course meals.

What would she do with the boy this time, she wondered, running through the rest of the day's schedule. She should probably just get on with things and he could join her. A thought flickered across her mind, prompted by yesterday's disagreeable time: could she? That had been *their* thing. Should she not protect that? Would he respect it or would he treat it like her jigsaw? The thought made her foot jiggle with nerves again.

She wondered again why she had offered to have him. What did she know about children? But the words had spilled out of her and now she was caring for a ten-year-old boy, just like that.

Billy and his mother had only been in the house a few days. The last tenant had barely made a sound: the dull hum of a television between their two living rooms, water running. The change had been sudden and very apparent: voices, sometimes raised, furniture moved and the unmistakable noise of the child's footsteps racing upstairs.

She had first seen the boy's mother after four days. She was dragging the overflowing bin onto the pavement next to Elsie's, barefooted, back bent over, wearing paint-spattered dungarees. Her dark brown hair was tied back in a high bun and she wore a headscarf knotted at the front.

She had smiled at Elsie, a tired, tentative smile. 'I'm Sam – Samantha,' she corrected. 'Just moved in.'

'I've heard you,' Elsie replied, glancing back at Samantha's house with its peeling window frames and rotting wooden gate. A small boy had appeared in the top window shouting, 'Mum!'

'That's my boy, Billy,' Samantha said quickly, chewing her lip as she looked at Elsie. 'I hope we haven't disturbed you too much, it's so quiet compared to where we've com—' She drew up short then, two pink spots appearing on her pale face. 'I mean, it's just quiet.'

'Mum!' the voice repeated.

'Coming,' Samantha called back. 'Probably wants to ask me when the TV is arriving. I've *told* him we can't affor— well, not yet anyway…'

Elsie couldn't place her accent, familiar from a television soap she rarely watched but often had to read about if the shop had run out of her usual newspaper and she was forced to buy a red top.

'I'm Mrs Maple.' Elsie nodded, straightening her bin. 'Well, I must get on.'

'Right,' the woman said. 'Of course, sorry, I'm babbling. Well, nice to meet you, we'll try to keep the noise down.'

Elsie paused, taking in this woman and the boy in the window above, the awkward half-sentences, her flaming cheeks, and something twigged. 'Is it just the two of you?' Elsie asked. She could spend a moment or two longer to talk.

Samantha turned a deeper shade of pink as she looked at her toes with their chipped orange nail varnish. 'Oh, um, yes,' she mumbled.

Elsie waited, her level gaze on her. Samantha didn't offer anything more. Did she have a husband? A partner? Had he left her? Had something befallen him?

'Would you like the rest of my bin?' Elsie asked Samantha, nodding to the black object.

Samantha looked up, eyes widening.

'My bin?' Elsie repeated as if Samantha hadn't heard her. 'It looks like you have a lot to throw away and mine is largely empty.'

'Oh, that would be…' Samantha seemed to relax, her face returning to its washed-out colour, a wider smile showing a neat row of white teeth. 'I got us a couple of things for the house and it all comes in a lot of packaging. Would you mind? Really?'

Elsie wasn't used to compliments, simply waving a hand. 'Silly not to,' she said roughly. 'Go ahead.' She turned to move back through her own doorway then changed her mind, facing Samantha again. 'And if I can be of any assistance,' she said, 'I am at your service.'

Samantha wavered next to the bin. 'Oh. I'll keep that in mind – thanks.'

'It's hard bringing up children on your own,' Elsie said briskly, chin tilted up. 'Help is here if you so need.'

'I…' With alarm, Elsie noticed tears filling Samantha's eyes, her voice growing softer, 'That is so kind, thank you. I'm sorry, not sure what's wrong with me at the moment. It's someone being nice, I think.' She laughed and swiped a sleeve at her eyes. 'Thank you, really, and lovely to meet you, Mrs Maple.'

'It's Elsie,' she replied, alarmed by the emotion from this almost-stranger. And anyway, she had to get moving or she'd be late sorting through the recycling: she needed to wash out the plastics. 'And I mean it, any time.'

'Well, thank you ag—'

Elsie was through her door before Samantha could finish.

'You'd like her, wouldn't you?' Elsie said as she moved through the kitchen. 'You'd say you'd wish someone had offered to help you like that.'

Only the tick of the kitchen clock replied.

So, she couldn't cancel Billy's visit. If she didn't babysit the boy, what would Samantha do? She'd lose her job in the restaurant and then what? There wasn't anyone else. Sometimes that was the case, and there really wasn't anyone to help. She thought then of the other woman who had been in the same position years before, who had shouldered everything on her own. That thought inevitably triggered other feelings too and she clicked her tongue. 'Must get on.'

Chapter 6

BILLY

Mum works for a Dick. Literally. She doesn't like it when I call him that but his name is Richard and that is an actual shortening of his name. And he is a dick anyway so even though she tells me off, she does it in the voice that sort of doesn't really mean it and her mouth twitches a bit like she might laugh.

He makes her work *all* the time and changes the rota at the last minute even though she has *told* him which shifts are better, the ones when I'm in school, but apparently there are loads of other people that want to work in the restaurant and Mum should be grateful he has given her a job for 'cash in hand' and then Mum goes quiet and agrees to do the shift, which is so unfair because then I have to go round to Mrs Maple, which is the worst!

I have to go after school today and I really don't want to, but Mum is still pretty cross with me after the whole fake illness thing yesterday so I don't say anything this time.

Mrs Maple is old like the grandma we don't see any more, Dad's mum who he called a 'bitch', which I know is bad but not as bad as the word he used to describe my other grandma. That made Mum cry and then a year later, Grandma died of cancer and Mum said we couldn't go to her funeral but she was sobbing really hard and I really think she wanted to go to that funeral. That made me sad. I haven't thought about that day for ages. Dad took me to Laser Quest after it happened and I forgot to ask more because I was too busy shooting lasers at him with the massive plastic gun. My grandma had been nice, even though Dad hated her. She always snuck me these chocolate wafer biscuits and once let me try some of her sherry. It was disgusting, but Liam thought it was so cool I had tasted it.

Mrs Maple seems to be busy all the time but she doesn't have a job. 'Come in, come in,' she says. 'You're later than I was expecting, I thought three thirty, you must have dawdled, so I've had to make a start.'

I wasn't sure what start she had made and she seemed to always be 'running late' or 'rushed' or 'hard pushed'. I couldn't understand it. She tutted because I forgot to remove my school shoes and had to go back to leave them by the doormat in a neat row next to hers.

She has deep lines between her eyebrows, probably because she spends the whole time frowning at me. It's not like I *want* to be at her stupid house with its flowery wallpaper and its faded velvet cushions and the sofa that smells of musty cat – and she doesn't even have a cat. She has about a billion china figurines – ballerinas, shepherd girls in weird hats lying with a hook and a lamb, a goose with a daisy, loads of bunnies, a soldier in a red uniform – and she dusts them when I'm there sometimes and then ticks her little chalkboard when she's finished.

The board is in the kitchen, next to the shelf with the whole family of china chicken eggcups that she also dusts. It's split into two columns. One has got all these timings on it and capital letters by it and she ticks them off. And the other column has a sun at the top and says things like 'Thinning' and 'Scarifying'. It doesn't make any sense.

She has straight grey hair that I think used to be brown because I saw an old photo where she was stood next to another lady, but the lady wasn't her, and that lady had brown hair too. Although the lady who I thought was Mrs Maple had a really lovely smile and sparkling eyes – which made me stare extra hard at the picture – so I'm not sure it's her after all.

Today, she ignored me for a whole ten minutes. I know because I had to wait on this strange high wicker stool in the kitchen that is way too small for me and so uncomfortable, some of the wicker bits poking into my bottom, so I just stared at the clock praying it would go faster. She was cleaning the oven, which looked so clean already. She was wearing yellow gloves and she tutted as she worked, then sometimes said things out loud but I wasn't sure she was talking to me: 'You always hated a dirty oven…'; 'Ship shape'; 'I'm taking care of things.'

Sometimes I replied and once she'd nearly hit her head on the grill, looking round, her lips almost disappearing as if I was a nasty stain she would soon be cleaning too.

It was so boring. I wanted to be busy because I kept replaying Daniel calling me a tramp as I had left school and I had wanted to turn around and use the bad word that Dad called Grandma but instead I just stuck my hands in my pockets and walked off. I didn't need more trouble and who would I have told anyway?

The clock finally reached the right time, four o'clock, and Mrs Maple snapped off the gloves, made the 'tick' on her board – *'Clean Oven'* – and then returned with a tray: two glasses of pear squash and two plates with two custard creams. The most gross biscuits.

I forced them down because she would always wait for me to finish and I couldn't seem to tell her I really didn't like them and basically it was a relief to do anything, even eat biscuits I hate, because if my mouth was full, I couldn't say anything silly that would make her forehead crease and I couldn't ask her questions because I never had anything to ask, like: do you like the goose and the daisy best, or the weird shepherd girl lying down?

'Right,' she said, another look at the clock, another 'tick', *'Tea and Biscuits'*, as she removed the polka-dot teapot to wash it.

'Do you want me to do that?' I asked. Mum always told me I needed to offer to help.

'No,' she said briskly, 'there's a crack in the lid.' She said it in a funny voice, like she thought I put the crack in, but I've never touched the ugly pot anyway.

'You could get a new one?' I suggested. 'There's that shop next to the hairdresser that sells them.'

I'd seen one in the window when Mum had gone in to buy a photo frame because she'd left all of ours in London. It had made her cry so she spent her first week's tips from the restaurant on two silver frames and sent off for two photos of us, but not Dad, which made me a bit angry, and she'd looked at me like I was the mad one and that made me angrier still.

Elsie stopped still at the sink. 'I don't want a new one.' She frowned again. I knew I should have stayed chewing on the last custard cream.

The silence went on and I wished Mum didn't work in the restaurant and that I was back in our old London home with Kayleigh who had let me watch TV after school and let me have crisps instead of the carrots and pasta Mum told her to give me. How had I ended up in this grumpy old lady's house? I hoped she wouldn't make me carry on with that stupid jigsaw. It was like a million pieces and she'd done, like, twenty-five of them and they were *all* blue.

'I don't have gloves for you,' Mrs Maple said. 'You'll be fine, I'm sure, it's not that long a time.'

I frowned, not completely sure she was talking to me. Was this one of those times when I should keep quiet?

She dried the teapot, returning it to its spot on the big wooden thing that she called the 'dresser'. In London we didn't have one, just kitchen counters like normal people, not a massive sort of wardrobe thing. She turned, like she was waiting for me to say something, a grey eyebrow raised.

'OK…' I said, not sure at all what I was agreeing to.

She smoothed her hair, as if she was a bit nervous. 'Well, come on then,' she replied, moving across to a set of hooks that lined the wall down to the back door.

Following her, I watched as she brought down a funny-looking apron dress thing that she tied over her clothes. 'Will your mother be cross if you get your school clothes dirty?'

I looked down in amazement, my sweatshirt covered in ink stains and juice I'd spilt at lunch and my grey shorts flecked with paint. 'She wouldn't notice,' I replied, realising as I said it that Mum would be embarrassed. 'I mean, she wouldn't mind.'

'Well, best wear this anyway,' Mrs Maple said, handing me an apron thing, edged with flowers and leaves.

I took a step back. 'I'm alright, thanks.'

'Don't be silly, it's just an old one, overalls to stop us getting soiled.'

What did this old lady think I wanted to look like? It was a girl's apron. My toes curled in embarrassment. What if someone saw me in it? It was bad enough being teased for my accent, but this would make it *so* much worse. A million years ago it had been pink.

'I'm really…'

'Come on.' Mrs Maple's lines deepened between her eyebrows as she shook it in front of me, 'Stop dawdling.'

But, oh God, I…

I took the girl's apron thing and Mrs Maple had to fuss and show me where to put my arms, which was all wrong, like putting on a coat backwards. She tied it too tightly at my waist, but I was too miserable to say anything. It came down below my shorts so I was stood there basically wearing a pink flowered dress, bad hair, the taste of custard creams still on my tongue, no friends in the world, hanging out with an old lady in a dark, narrow corridor full of old boots. I just wanted to tear off the stupid thing and run straight out of there and back to my old life.

'That should do it,' she said in a satisfied voice as if I looked fine, which I did not. 'Well, come on then.' She paused at the back door, fumbling with the key to the lock at first. 'No time, must push on,' she said aloud.

Why was she faffing around? She had dressed me in the pink thing and now she was wasting time just staring out of the small panes of glass. What was out there? Some rubbish tiny patch of outdoor space she would make me clean? A shed full of more figurines to dust? A tank of actual newts? My heart sank as I ran through the options.

'It's OK, it's fine. He'll be careful.'

She was talking to herself again. It was well odd and before I could ask who she was speaking to, she had taken a breath and had opened the back door. Her body blocked out my view as I followed her out, and as she stepped to one side, for a second the sunlight blinded me. Then, as my eyes got used to it and I looked around at what I could see, I couldn't help but let out the most enormous gasp.

The house was small but the garden was massive. *Huge*. Although it was only as wide as the house it went on for miles. There was a glass shed at the bottom of it and that seemed like half a football field away.

And the whole strip of bright green grass was lined with flower beds bursting with different colours: it was like a normal film that suddenly turned into a bright cartoon.

Gaping, I moved onto the patio, some weeds poking between the paving stones and as I looked closer, I could see other things that were a little bit wrong: the tilted fence panel, a broken stone pot that needed moving, a ladder resting on its side, a panel missing in the roof of the glass shed.

Mrs Maple was fussing over a set of pots nearby, bursting with thin green strands topped with purple flower heads. They gave off a really strong scent, familiar but I couldn't name it.

'Lavender,' she told me as I approached.

'Oh right, it's nice,' I said, surprised to see her face move into a totally different expression than her usual one. She was smiling, her eyes crinkling with the compliment.

'Isn't it? Such a wonderful scent.'

'So…' I carried on, looking at her, forgetting for a moment the pink dress and Daniel and Dad being miles away from home, just noticing the sun on my face, the bright colours around me. 'What are we doing?'

'Well, today is weeding. I'll show you what to pull up and we can make a start. You don't have gloves so perhaps you should stick to the ones here,' she said, waving an arm to the patio. 'Pull up any of them that you see in between the cracks and don't leave any of the roots behind, that's the key.'

'OK, I can do that,' I replied, staring round. I could already see loads.

'Excellent.' She smiled again! This was getting so weird.

Kneeling on the stones, I moved around, carefully tugging on the ones I could see. Some were stubborn and broke off in my hands, others were pulled out easily. It felt really good, feeling them come out whole, thin, white roots waving in the breeze. My pile started to grow as I chucked one on top of the other, carefully moving to the next stone and the next, enjoying doing something easy, without thinking too much, on a nice warm day. It finally felt like summer would be here soon.

Mrs Maple was bent over a flower bed. She took a long time pulling each weed up, rubbing her knuckles when she thought I wasn't looking. I wondered if I should offer to do it for her. She was bent over again now, one hand on her lower back. Then she gasped, loudly, and I jumped up, a frown on my face: that hadn't sounded good.

'Are you alright?'

She held a finger up, nodding slowly. 'Fi— Ow!'

As I went over, I noticed tears in her eyes, the blue brighter because of them. I didn't know what to say. I hated it when Mum cried, it made me feel like my tongue couldn't fit in my mouth.

Mrs Maple winced, 'F-fine, thank you, Billy,' she said stiffly, rubbing at her back again. 'I just get the odd twinge.'

That hadn't looked like a twinge to me. I sort of stayed next to her, looking around her enormous garden, at the number of flower beds, the number of plants, the amount of work she would be doing, and frowned. Poor woman, it was a lot. 'Can I get you a glass of water or something?'

'No, no, stop fussing.' She was back to her normal voice, one that had me rushing over to the patio to carry on my weeding.

We worked together like that for a while. I cleared the patio, my hands dirty, soil under my nails. Mrs Maple looked delighted, beaming.

'You did that so quickly!' she said, placing a hand on my shoulder. 'You are a wonder!'

I bit my lip, embarrassed to be so happy with the compliment. Something about Mrs Maple had changed in this garden, as if it contained a bit of magic.

'Let me fetch you a trowel from the greenhouse and you can help me with the beds. We don't have much time.'

'What's a trowel?'

Mrs Maple laughed then, the first laugh I had ever heard from her. My eyes went wide at the noise: a soft chuckle, deep from her stomach. It made me grin.

'It's a small spade, good for digging out the weeds.'

'Right!' I smiled. 'Well, I can get it,' I offered, realising she was pointing to the glass shed right at the bottom of the long garden. Mrs Maple looked exhausted. Did she do all this on her own every day?

'Lovely,' she smiled back and something small shifted between us. 'I'll make a start on your dinner: I bought sausages.'

'Sick.'

'Oh, no!' She froze. 'Is that bad?'

She never really looked worried about what I thought about things so I laughed at her face. 'No, no, sick is good, you're alright…'

'Sick,' she repeated, smiling as she said it, 'how strange.' Then she laughed again. I couldn't help my eyes get all big: who was *this* woman?

Stomach rumbling at the thought of the sausages, I set off, the shadows really long now as I headed over the grass towards the greenhouse. We'd been out in the garden for ages. Mum was going to be back from her shift soon and for the first time I didn't mind if she was late. Normally I was staring at that clock in Mrs Maple's kitchen but being in the garden felt different. As I moved past the flower beds I admired all the different colours and shapes. A fence panel with ivy clinging, a small treetop heavy with dark green leaves, funny cone-like pink flowers. The garden was so busy with plants, trees, pots, bees buzzing.

The greenhouse was a dusty mess, filled with a strong smell of damp: broken pots, slanted shelves and tools lying abandoned. A lot of the things on the floor looked heavy and I wondered how Mrs Maple managed them on her own. Stepping carefully over a smashed flowerpot, I saw what I thought was the trowel. Mud clinging to its surface, I picked it up and took it back outside.

Mrs Maple was still inside, a black outline in the orange square of her kitchen window. It would be dark soon but I didn't want to stop just yet. There was a patch close by, underneath a tree in the corner of the garden, that was covered in weeds. In fact, compared to the rest of the garden, it looked sad and neglected. I headed across to it, wanting to test out the trowel.

Bending down, the pink dress protecting my knees from the dirt and pebbles in the soil, I pushed the trowel into the earth. Some of these weeds were huge and I wrenched them free, building up a sweat, amazed how much further I had to go. Sinking the trowel in again, I frowned as it hit something solid. A large stone? I tried again, a few inches from the first spot. The trowel couldn't get through. There was something there blocking it. On a third go I hit something that sounded like metal. It definitely wasn't a stone.

Frowning, I scooped some of the soil away, realising the object was large. The trowel kept striking the metal as I slowly cleared the little area, soil piling up next to me. It was something metal, rusting in places: a red tin.

I could hear Mrs Maple calling my name from the other end of the garden: 'Billy, teatime!'

'Coming!' I yelled back, my heart beating faster at the thought that I had discovered something. This felt like in the films I'd seen, a tin full of gold or treasure. It might have been there for a hundred thousand years. I had to know. I pushed the trowel in again.

Mrs Maple had started to walk across the grass towards me, the house a big black shadow behind her.

'Billy? What are you doing there…?' she called as she moved nearer.

'I think I've found something,' I replied, gently smoothing at the surface of the tin, wiping away the soil, and lifting it out of its hole. It was heavy, things sliding around inside, and my heart started to race. This was so cool! Soil trickled from it as I placed it on the ground next to me.

It was a battered, rusty, red square tin, quite large, with letters on the lid: 'H' and a faded 'P'. I ran my finger over a worn '&' and felt excited at the thought of opening this great mystery.

'Let's get you inside, I've made your tea.' Mrs Maple was close now, almost standing over me as I looked up, and I almost forgot where I was for a moment because all I could think about was the tin of treasure. The sun had practically sunk and it was only when she moved closer I could see the colour had drained from her face.

'I found it,' I said brightly, scooting around to lift the tin to show her.

Mrs Maple put one hand to her chest, stepped backwards, half-stumbling. 'But how…? I…'

Chapter 7

ELSIE

She frowned as she peered out of the window, seeing him hunched under the tree in the corner next to the greenhouse. Practically scalding herself on the saucepan, she abandoned the sausages, where they popped and hissed behind her. He was kneeling in the dirt with the trowel. She fumbled with the door handle to the garden, ignoring the pain in her hip as she moved down the lawn towards him. What was he doing?

They had been having such a lovely time. She had been so worried about allowing Billy in the garden, joining Elsie in a place that meant so much to her, that meant *everything* to her, to them. Two peas in a pod they'd been, spending their days outside in the garden together. For years, whatever the weather, they knelt side by side, back and fingers aching with their efforts, exchanging smiles, discussing the things they would plant, watch grow. The idea of allowing someone else out there had taken her breath away. What if it ruined the memories? What if he hadn't cared?

But something about entering the garden with Billy had changed things between them. She had adored the shocked awe on his face as he had stared around at the space she nurtured daily. And to have company again there felt so natural. To have Billy there, no longer a nuisance but a help, felt just right.

She had been so upset recently, having to move inside, away from her beloved garden, forced to take painkillers, abandon jobs that were becoming too difficult. The ladder lay on its side where she had dragged it, wanting to clear the drain of leaves, unable to continue as her hip seared with pain. The heavy stone pots that she used to empty and manoeuvre seemed ten times heavier these days. The large spade seemed too daunting a prospect. A rake to scarify the lawn an impossible feat.

She had been frightened that soon some jobs would be completely beyond her, that the place would fall into neglect. That would be the greatest betrayal. The garden used to be a comfort, a release from her thoughts and feelings, but recently she had left it quickly, feeling less able these days, then seized by fear for the future, rage that her beloved place was becoming the source of her worry.

Taking Billy out there had changed that, giving her a tiny flame of hope that things could be different, that she had some help and some company, after so many years alone.

The garden had been getting out of control, weeds springing up faster than she could remove them, the grass needing mowing urgently, the ancient lawnmower in the shed unwieldy. Perhaps, she'd thought as she watched him pull at the weeds, moving carefully and quietly over the patio as instructed, calling out to her excitedly, perhaps they could revive it together? Certainly, she felt less awkward, conversation no longer stilted as they worked together companionably.

The sunlight had all but disappeared by the time she made it over to him. He had dug something out of the earth, it was there next to him lying on the grass. She placed a hand on her stomach: what had he found?

She told him dinner was ready, to get away from there. He looked surprised, getting up, showing her what he had discovered, passing it to her like an excited puppy with a bone.

She couldn't believe her eyes. After all these years.

He pestered her and pestered her. 'Can we open it?'; 'What do you think's inside?'; 'Oh my God, I saw a show once where this man found treasure in his garden and he bought a yacht and his own whole island and stuff…'; 'Let's open it now.'

He'd kept going as they moved inside, as the smoke alarm started wailing, a knock on the front door and she had snapped at him.

The sausages were burning, steam filling the room as she jabbed helplessly at the smoke alarm with the end of a broom, missing each time.

Another knock and Billy's mum Samantha was at the door, Billy streaking past. Samantha's smile quickly disappeared as she took in the expression on her son's face, as he shouldered past her without so much as a hello.

'Say thank you to Elsie, Billy,' she turned, frown lines appearing, realising that something had put her son in this mood. 'Billy…' she called.

She twisted back to Elsie, 'Sorry, I don't…'

Elsie hadn't been given any time to catch her breath but she didn't know how to make things better, her chest still heaving from the angry words she had fired at him, from the feelings that had risen up in her.

Billy was out on the pavement and through the gate, still only a couple of metres away. 'I've got my key,' he was saying as she looked across the low fence at him.

'Billy, don't be rude.' Samantha watched as he turned the key and stepped inside their house, spinning back to Elsie. 'I'm sorry, I'm not sure, he's not normally, um... he's, well things are... difficult for him right now. But...'

Elsie realised then that Samantha thought Billy was upset about something at home when it had been their row of course that had caused his reaction.

'I burnt the sausages,' she said distractedly.

'Oh, I've got things. It's not a problem, you are sweet for watching him. I hope he wasn't too much bother... I'm not sure why he just left like that, he has been...'

Elsie hadn't meant to shut the door so quickly, throwing a hurried, 'It's fine, goodbye', Samantha's confused face disappearing behind it. She couldn't listen any more, didn't want to hear explanations when she knew exactly why Billy had been so angry. She shouldn't have snapped at him, but he should have listened to her.

Moving back into the kitchen, she glanced in the direction of the tin, feeling the same tug whenever she thought of it all those years ago in the place it had lived, in that very room: such a familiar item. Billy hadn't understood its significance, not knowing his questions were like individual bullets firing through a wall she had built years before.

'Why can't we open it?'

'Billy, please, it's nothing.'

'Why won't you look inside?'

'It's obviously old, it will be dirty.'

'What is it? Do you know?'

'Don't be silly, how would I know what it is?'

He wouldn't drop it – loud, insistent, until she had turned and spat at him, 'Enough.'

He had stepped back, fallen deathly silent, eyes to the ground.

'Stop asking me.'

He had looked utterly downcast, biting his bottom lip, tears pricking his eyes. Yet she hadn't stopped.

'I *told* you to leave it… Why couldn't you *listen*?... How *dare* you.'

Then the wail of the smoke alarm, a knock too: his mother at the front door. He had moved wordlessly past her inside.

She looked across now at the tin on the dresser: the trigger to all of this mess. Some of the red had peeled away, leaving rusty spots on its surface. She remembered that tin as it had once been and a fresh stab of pain sliced into her. She knew Billy wanted to open the tin. It was understandable – which young boy wouldn't want to open something they'd discovered buried, long-hidden? She *didn't* want to open it though.

That tin had been her mother's – and she hadn't seen it in twenty-eight years.

*

I remember showing you a painting of the river I had been working on for days, frustrated that I couldn't seem to capture the exact feel of the place, layering the paints on top of each other in the hope it would start to take shape, starting again until finally it began to resemble the image in my head.

A favourite spot of ours, halfway to Mapledurham, in the small copse we discovered hidden from view of the path. The ground flat, the bank dropping away steeply into the water, the reeds so thick the surface glowed green.

I'd been nervous as to what you might say – would you think it was a rubbish effort? I had sat for hours on the bank, legs dangling over the side, the grass tickling my thighs, the sun hot over my head as I immersed myself in the scene.

All those painting lessons at the kitchen table, the paintbox filled with different coloured promises sat next to the red biscuit tin on the dresser, always to hand, but this felt different. A painting I was keeping secret until its grand reveal. I'd hidden it under my bed for the week, worried it would be discovered. Now this was the moment you would look at it.

Had I captured the willows bending gently towards the water, their leaves trailing on the surface? Had I caught the silvery dashes in the centre of the river that danced when the sun beat down? Had I caught the soothing calm of the green hills beyond? The gentle put-put of a barge moving past?

I shouldn't have doubted how you'd react. You were always kind to me, always encouraging any talent. I hadn't had to wait long…

'Elsie, this is—' You had broken off to study certain aspects more and I'd been so grateful you were taking in every inch of the familiar scene. 'It's like we're sat here,' you'd said, your face crinkling as you looked up at me. 'Like we're the only two people in the world that know about this place.'

And that's what I had thought too, that was the future: just the two of us sitting on the banks of the river, looking at the beauty all around us, peaceful. Two peas in a pod.

And that thought could not have made me happier.

Chapter 8

BILLY

I thought she was going to have a heart attack. Her face went completely white and her eyes were all googly as she looked at what I was holding. It was just a tin. Did she not like gold and diamonds and buried treasure? Then she snatched it off me, didn't even say why, and just turned back to the house. I knew she was a total misery. All those smiles and chuckles in the garden before were not really her. *This* was her.

I followed her and I was just asking her a few questions and she'd turned and shouted right at me, when I hadn't even done anything apart from find treasure and it was so unfair. Then the smoke alarm went off and the door went and Mum was early, thank God, and Mrs Maple went in but couldn't get the broom to make the alarm stop, but I wasn't going to help her because she'd only shout at me again. And I thought Mum might get it but she didn't give me any time to explain, she just followed me back to our house saying how embarrassed she was because I'd been so rude to Mrs Maple and I couldn't just do things like that and she thought Mrs Maple was this nice lady and that was totally unfair too.

I went up to my bedroom, threw myself on the bed and screamed into my pillow because everything had gone wrong and it had all happened so quickly. The garden had been good and I'd been so excited about that red tin. I should have just opened it when I was on my own and then I could have kept all the gold to myself anyway. Mrs Maple didn't deserve anything. It was like she didn't even care about looking in it. Who doesn't want to see what's in a buried tin like that?

Mum made cheese on toast for tea even though it was late so I had to go to the kitchen but then she started on me again.

'You can't get so angry all the time,' she said and it just made me feel angry all over again.

She didn't even want to hear my side of it. I got the whole blame and she told me, 'You'll have to go back tomorrow and apologise to Mrs Maple.'

'I'm not going back there.'

'You are.'

'No way!'

'Billy, this isn't a debate.'

'I'm NOT going back there.'

I pushed the plate away then and I didn't mean it to slide off the table but it did and it smashed into pieces, which was sort of how I felt inside, all jagged, but Mum went mental before I could say sorry or clear it up, shouting that we didn't have lots of new stuff and I couldn't just break things and God, Billy, what was my problem? Then when I had gone to help, she had screeched at me to get away and I didn't even want to be there anyway and cheese on toast wasn't even a proper dinner, and I told her that and that I hated her and ran back upstairs.

Mrs Maple could probably hear Mum crying from her kitchen. I could hear her from my bedroom even though I pressed my head right into my pillow and squeezed my eyes shut and it was so unfair that *she* was crying. I just wished I was back in London and Dad would be there, asking if I wanted to play Forza Horizon 4 on the Xbox and he would call me 'good lad' and listen if I wanted to complain about Mum and never made me feel bad about that – 'Women, you can't understand them, just let her go on.'

And I wished he was here to say that to me and help me escape from this stupid new house in his car that had crisp packets on the floor and smelt of the last owner's dog but at least it would get me places. Away from here.

Why had she brought me to this stupid village where we didn't know anyone? And she wouldn't even let me have a mobile so I couldn't call Liam and tell him what was going on. Did he miss me? Did he notice I wasn't there? Did he have a new best friend now? I bet he did and I bet he'd forgotten me already. I had nobody and even worse, Daniel was making everything a hundred times harder.

All these thoughts made me start to cry too so we were both crying and then Mum was suddenly at the foot of my bed, stroking my back and saying 'Shush!' like I was small again and had scraped my knee. I was glad she was there and it made me cry a bit louder because everything just sucked and everything was wrong.

'I don't want to go back there, she's horrible, she shouted at me,' I said, my voice all muffled in the pillow.

'Billy, please, it can't be that bad. What happened, anyway?'

I turned on my side and I told her, 'I found this tin in her garden… Her garden is huge and this tin was buried… but she shouted at me and then you came… I don't want to go back there. It's horrible, it's like a house from the olden days… I want to go back to London… Liam said I could go camping with him this summer 'cos they go to this lake every year and now he won't remember me and why can't we see Dad? Maybe he'd say sorry, and…'

Mum had tears rolling down her cheeks. I struggled to sit up and it was all spilling out of me but she didn't really talk back, just sat there listening until I sort of ran out of stuff to say. Then I lay back down feeling empty and tired.

'Get your pyjamas on, OK, and clean your teeth.'

'I don't want to go to Mrs Maple's any more. Please, Mum.'

She sighed, standing up, holding out her hand to me. 'I don't know. I'll see wha—'

'*Please*, Mum.'

'I'll look for a babysitter,' she said, her voice quieter now. 'Alright?'

I nodded, sniffing, wiping my nose, which was wet like my cheeks.

'Sorry about the plate. I didn't mean to.'

She sighed again. 'I'm sorry I shouted at you. I know it hasn't been easy…'

And for the first time since London I felt like she was back to being Mum, and it made me want to hug her, but she had moved towards the door of my bedroom, her body a bit slouched like she was tired.

'Pyjamas,' she said again and I reached under my pillow and got my pyjamas like she told me to.

Nothing was fixed but at least I wouldn't have to go back to Mrs Maple's house, treasure or no treasure.

Chapter 9

ELSIE

'I know I shouldn't have shouted at him,' Elsie said to the walls. She was sat at the top of the stairwell of her house, talking to the closed door opposite her bedroom. She had finished the weekly clean, a can of furniture polish and a yellow duster gripped in her hands. It always felt strange after she'd been inside the room, the smells and sights unchanged in twenty-eight years. She had pulled the door closed and sat immediately on the top step, not wanting to go downstairs just yet even though she needed to tick the chalkboard.

'I was surprised, I didn't have time to think through my reaction.'

There were no comforting words back and Elsie squeezed the duster tighter.

She replayed yesterday afternoon again. She hadn't felt that comfortable in her garden for months. She hadn't realised how much she craved someone else to share in her love of the outdoors, the haven that she and her mother had lovingly created together. But now she needed to fix things with Billy.

She gave a last glance back at the closed door before she stood up. Would she ever spend more time in that room beyond just the hour cleaning, she wondered. Would she ever have the courage to face what was inside?

'It's hard,' she said aloud.

Billy had been the first person to make her believe one day she might have the strength to do it, if she could change. He had such a lot of worries and yet he seemed to always be polite, in good humour. He didn't deserve being snapped at. There were moments when she saw the woman he must see, the hard-edged old lady who lived next door: prickly, difficult. She didn't want him to think of her like that. She didn't want him to see what everyone else saw. A thought struck her and she stood quickly, moving through the house to fetch her handbag.

She hadn't had her customary tea and custard cream, she realised on the way down the high street. She had been so distracted by her idea she had only grabbed her coat and had forgotten her mother's beloved blue silk scarf. She would normally have turned back but it didn't seem worth it and she picked up her pace, barely feeling the ache in her hip.

She was almost there when she saw her, the red cropped hair even brighter outside, dressed in a tracksuit, holding two small hot pink dumbbells, wiggling her way down the pavement on Elsie's side. It was too late to cross the road; perhaps she wouldn't stop.

She stopped. 'Elsie,' she said, still pumping the dumbbells up and down as she trotted on the spot, her cheeks pink and clashing with the shade of her hair.

'Hello, Jun—' Elsie tried to smile, get it all out of the way quickly so she could get on.

'I'm on a power walk. I do them twice a week, Elsie. My friends say, "June, how do you find the time?" but do you know what I tell them?' She puffed.

'What do y—'

'You have to put your own oxygen mask on first. Do you get me, Elsie? Self-care is so important. Well, I best get on, we don't *all* have the luxury of time,' June said, shifting a dumbbell in her hand.

Elsie smiled through tight lips, trying not to look cross, but she had somewhere she needed to be too. Just because she wasn't carrying strange coloured weights didn't mean she wasn't on her own mission. Before she could say anything else, June had left, her bottom waggling from side to side as she disappeared up the road.

Elsie breathed out slowly. That woman! Put your own oxygen mask... honestly. She had almost forgotten what she was there to do.

Fortunately, moments later, she had what she had come into the village for and felt much brighter for it. Clutching the bag to her chest, she stared across the street, seeing the white peaked hat of Mr Porter bustling behind the counter of the butchers. It wasn't the right day for her visit there but she remembered Billy's comment about living on plain pasta. Meat was expensive, Elsie thought, as she crossed the road.

'Elsie,' he said, looking up, handing a pie in a paper bag to his last customer. 'Good to see you, you look well. Darren, look who it is!'

Darren looked up and gave Elsie a wary smile.

'How can we help today? I've got a fresh batch of steak and mushroom pies in? Or one of the Scotch eggs you like... the bigger size?'

'Some diced chicken, please,' Elsie said, touched that he appeared to remember some of her favourite items. That thought made her add, 'And a Scotch egg would be lovely.'

Mr Porter beamed. Elsie fumbled for her purse, accepting the bag with a quiet, 'Thank you, Mr Porter.'

'Honestly! It's Stanley! You take care of yourself, Elsie. We'll see you in here soon, I hope,' Mr Porter said as she blustered out the door.

'Thank you, yes, thank you, Stanley.' She stumbled over the name, always formal, always perfunctory. Anyway, she really did have to get back, she didn't want to waste a moment longer.

Clutching her prize in her hand, she hurried home, past the post office, past the library. Scarlet had given her a wave from the window and Elsie, hesitant at first, had returned it. That was a good sign perhaps, people could be nice. Surely Billy would give her a second chance? She swallowed as she passed her own house and headed straight to next door, a trembling hand reaching for their doorbell.

'Would you mind if I came in?' Elsie felt her heart hammering as Samantha appeared in the doorway. She didn't look impressed. Two deep lines between her eyebrows appeared as her eyes narrowed. She crossed her arms, not inviting Elsie inside.

Elsie licked her lips, cracked and dry. 'I got you some chicken,' she announced. Samantha's mouth twitched but she didn't budge.

'I've come to apologise,' Elsie blurted, gripping the bag tightly in her hand. 'Please.'

Something shifted in the younger woman's eyes and she stepped to one side, a hand indicating Elsie could step inside.

'Thank you,' Elsie said, squeezing past her.

There was no porch, the door led directly into the living room, a small square room with not even a lampshade over the bulb. In fact, as Elsie looked round, she realised how bare the place really was: hardly anything in it at all.

There was an old sofa in faded burgundy that had seen better days, holes in the arm rests, no cushions. No pictures on the walls, a single hard-backed chair, no trinkets, frames or even a television. It was so stripped back it made the small room look cavernous, and there was something temporary and depressing about the scene, so different from her own house crowded with memories. For a moment Elsie forgot what had brought her there.

'So,' Samantha said, 'Billy told me you shouted at him.'

Elsie flinched at the coldness in her neighbour's voice, at the directness of the sentence.

'I… well, "shouted" might be going too fa—' Elsie felt her usual defences go up and then swallowed, remembering the little boy's face in the garden, his enthusiastic excitement that had morphed into something else. She dropped her head and nodded, ashamed. 'I did. He really didn't deserve it.'

'Why? He's only ten and he's got so much on his plate right now.' Samantha was clearly cross, swiping her fringe out of her eyes. She really needed a haircut. Oh goodness, Elsie realised, perhaps she couldn't afford to treat herself.

'It was… I… The thing is…' How could Elsie explain the swell of emotions that had risen up inside her as she'd realised what Billy had found? How could she justify the way she had spoken to him? She didn't really remember what she said: one minute she had been lost in a sea of thoughts and feelings, old scars now livid and open, the next all she could hear was his voice asking the very questions she didn't have answers to. Then she was spinning round, wanting him to stop so she could think, get away, be alone and she had twisted round to face him, opening her mouth, angrily silencing him.

'I am truly sorry, I treated him badly.'

Samantha didn't say anything, arms crossed again, eyes not quite meeting Elsie's as she battled with whatever she was thinking.

'Please, I want to make it up to him, and you,' Elsie said, holding out the small bag she had been clutching. 'I wanted to give him this – is he here? Would he see me?'

'He's at school.'

'Of course,' Elsie replied, her hand dropping to her side. 'Silly, of course he is.' Her smile was weak, sad.

Samantha stalled, nodded at the bag, 'What is it?'

Elsie felt a small opening, a chance to fix things. 'Gloves,' she explained, holding up the bag. 'For Billy. I didn't have any in his size so I went to the DIY shop this morning. He seemed to like the garden…' she trailed away.

Samantha took a breath, her voice soft, her eyes less suspicious. 'He told me.'

Elsie felt her chin lift, 'Did he?'

Samantha nodded slowly, relenting a fraction. 'He told me you had every kind of flower and there were even fruit trees that would grow things he thought might become apples. He got quite carried away.'

'He really did seem to like the place,' Elsie said, a small smile on her face. *He had noticed the trees?* She hadn't realised he had spotted the fruit trees. He might have meant the plum tree in the corner that she was late to prune. 'I would love to teach him more. If you would allow him to come over again?'

Samantha's expression changed again, a cloud descending. 'I… I'm not sure. He really… Look, I do understand. I know you're probably not used to young children, but, well…'

'I will try harder,' Elsie replied, a note of desperation entering her voice. 'I know I can be… difficult. I'm not used to children, well, not good with people generally, I…' Why was she fighting so hard for this boy who only a week or so ago simply represented disruption and chaos?

'It's not that I'm not grateful, it was kind of you to step in and take him those other times. It's let me do my job, it's just…'

'I really do want to,' Elsie said, 'I need to make it up to you both.'

Samantha sighed, twisting her hair into a low bun. 'To be honest, I've been looking but it seems round here babysitters are a rare breed. I searched online again this morning, but people aren't exactly hammering down the door to look after my kid. Not at the times I need them, and who knows when Rich will decide to change my shifts again.'

Elsie's heart swelled with a tiny sliver of hope, a feeling that also surprised her: she hadn't realised the impact Billy had made. 'Well, I am available and would love the chance.'

Samantha's face fell, an embarrassed blush forming. 'I told him he didn't have to see you again.'

'I understand,' Elsie replied, her heart sinking with that knowledge. How awful that the little boy had said those words. What had possessed her to be so cruel? 'But,' she started, for the first time in her memory wanting to do something for someone else, 'you do need someone to look after him?'

Samantha didn't respond to her question.

'I am happy to have him whenever you need.'

Still Samantha didn't say anything.

'I know I was unfair to him and I do feel dreadful. I really won't ever do anything like that again, I assure you.'

Finally, Samantha looked up. 'I'm not sure he'll be that keen, to be honest…'

'I imagine not. I was very harsh with him and I will make sure he understands that it was unacceptable and absolutely all my fault.'

These words finally altered something in Samantha's demeanour. Her shoulders dropped and her face opened up. 'He said something about finding a tin, a box of some sort?' she asked tentatively. 'I didn't really understand what he found but Billy has always been a curious little thing.'

'Sign of intelligence,' Elsie said, relieved that Samantha appeared warmer with her.

'Well, he has mentioned it more than once,' Samantha carried on, 'He thinks it might have been left there by pirates.'

Elsie leapt on her chance with both hands, despite everything. 'Well, you tell Billy if he agrees to come back, we can open the tin together,' she said, swallowing down the instant surge of anxiety triggered by the rash statement.

'So, there is a tin? Well! Maybe he's right and you'll both find gold. God knows, we could do with some of that!'

Elsie wasn't really listening, the nerves fluttering in her stomach at the thought of what she had started. Still, at least the promise would get him there. She would let him open that tin: what was the worst that could happen?

Chapter 10

BILLY

'You said I didn't have to go back there.'

'I said I'd look for a babysitter.'

'That's the same thing.'

Mum went quiet, which she always did when she knew I was right. Not that being right meant much. She was making me go back to Mrs Maple's. She hadn't said anything all weekend and now we were about to leave for school and she was springing it on me.

'No way!' I said, stopping, one black school shoe in my hand.

'She feels terrible,' Mum replied. 'She came round and apologised while you were at school and look,' she held out a pair of large, khaki green gloves, 'she bought you these, they're brand new, for the garden. She said you'd been so good in her garden – that's nice, isn't it? She obviously likes you, Billy.'

'Funny way of showing it,' I said, remembering the way she'd turned round in her garden and shouted at me.

'I'm sorry, alright?' Mum sighed. She did that a lot now, her face paler, her cheeks thinner; she looked funny without her bright orangey lipstick which she never wore any more, 'I did look but there isn't anyone around here who wants to do the kind of hours we need, and, frankly, Billy, we can't really afford it.'

What could I say? I knew something was going on. Mum was counting things at the supermarket checkout and she made me take back the box for the fajitas and the chicken breasts, and we'd had cheese on toast again last night and we still don't have a television and I'm not stupid.

'I could stay here on my own.'

'You're not old enough,' Mum said, but not angrily.

I scuffed my toe on the floor. 'What if she yells at me again?'

'She won't.'

'What if she does?'

'Well, if that happens, you tell me and you really won't have to go back there.'

I looked up. 'Where would I go?'

Mum paused. 'We'd work something out.'

I was quiet, not sure what else I could say.

'Everyone deserves a second chance,' Mum said, 'don't you think, Billy?'

'What about Dad?'

She reared backwards. 'What do you mean?'

'You're not giving him a second chance. Does he even know we're here?'

'Look, Billy, it's complicated. I… I know maybe I should…' She was fiddling with the sleeve of her sweater and she wouldn't look at me. 'You don't know some… it's just…'

'Don't bother,' I replied, knowing I was being rude. It wasn't like I expected to get a straight answer from her anyway. I felt a bit sorry for Dad: he must be *really* missing us now. He never said it, but Mum always told me how much he loved me even if sometimes he didn't show it either.

'If it doesn't work out at Mrs Maple's,' Mum said, 'maybe you can go round a friend's house another day? From school?'

I thought of school and my total lack of friends. Yeah, great, I could head round Daniel's or Javid's or Max's – hey, guys, want to hang out? They'd sneer and make stupid comments about my clothes and my voice and I hadn't even told Mum, who'd probably want to come in and talk to the teacher, which would only make things a million times worse.

'Yeah…' I said.

'It's only for a couple of hours after school today. And if you hate it, well…'

'Fine.' I slouched onto the sofa, which smelt of cat hair and damp. I missed our flat and the soft grey throw that Mum draped along the back of our L-shaped sofa that meant I could lie right out with only my feet poking over the end. God, I hate this stupid house.

'I'm sorry, Billy, I need this job. Rich said—'

'I said fine,' I replied, shoving my shoe on, 'I've got to go.'

'I can walk round there with you after school, if you like.'

'I can get there alone, it's like two seconds away,' I replied, watching her slink back.

She nodded dumbly. 'Alright, fair enough. I am sorry, Billy. I'll pick you up once my shift's finished at 6 p.m.'

'Whatever.' I picked up my rucksack and barely looked back at her. Normally she forced me to give her a kiss on the cheek, or a high five if I really wasn't in the mood, but this morning, she didn't say anything, just let me leave.

I was halfway to school when I realised I'd left my PE stuff at home but there was no way I was going back now. I'd just have to pretend I was ill or hope they'd let me sit it out anyway. I was crap at PE at this school. They didn't play football this term, we were doing tennis on the court, and I've never played before but I think Daniel has his own court or something because he's amazing at it.

Thinking about Daniel only put me in a worse mood as I turned up to school, joining the queue into the classroom. No one said 'Hi', although Becky looked over and smiled at me but I was standing next to another girl who was a twin and I couldn't remember which one so she was probably smiling at her.

In the end they'd found me spare PE kit, which was gross and smelt of someone else's BO, even though Mr Williams said it had been washed. Javid and Max were clutching their sides cracking up in the changing room as Daniel walked past, calling me a tramp again.

'Although they're nicer than your normal clothes,' he'd said, swinging the tennis racket round so it hit me in the calf.

I'd been about to go for him but Mr Williams had come in then and told us to hurry out onto the court.

The whole session was rubbish as we all queued up to hit the ball and I kept missing it, hearing the sniggering behind me every time.

'You're alright, Billy, you'll get there,' Mr Williams called, but only because he was paid to say that. I was rubbish.

The day went really quickly, probably because I was dreading the short walk down the road and into Mrs Maple's house. No doubt she'd be sitting there surrounded by her weird china stuff, finding more pieces of blue for her impossible jigsaw.

Mrs Maple answered the door the moment I pressed the doorbell, even though it hadn't made any noise, as if she had been waiting right next to it for me to arrive. 'I told you he'd come,' she added over her shoulder as if someone else was there. She's a bit strange.

She was wearing a smart dress and a silver necklace and I think she'd put some make-up stuff on her face because her lips and eyes looked a bit different.

'Billy, I'm glad you came,' she said as I shrugged off my coat in her little porch bit to put on the hook 'cos if I didn't use it, she'd only nag me to.

I didn't say anything, it wasn't like I had a choice in the matter. Soon I'd be old enough not to need anyone looking after me. I reckon I'm grown-up enough anyway. Mum always told me I was mature for my age, but apparently the police could arrest her if she left me on my own.

I remembered my shoes too and bent down to slide them off.

'You can keep them on, it's fine. I can vacuum when you leave.'

'S'OK,' I muttered, not wanting to give her any reason to get angry at me.

I padded after her into the kitchen where, surprise, surprise, the polka-dot teapot was sitting on the table next to a plate of custard creams. *Great.*

'I thought you'd want a snack after school. It's not really teatime but I thought I could make it now. For you,' she added, a smile on her lips that had the soft shiny pink stuff on today.

'Thanks,' I said, still not really looking at her, just sliding onto the kitchen chair and reaching for a biscuit. I wanted to hold my nose as I nibbled it but forced it down in two big bites.

'Oh, you are hungry, do have another.' She pushed the plate towards me.

Oh, man…

I picked up a second, holding it in my fist and hoping she wouldn't notice if I put it back later.

'Pear squash?' she offered, placing a glass on the table.

Then I noticed the red tin on the counter behind her. She had moved it from the dresser, wiped the soil and it was just sat there, waiting.

She saw me looking: 'I haven't opened it.'

I bit my lip and looked away, not wanting to get her cross or look like I cared. But my eyes couldn't help flickering back. I felt the same curiosity that I had the other evening, remembering when I had hit the surface with the trowel, the strange clunk it had made, the excitement when I'd realised there was something buried, hearing the contents slip and slide as I lifted it out.

Mrs Maple was sort of wiggling her hands. She sat on the chair at the head of the table, then stood up again, then sat back down again. It made me frown as I watched her. She finally settled and looked at me. 'I'm so sorry for shouting at you the other day, Billy. It was, well, it was unforgiveable. How were you to know?'

Know *what*?

'And I hope you got my present? The gloves? I hoped you would want to wear them for when we garden again? You seemed to enjoy it befo…'

She trailed away before I could add, 'Before you shouted at me?'

'They're at home,' I said, not wanting to cave, but then it felt rude, not saying anything about the present. 'But thanks,' I added, my voice low and quiet.

That word seemed to relax her, her smile wider. 'There's no need for you to thank me, it was the least I could do to show you how sorry I was. We could get out there now if you like?'

I looked up. 'You said we could…'

Mrs Maple swallowed. 'I know I promised,' she said, looking away, as if she was talking to the walls again and not me.

'I did.' She took a breath and I realised her hand was shaking as she reached for the polka-dot teapot. 'Yes, I did, the tin.' Her voice broke on the word and I realised she was nervous. Was she worried about being with me too? The thought made me soften a bit. She had apologised and given me the gloves and she did seem sorry; she was being quite friendly, like she'd been in the garden before it all went wrong.

'I did promise your mum we could open it together.' She took a breath and looked straight at me, 'So we should, yes, that's fine, yes...' she said, one hand crossing over the other.

I licked my lips, wanting to silence the voice in my head shouting 'YES'. Shrugging, I put my two hands in my lap. 'OK,' I said. Inside my stomach was doing little flips. There was definitely treasure in it.

She stood up slowly. 'It's alright,' she said aloud. I frowned, not sure who she was talking to.

She stood at the counter for a second, her back to me. I was leaning forward in my chair, almost toppling onto the floor. I'd a hundred per cent forgive her if she shared the gold. Oh my God, that would totally help Mum out! No more counting the money at the till, she could buy a million chicken breasts.

'Right. Well, here we go...' Mrs Maple's voice sounded funny, higher, her shoulders tense as she lifted the tin from the side and carried it carefully over to the table. 'Here it is,' she said, placing it on the surface.

I stood up, my heart starting to race as she looked across at me.

'Would you like to open it?' she asked and, eyes wide, I nodded at her. 'Go on then.'

She pushed the tin towards me and I placed my hands on it. It felt cold, the spots of brown rust still there. Mrs Maple sat back down, her hands gripping the wooden armrests of her chair as she watched me.

The tin's lid was stiff as I hooked my fingers and pulled. Nothing happened. Then with a scrape something came away, tiny red flakes from the tin fluttered to the table and some stuck under my fingernails. A tiny noise, a small pop, and the lid was in my hand.

I was holding my breath, waiting to see what was inside: the glint of silver or gold.

Nothing shone.

The tin was almost full, something woollen lying folded on the top, squeezed into it. I pulled it out, heard Mrs Maple suck in her breath. A small rectangular white knitted square, it would barely cover my legs if I sat down.

'What's this?' I asked, holding it up – too small for a blanket or rug.

Mrs Maple rubbed at her neck before answering. 'I'm not sure,' she said vaguely.

I set it to one side, excited to see what it had been covering, frowning as I stared at the items beneath it.

No gold coins, no silver coins, no diamonds. But then my hand reached in and I pulled out a necklace – some round shiny cream stones.

'Pearls,' Mrs Maple said, her own hand fiddling with the silver chain at her throat. She looked frightened, her face frozen, as if it was a bottle of poison. It was just a necklace.

There were other things: a small cardboard ticket thing, a name printed on it; a black-and-white photo of a man with a moustache turning to his right and staring off into the distance, 'Bernard, 1956' written on the back in purple ink; a pack of playing cards; a postcard, the writing too slanted and small to make out, signed only as 'H', the tiny date squashed at the top, 04/06/58; an oval hairbrush with pink flowers painted on the outside. A picture drawn by a child: two stick figures holding hands.

So just junk, really.

There was a small paper bag: the last hope. Maybe that was where the sapphires and rubies were and I felt my heart hammer, seeing different coloured circles inside. I spilt them out on the table but it was just a lot of boiled sweets, all wrapped individually: red, green, yellow, purple.

This was rubbish. Just bits and bobs, not even new things – the brush looked really old and like something a grandma would brush her hair with, and there was no way I'd be eating any sweets that came out of the ground.

Disappointed, I looked inside the tin for one final time, hoping I had missed something. Lying on the bottom of the tin was a white card with a date on it: '2nd March 1950'. Turning it over, I realised it was another photo. This one was of a baby lying in a funny-looking basket, all tightly wrapped in a blanket. I peered closer: it looked like the white knitted thing in the tin. Weird. I put it down and sat back, mouth turned down.

'Well,' Mrs Maple said, reaching across, 'that's it then.'

She picked up the photo of the baby, glancing at it briefly.

I looked up. 'Hey, I think that baby's wearing this blanket.'

Mrs Maple seemed to go very still. 'Oh, oh yes, so she is.'

I leant forward. 'She? Is it you?'

Mrs Maple placed the photo back in the tin, her hand shaking a little, but hands on old people often did. I wasn't sure she heard me. 'It's our old biscuit tin,' she said, her voice fast, high.

I looked up quickly.

'Huntley & Palmers biscuits, hence "H" and "P",' she said, looking brighter and tapping the lid so it made a funny metallic noise. 'It belonged to my mother. We used to have our custard creams out of it – until we got a new one, that is.'

'It's a biscuit tin. Why'd she put it in the garden then?'

Mrs Maple turned away from me. 'Oh, I haven't the first idea. Speaking of biscuits, we could have another one now if you'd like?'

'No, I'm alr—'

I was about to ask her more when I saw something folded on the bottom of the tin. Pulling it out, I smoothed it out on the table.

'What's that?' Mrs Maple asked, stepping towards me again, peering over my shoulder.

'It was folded at the bottom.'

'Was it?' Mrs Maple's eyes rounded.

It was a map, neatly drawn and coloured with watercolour paints. There were winding roads, tiny houses, the river slicing through the page, curving off to the left, little green trees in clusters, everything labelled with different words: a butcher, a chemist, a sign for a train station, arrows going to other places.

'This bit is the village,' I realised aloud, recognising some of the places mentioned, then frowning at words I didn't recognise.

'What's Brendan's?'

'It was a cobblers. It's been closed for years now,' Mrs Maple said, her voice robotic.

'And there's another village, and Reading,' I kept looking, 'What's "ABC"?'

'A cinema.' She had a strange look on her face as she stared at the map too.

'It's like a treasure hunt,' I said excitedly, starting to believe that the tin really would make us rich. 'It's leading us to all these different places. I wonder why?' I frowned, looking up. It seemed odd to have this map in the tin with no explanation as to why. Maybe the other items meant something.

'What do you think it means?' I asked.

'Hmm… it is peculiar,' she said, eyes sliding from my face as she went to take the map back. 'Well, let's put it all away.'

'Maybe it's like a mystery we need to solve,' I said slowly, returning to the items on the table.

Picking up the photo of the man, I stared at it. Maybe he was a spy or something and he'd buried it in the garden? 'Who was he?' I asked.

Mrs Maple licked her lips, her finger and thumb rubbing together. 'He was my father,' she said.

'Cool!' I stared back at the man and suddenly I could see a similar-shaped nose, something in his faraway expression that was just like her. 'What did he do?'

Mrs Maple took the photo from me and tipped her head, 'He worked in road construction.'

My shoulders dropped. Not exactly a job for a spy.

'He died before I was born,' she said, her tone soft as she returned the photo to the tin.

'What of?' I knew it was probably rude to ask but this could be an important clue.

'In a motorcycle accident, he loved them apparently. So, I never knew him.'

'That's sad. I miss my dad sometimes, even though…' My throat felt funny, tighter, and I stopped. I could feel my face getting really hot and wanted to change the subject. 'So, was all this stuff his? Did he take your mum's tin and bury it, maybe?' I asked, looking at the things in front of me. They didn't seem like things a man who built roads would own though: a necklace, a flowery brush, an old postcard with a deep orange sunset peeking above a massive rock, all flat on top.

'No, no, not his – no.'

Why did I get the sense Mrs Maple was holding out on me?

'So, your mum did?'

Mrs Maple didn't answer and I picked up the map, studying it again. There must be more clues here. 'We should visit these places.'

'I'm not sure…'

'It might be fun. I haven't gone anywhere since we arrived, and maybe we'll find out more…'

'Maybe…' Mrs Maple said, her voice uncertain. She seemed in a mysterious kind of mood. 'We could.'

'I've literally only been to the school and that totally sucks.'

'Does it?' Mrs Maple looked surprised and I felt myself get hot in the face.

'Well, it's OK, I haven't really… some of the kids, you see…'

'Has it not been an easy start?'

'Well, sort of, I mean…' It was my turn to look a bit shifty.

Mrs Maple stared right at me with her pale blue eyes, 'You can tell me, you know.'

Something about her expression made me want to talk. Mum had been so distracted she barely noticed I didn't want to go to school, and I didn't talk about any of it when I got home, just headed straight to my room and flipped through a textbook because there wasn't even any TV to watch to help me forget.

'A couple of the kids aren't that nice,' I admitted, 'but I can handle it, it's fine.'

Mrs Maple rested a hand on my shoulder. Her touch made me jump a little but there was a kind look in her eyes. 'I'm sorry to hear that, Billy. I never went to school, I was home-schooled by my mother, but I imagine that might be difficult.'

'What's home school?'

Mrs Maple's eyebrows lifted. 'What it sounds like. I stayed at home for lessons. My mother taught me everything, even arranging the examinations I'd need to take.'

'Were you sick?' I asked. I didn't know anyone who didn't go to school. I thought it was the law – Mum was always telling me I'd get in trouble if I didn't go.

'No,' Mrs Maple said, her words slower, 'No, I wasn't sick. My mother felt that she could give me a good education.'

'She must have been clever then.' I didn't want to be rude to Mum but I wasn't sure she'd be able to tell me everything I needed to know. Last year, she'd helped me with my maths and I'd still got all the answers wrong.

'She was a wonderful teacher, she taught me all about literature and history and we did scientific experiments at this kitchen table.' Mrs Maple looked off into the distance, a small smile on her face.

'That sounds cool. And no PE,' I added. No PE and no Daniel and his mates. That sounded even better, though our home wasn't exactly filled with anything interesting.

'And no other children,' she said, and then she stopped looking happy and her mouth joined together in a thin line. 'I'm sorry you're finding school difficult,' she added quickly, that funny look on her face, like she'd been about to say more.

There was a silence which got a bit awkward and I looked back at the map for something to say. 'So, can we go to the cinema next time?' I pointed to the tiny square in the top right of the map, a small label saying 'ABC'.

Mrs Maple took a breath. She seemed almost worried. Maybe she didn't like the cinema or thought I would just want to see films she'd hate, but then her face cleared.

'Why not?' she said, a small smile appearing on her face, 'I suppose it might be fun.'

Chapter 11

ELSIE

Why had she agreed to it? Would it simply be an excuse for an excursion, something light-hearted, a chance to take a trip down memory lane with someone by her side? Billy had seemed so lost in the little village, missing London, his father, his best friend and this was an opportunity to show him some of the places that had once meant so much to her. And yet...

She turned over, readjusting herself on the pillow, her hip hurting, turned back again. She couldn't sleep.

She recognised many of the places, spots where they'd spent time together. But not all of them held happy memories. One small square meant so much more. She pushed her fist into her pillow as she tried again to get comfortable. She couldn't stop thinking about it though, the tiny details painstakingly painted in miniature. Elsie exhaled in the dark. She didn't want to think about these things, she'd carefully constructed her day around small rituals that made the time pass, lessened the pain. Would enough time ever pass? She thought then of previous trips to places on the map, her chest aching with the images that she conjured.

She lay awake, staring at the ceiling of her small square room. It was no good, she knew she would be restless all night; perhaps a mug of hot milk would help. She reached to switch on her lamp and swung her legs over the single bed, padding across to fetch her dressing gown from its hook. Opening her door, she stood stock-still, not wanting to move over the threshold.

The door opposite was closed, as it always was, the marks in the wood so familiar to her after all these years, the swirl of the grain above the doorknob like a large brown eye, a small dent in the middle of one of the wooden panels where a workman had lost his grip on the wardrobe he'd been carrying. She stood in front of it, her hand reaching out to place a palm on the door.

She could push it open, she could move inside, sit there for a while, and yet she stayed, frozen in the stairwell, the bulb overhead dull, the house breathing in and out. A cough through the walls from next door made her startle. The moment passed and she moved carefully down the narrow staircase, one hand on the banister.

She kept the kitchen in darkness, the fridge throwing a shaft of light onto the floor, flashing up the items on the dresser. A hint of red. The inside filled with all those things. All those secrets. She grabbed the milk and moved across to the oven.

The gas flared into life and she warmed her hot milk, stirring slowly, her reflection pale in the window opposite, the garden in darkness beyond. The red tin sat on the dresser behind her; she could feel its presence as she poured the steaming milk into her mug, switched off the gas, returned the milk carton to the fridge.

She took a breath and picked the tin up, carrying it across to the kitchen table and placing it down gently. Biting her lip, she wrapped her dressing gown tight around herself and sat down.

The lid came away easily and she stared at the top of the small pile, picking up her mug and taking a sip. She was comforted by the warm milk, a taste from her childhood, her mother's hand on her brow, soothing her back to a dreamless sleep. 'My Elsie,' she would whisper in the dark, 'my precious girl.'

Elsie swiped at her eyes, a whisper in the room, 'I was your Elsie, wasn't I?'

Her eyes were dragged down to the blanket that lay folded on the top. She lifted it out, set it to one side, a tremble in her hand.

It uncovered the bag of boiled sweets, the bright discs inside a shot of colour. Her mother always set aside the green ones for Elsie, her favourite. Elsie knew they were her mother's favourite too but that never stopped her passing them straight to her daughter. The thought lifted her mouth but then she saw the photo underneath and the smile slid from her face.

The face of her father stared up at her, his expression serene as he gazed to the side. She hadn't thought about him in years. She traced the picture as she sat there, a man she had never known, wondering at the sound of his voice, his accent, his smell – engine oil, perhaps? Woodsmoke? Did he have big hands? Would he have grown a beard in later life? What type of father might he have been; what might have changed had he lived? Everything, she thought sadly, as she placed the photo to one side.

Her mother hadn't talked about him a lot. Elsie hadn't realised that was strange. Devoid of school friends and playmates and relatives, she wasn't used to chatter from other children about their fathers. It was simply her and her mother: two peas in a pod.

As a teenager though, Elsie had grown curious. Who was the man who made up half of her? Her mother had met him at a tea dance, apparently, in 1955. Their first dance was to 'Secret Love'. Yet it wasn't one of the LPs in her mother's small collection. Her mother told her that he loved tinkering with machines, his hands and forearms permanently smeared with black streaks, making her laugh when he held her face in his and left marks on her cheeks. He could be quiet, detached, leave for long walks. He was excited about being a father. He didn't have siblings, only parents who lived in Norfolk, who visited them once. They didn't approve of the match. And then he had gone out on a wet day, his motorcycle had slipped from under him and he had died there in the road. Her mother had stayed in the house they had bought together and two months later, she had given birth to Elsie at home: 'The most wonderful thing that ever happened to me.'

Elsie picked out the square of yellowed paper, the childish drawing she must have drawn more than fifty years ago, two stick figures holding hands. Two peas in a pod.

Had it been the most wonderful thing, she wondered, as she stared down at the red tin, the china paddle brush, the blanket and the black-and-white photo of a baby. Had it?

*

Everyone should be loved like this, have a person who is interested in every small moment, every thought, every memory. Who sits back and listens, asks questions; an excuse to learn more. It is life-changing to get the sense that you are that important to someone. That is always what you did for me: let me think that I was endlessly fascinating even when I was just boring you about the weather, the spring bulbs I'd planted, our trip to the village pantomime.

We would sit and talk about the past, and the future. We would make plans.

There was that day, in the house, when we had pulled the LP collection out, you browsing the big, black records before selecting a favourite. The scratch of the needle as the turntable started to spin, the crackle at the start of the track and then the whole room filling with the unmistakable opening notes of 'Twist and Shout'. You pulled me up off the sofa with two hands, dragged me into the middle of the carpet and, watched by a hundred china figurines, you taught me how to jive. The unfamiliar sight of you shaking your hips, twisting your feet and body lower, lower, lower to the music as you showed me different moves.

I felt self-conscious at first but your expression was so carefree and enthusiastic that I followed your shouted instructions, let you set the needle back to the start, felt tiny beads of sweat at my hairline as we twisted, jived and danced like lunatics in the middle of a room where I knew every mark and item but didn't recognise this new me.

How I felt like I could burst with the thrumming beat of the song, the happiness of the moment. You had crooned in a terrible, too-high voice and I felt an ache in my stomach as I laughed and laughed, stopping to grip my sides. Imagining in that moment a future where we'd do nothing but be together, playing records and jiving in our living room without a care in the world.

Chapter 12

BILLY

I wasn't in the mood any more to go to the ABC cinema on the map, panicking when I realised someone might see me with an old lady. That was all I needed. But Mrs Maple was already standing in her porch dressed in her coat when Mum dropped me off with a wave.

'I'm taking my reading glasses,' Mrs Maple announced as she closed the door, 'and a few items we might need.'

She was talking faster than normal, her fist squeezing the handle of her cream leather bag, which was massive and full. I wondered why she was being weird and what she thought she would need for a trip to the cinema.

'Are you going like that?' she asked, her mouth a thin line as she looked at me.

I glanced down at my jeans, a hole in the knee, my faded T-shirt, and gave a small shrug, not wanting to admit that my choice at our new house was made up of one other pair of trousers and about three T-shirts, most sat in the laundry basket. We'd left my favourite navy T-shirt with a pin man on the front in London and Mum said Dad wouldn't be able to send it. That had caused another row.

It was why I was in such a bad mood. I didn't know why I was so angry sometimes. And Mum had barely noticed anything going on at school. Yesterday, I'd been walking out of the gates with Becky. She'd been telling me about a group of them who were going to hang out down on the meadow that weekend but then Daniel had appeared with Max and Javid close behind and he'd followed us down the road making kissing noises so Becky got totally embarrassed and didn't tell me what time, just turning down a road even though I didn't think she lived down that one.

'Well,' Mrs Maple said, fiddling with the collar of her coat, 'let's head off. If we leave now, we should make the 11.17 a.m. train. I wrote out the outgoing and return times from the schedule outside the station yesterday.'

'OK.'

'And I packed some snacks. For the journey.'

'How far is Reading?' I asked, thinking it was close and wondering why we would need snacks. Mum had popped there when I was at school, something to do with a solicitor. It sounded well boring and she hadn't explained much about it anyway.

'Eight minutes.' Mrs Maple flushed. 'But they are to last all morning.'

'Alright...' I said. My stomach rumbled. Snacks or not, I hoped she'd buy us popcorn. Mum and I had had more toast for breakfast and shared a banana before her shift, although she'd said she'd get some tips today and had promised to buy us pizza later on.

We walked to the train station in silence, skirting puddles from heavy rain in the night. The café was pretty busy, steamed-up windows hiding most of the faces, and my heart raced as I prayed no one from school would see me. The florist, the small supermarket... each time I felt my chest tighten. A lady was peering at us out of the chemist window and Elsie muttered something as she noticed her too.

'Oh goodness! Billy, walk quicker.'

Too late, the lady with the crazy coloured hair had stepped into the street. 'Elsie, I thought that was you.' Her eyes were smudged a bit underneath and she kept staring at Elsie and back at me. 'And this is…?'

'Billy.' Elsie sighed and I wondered how they knew each other. Probably an old lady thing, but now I thought about it, I'd never really seen Elsie with friends or anything – it was always just her.

Not that I thought she was friends with this woman, who had sucked in her mouth. 'Billy. I haven't seen you before. A relation?' she asked Elsie and I wasn't sure what she was getting at.

'Neighbour,' Elsie replied quietly.

I could see she was sort of struggling so I piped up, 'We're going to the cinema!'

The woman's eyes got even rounder. 'The cinema in the day, what a luxury! Some of us have to get on.'

I didn't like her.

'We need to catch a train,' I said, realising Elsie had gone quiet and tugging on her arm. 'Come on, Mrs Maple…' And when we were far enough away, 'Mrs Maple, who was *that*?'

'A busybody,' Elsie muttered and that made me laugh.

'Not a fan?' I giggled.

Elsie blushed. 'Get on.'

Finally, we reached the station, where a man sat on the nearby bench with his nose in a newspaper and a couple of older girls I didn't recognise were all waiting.

'Made it,' Mrs Maple said, giving me money for the ticket machine. 'Two day-returns, off-peak apparently. Will you sort it? It was a man in a booth in my day, not this confusing thing,' she added, staring at the screen and the card slot.

Shrugging, I pressed the right buttons, pushed the coins through and the machine spat out our tickets.

'You're a good boy,' she said in a delighted voice as I handed them over. 'I shall keep them in case there is a ticket inspector.'

The train appeared, the carriage half-empty, and we shared one of the tables. Within a minute Mrs Maple got out a small Tupperware box from her cream bag which she opened and passed to me. I peered inside, heart sinking at a few sad-looking raisins and four custard creams.

'I'm alright,' I said, passing it back and patting my tummy. 'Big breakfast,' I explained when her face fell.

Reading was busy: smelling of engine oil and coffee, cigarette butts on the pavement outside the station. A cyclist passed, a taxi horn blared up ahead and Mrs Maple was talking to me as I stared around at the Saturday shoppers, a child crying with his mum, a man in a sleeping bag in a doorway.

It looked a bit like a part of London and I felt my throat thicken. Bending down, I pretended I was doing up a shoelace.

'The station, well, I knew they had modernised but… and the cinema used to be… it is rather… gosh, that is…'

I straightened, realising Mrs Maple was seriously confused. The lines on her face deepened as she started to walk, stopping to stare down the side streets before heading back the other way. We should have brought the hand-drawn map along.

Swallowing my homesickness, I caught up with her. 'Mrs Maple, are you alright? Are we heading the right way?'

'To be honest,' she admitted, moving us into the doorway of a closed-down furniture shop, smeared glass and dust beyond it, 'I haven't the foggiest where we are. Reading town centre is transformed. I… It's unbelievable. I can't recall a thing.'

'Alright, well, we can ask someone. Someone in the station, perhaps?'

'What a good idea, I hadn't thought of that. They are bound to have an Information Desk.'

In the end it was the homeless man in the sleeping bag who helped us out, Mrs Maple stopping in front of him. 'Young man, could you assist us? The last time I was in Reading John Major was Prime Minister.'

I almost dived behind her.

The man sat up. 'Course. Remember the Town Hall?'

'Yes,' Mrs Maple said, the first smile since we'd arrived.

'Well,' he pointed, 'keep that on your left and follow the road down and through to the Oracle shopping centre…'

He continued, Mrs Maple nodding and thanking him, dropping a folded five-pound note in his cup. 'What a very nice man,' she said as we moved away, my mouth dropping open as I followed her. Where was Mrs Maple the battleaxe? The man had grinned at her! Told her to have a lovely day!

'Is that really true?' I asked as we moved through the streets, the people thinning out as we headed down the hill, around the corner and over a bridge, the river grey beneath us.

'Is what true?'

'That Reading's eight minutes away from the village but you haven't been here since, like…' I wasn't sure about John somebody. 'A long time ago.'

'Oh, look,' Mrs Maple said, bringing her hands together, 'we must be close.'

A row of chain restaurants the man had mentioned appeared and there, on the end of the block, stood a huge Multiplex cinema, adverts flashing up on screens, a row of cash machines to the side.

'So, when the map was drawn that was a long time ago…?' I asked, curious who had drawn it and why.

'Yes, a long time ago now,' Mrs Maple said, a frown appearing, wearing a look as if she didn't want to talk about it.

'So, who drew it then?'

'Hmm…' She could *totally* hear me.

'Who drew the map?'

'Oh, look, there's a John Lewis.'

'Because maybe the map is trying to lead us somewhere?'

'My mother drew the map,' she finally said, looking at me.

'Your mum? Why?'

She lifted one hand and rubbed at her neck. 'I'm not sure.' I gave her a doubtful look. It was like when she told me it had been her mum's tin. What was the big secret? Why had her mum filled biscuit tins with strange things and buried them?

'Well, she must have had a good reason.'

'I think,' Mrs Maple said slowly, her eyes not quite meeting mine, 'she must have wanted me to revisit all the places we had gone as a child.'

'But why?'

'Oh look, a cinema,' she cried, pointing over my shoulder, 'and although it isn't the one we frequented, we could go in?' she said, turning to me. 'It is a cinema at least.'

I thought of the map, the building in the top right labelled 'ABC'. The whole point of our journey. If she wanted to revisit the past didn't it mean we should look for the other cinema? Why was she acting so odd?

'We could try and find the old one?'

Mrs Maple waved a hand away. 'No, no, let's watch something,' she said, a new energy in her. 'No need to always live in the past.'

Shrugging, I agreed – there was a massive thick grey cloud above us and I didn't want to be running around lost in the rain.

We chose a film, a comedy with talking dogs which normally I'd say was too young for me, but Mrs Maple didn't want to watch an action movie that I thought looked good.

'It's a 12 certificate,' she said, one eyebrow arching in my direction.

'The dog one then,' I replied, aware of a group of older lads looking over in my direction, suddenly just wanting to get into the darkened room.

She rolled her eyes, a small smile on her face, 'That's a better idea. Honestly, Billy, you'd get nightmares.'

'Mrs Maple, I'm ten, not six.'

'All the same…'

I watched 12s all the time, even 15s when Dad was home, although Mum did get really angry with him once when I had woken in the middle of the night screaming about zombies.

Mrs Maple bought the tickets and a huge tub of sweet popcorn and asked me if I wanted a drink too. The Coke would last me all day.

'Aren't you getting something?'

Mrs Maple tapped her nose. 'I packed my peppermint tea in a thermos,' she said, looking at her wrist. 'And look at that, it's almost time!'

Time for what I wasn't exactly sure but I wanted to sit down and make a start on my popcorn – a couple of pieces had already fallen and bounced on the carpet. The talking dogs couldn't be that bad.

The cinema was cool, with plush leather seats and loads of leg room, and it was pretty empty as we moved into our row, the screen large and looming in front of us.

'It is enormous,' Mrs Maple said, eyes boggling at it. 'The screen's about ten times the size I remember.'

It was weird seeing someone so amazed by normal things. It was obvious that Mrs Maple really hadn't been out and about much. It made me feel a little bit warmer towards her.

'These are our seats,' I said, letting her sit down.

I pushed myself back in the leather, pressed the button on the armrest to make it tilt and as it started to move, Mrs Maple leapt up again. 'How are...? What the...? Oh!'

It had clearly blown her mind.

'Alright?'

'But...' Then she realised I had made it happen and stared at me, wonder in her voice. 'Show me how to do that.'

'It's that button there,' I said, and, as she went to sit, I pressed it and the leg part went up and that toppled her into the seat. Before the film had even begun I was clutching myself laughing as Mrs Maple, legs stuck right up, squirmed like a beetle that couldn't right itself, calling out in her seat, 'Enough now, Billy.' Then, as the tilting stopped and she realised I was chuckling, she started to laugh too. 'Oh, what do I look like?' she said, dabbing at her face.

We had to be shushed when the trailers began.

Chapter 13

ELSIE

She had hardly slept the evening before fretting about the upcoming trip to the cinema. Setting aside her nerves of the day itself: the strange prospect of returning to her past, a whole day with Billy, she was nervous it might encourage him to find out more about the things in the red tin. Would he start to ask more questions? Would he want to explore every place on the map? That would be impossible and Elsie stayed awake worrying at the thought. Then just as she'd dropped off she had woken, convinced she could hear crying through the walls of next door.

Today, she felt sluggish as she made her bed, leaving her room to pause, as always, outside the door opposite, one hand reaching for the doorknob, the brushed brass. Her fingers paused centimetres from it. She felt a painful lurch inside her, the room such a physical reminder of her grief. 'I'm not being silly,' she said, starting down the stairs, defensive.

She needed to get ready. A promise was a promise and the poor boy must have been getting bored: she knew her life wasn't exactly suited to an energetic ten-year-old child. And she still felt guilty for shouting at him in the garden; he had accepted her apology with grace. She was surprised how relieved she had felt that she had the chance to make things right.

Today, she should be continuing the jigsaw, there were some complicated clouds to complete. She gulped down the anxious feeling she got every time plans changed. She'd had time to prepare at least and that always made her feel better, more in control of things. She had written down their itinerary the day before, bought snacks for the travel, a thermos for her peppermint tea. She had polished her reading glasses and had packed her bag early that morning, triple-checking she had everything she might need. She was just popping in a plaster just in case the walk gave her or Billy blisters when there was a knock on the door.

Samantha was already halfway down the road to her shift, a wave goodbye as Billy slouched inside. He was rather scruffy and she was a little disappointed he hadn't made more effort for their big adventure. He had scowled at her when she had politely asked about his clothing, so she didn't push it.

Attending the cinema with her mother all those years ago had been quite the occasion. They would wear their best clothes and would only go once or twice a year and she would spend the months afterwards re-enacting everything she could remember from the show. She remembered her mother had to ban her from singing 'Sixteen Going On Seventeen' for a month because she sung it so much after watching *The Sound of Music* in 1965. Elsie knew it wasn't like that any more, the kids these days had DVDs and streaming – Billy had told her, it was one of the things he missed about London. To her though the cinema was where magic happened and she had been transported to a glamorous world of technicolor.

Would the cinema be the same? ABC Reading? She licked her lips, nervous to be returning. She felt a wave of grief almost cripple her as she started down the road to the station. She was jittery by the time they arrived in Reading, the whole place another world. The station itself was a futuristic maze of escalators, shops, lifts and more in places that hadn't even existed all those years ago.

In many ways the changes made her relax a little, unable to reconcile the setting with her memories. By the time they found their way to the cinema she was feeling more confident. The sad nostalgia that so much had gone was replaced with an amazement at the changes. The slick, streamlined buildings, the cycle lanes, the lights, the glossy department stores... none of it how she remembered. And she felt as if she could start enjoying the day, not worried about being floored by a memory any more.

She had a wonderful time. She had never really thought of herself as a dog person but after that movie who wouldn't be?

As she pulled back the curtains in her bedroom the day after their trip, she felt so much lighter. Billy was due to appear after school, his mother agreeing to extra shifts for her hard-nosed manager Richard, who sounded rather charmless and kept changing things at the last moment. Elsie had written a 'To Do' list for the garden and after their successful cinema outing, she was hopeful that things might be a little easier with the boy. Certainly she had to admit to forming a small soft spot for him.

The tell-tale fire-engine red of the tin flashed in her peripheral vision as she made herself some tea. She thought of the items inside, the string of pearls that her mother had worn. How she had loved them. She hadn't been too fussed by appearances but had always looked smart, even when it had just been them on their own in the house.

Billy was quiet as he appeared, pulling off his school sweatshirt in the porch, perhaps wanting to leave the day behind him, to shed school. It was clear he wasn't happy there, his mouth downcast as she politely enquired after his lessons.

'Fine,' he mumbled, accepting the glass of pear squash, a sad expression on his face as she handed him his own plate of custard creams. She didn't probe further; perhaps he would open up more in the garden. She was excited to get back out there with him.

Billy seemed distracted today though, swinging his legs back and forward on the chair, barely touching his biscuits. It wasn't quite time for the garden and he was fast losing patience, spinning his teaspoon on his plate so that she almost snapped at him to stop it. Instead she got up.

'Cards?' Elsie asked, remembering the pack in the tin, half-forgotten games merging into one.

'Alright...' Billy said, even more dejected, hands in his lap.

They played cards – Strip Jack Naked, a two-player game – but Billy, after his initial amusement, didn't seem too enamoured, and Elsie regretted having asked him. She should have just ignored the timings and gone to the garden with him. She had loved to play cards with her mother, had played endless rounds, pestering her, and when her mother was too busy using the pack to line up rows and rows of cards in a game of patience.

'Is it time yet?' Billy asked, chin in one hand, not even hiding his boredom as he placed down another King.

'That's three cards I owe you,' Elsie replied brightly, not liking things disrupted, because then everything would be all out.

'Shall we check out another place on the map, see where it leads us?' Billy asked, standing suddenly, his cards forgotten.

Elsie couldn't help a worried look at her watch. 'I thought we were going to select some new spring bulbs.'

But Billy had already moved across to the dresser. Elsie had left the map out, forgetting to put it back in the tin, staring at it for an age, her tea long cold that morning.

'How about here?' Billy pointed to a square in a small patch of bright green, like a chopped-up field, houses in a semi-circle around it.

Elsie moved round to see where he was pointing, her mind already filling with images from the past, how that map triggered them.

'Well, I'm not sure,' she said, biting her lip.

'Come on, you can show me how to get there. Mum keeps telling me I need to get to know my new home.' He half-spat the last word and Elsie felt a pang for this boy who seemed so at sea, his accent a constant reminder that he was from somewhere else.

'Come on, Mrs Maple,' Billy pleaded, seeing her waver.

She thought of her enjoyment at their trip to the cinema. Some of this map was clearly meant to be a wonderful walk through special memories. 'On one condition,' she said, putting one finger in the air, 'you must call me Elsie.'

He screwed up his nose.

'I'm serious.'

'Alright then,' he said, energy restored, 'come on, Ells.'

Elsie made a face, 'No, no, that won't do!'

He burst out laughing at her horrified expression and the stilted atmosphere of the past hour melted away.

'Come on, you horror!' she said, reaching out to ruffle his hair.

They both looked surprised at the action.

It was a beautiful afternoon, the days longer now, the temperature rising. They moved down an alley edged by lush green bushes, dodging stinging nettles and brambles as Billy told her a little more about London and a boy called Liam who had been his 'best mate'. He told her that Liam had saved money up to buy Billy a new tyre for his BMX bicycle and pretended his mum had given him the money. Liam sounded like a nice boy. Getting outside seemed to loosen Billy's tongue and he stopped intermittently to point out things he'd seen.

'Eagle!' he cried.

'A red kite,' Elsie corrected.

'A bee!'

'Wasp.'

They emerged from the path, the village behind them, fields and woods stretched out before them. On their right was a field of allotments: spades sticking out of the ground, water butts, small sheds, the odd lone gardener.

'What are they doing?' Billy watched a man in a beige sunhat carry a watering can back to his patch.

'It's the village allotments,' Elsie replied, moving through the gate to the field behind. Billy, however, had stopped dead on the track, gazing around at the different sections. There were radishes, lettuces, rows of asparagus, seemingly bare patches, holes ready for something to be sowed. 'Billy?'

'Coming,' he started, joining her at the gate. 'Hey, a rabbit...' he said, pointing quickly as a rabbit peeked out from the hedgerow and then dived back inside.

'You'll probably see a few of them.'

They skirted the back of the allotments, Billy amazed at the sight of twenty or so chickens scraping and strutting over an area of dirt, laughing as one rushed up to the wire fence to stare at him. It gave Elsie the seed of a thought.

They were headed to the old pillbox, the square on the map that Billy had pointed out. A place Elsie had played in as a child, hiding there as if it were her personal den. She watched now as Billy ran through the long grass, chasing another rabbit that bounded away from him.

'It's like the zoo here,' he said, eyes wide, taking in the field of cows beyond, the birds circling overhead.

Elsie realised his world of concrete, endless streets and countless people was a hundred miles away from this view: the different shades of green, the dense wood beyond, the hazy blue sky, enormous overhead. For the first time in a long while she could see it through fresh eyes and she realised how she had always taken it for granted: how lucky she should have felt, growing up in this beautiful countryside. She had always focused on the smallness of it: the two-bedroomed house they lived in, the handful of shops on the tiny high street, the same bench they fed ducks from, the feeling that life ended at the edge of the village.

Billy was fascinated by the pillbox, Elsie explaining the concrete structure had been built in case of a German invasion in the Second World War. His eyes were wide as he contemplated a world of guns, spies and battles, so far removed from this sleepy, sunny day.

'The doorway is blocked up now but I used to play around here, imagining screaming from the enemy that arrived on the Thames. Mother taught me all about the Second World War: the preparations for an invasion, a German army, they dug anti-tank ditches all the way along here, stretching right into Theale…'

Billy followed her arm, mouthing 'Cool!' as he moved around the dull block, an eyesore in this rural stretch.

Whispering, Elsie told him to stand still and he froze as if she had spotted the approaching German army. 'Muntjac,' she said in a hiss as close by, a baby deer peeked out from behind a cluster of trees. Billy followed her gaze, his excitement palpable from the drawing in of his breath. They watched as the deer picked at the ground, oblivious to its audience before a cry overhead startled it, neck raised suddenly, bounding back to cover.

A woman in large sunglasses, her blond hair tied up, was approaching, pushing a pram along the narrow, flattened grass of the path. Elsie realised she recognised her as she moved closer. Billy was off again, racing around the pillbox pretending to fire machine guns, theatrically throwing himself in the long grass: he obviously needed to blow off steam. Where were his friends, Elsie wondered sadly, realising that he looked just as she had at that age: enjoying the day by escaping into his mind. How had that worked out for her?

She was miles away as the woman passed, muttering a quiet, 'Hi.'

It was Scarlet, the librarian who always tried to help and waved at her in the street. Elsie felt a strange sensation of seeing someone out of context. This woman was walking along dressed in a bright pink vest top and jeans when normally she was in something a little more staid, sat at the desk near the library entrance, squinting at the computer screen or organising the returned items. Her hair was up in the high bun again. Elsie realised as she looked at the woman and then the pram that this woman who had spoken to her every week for the last year or two had a baby. And Elsie had never even thought to ask. It would explain why she hadn't been in the library for a few months last year.

'Hello,' she replied, shame making her embarrassed.

'It's lovely out here, isn't it?' Scarlet said, pausing and adjusting a blanket over the body of a chubby-faced baby on the edge of sleep. 'Is that your grandson?' She smiled, looking at Billy star-fished on the grass, staring up at the scud of clouds overhead.

'No,' Elsie said, the shortness to the reply making Scarlet shrink back a fraction. 'What's the baby's name?' Elsie indicated the pram, trying to fix things. Scarlet had always been nice to her, polite and never badgering, pointing out that month's recommended reads but otherwise staying silent. She must have guessed that Elsie didn't know she had had a baby.

'Harry. I've always liked it.' Scarlet smiled, barely any lines appearing, her forehead completely smooth.

'A lovely name. Fit for a prince!' Elsie said, frowning inwardly at her own terrible joke. 'How are you finding him?'

Scarlet sighed, a sneaky look at the pram in case Harry took offence. 'It's been good. I mean, not much sleep, but he is a sweetie.'

'He looks it,' replied Elsie. Harry rewarded her by waking and giving her a bashful smile.

'He's a flirt, like his dad.' Scarlet laughed.

Elsie hadn't even known Scarlet had a partner. She must remember to ask after them next time she was in the library.

'Well, I hope you enjoy the sunshine. I love these warmer days,' Scarlet said, tilting her head towards the sky, her skin peachy in the light.

'Me too. A great time for the garden.'

'My mum loves gardening,' Scarlet replied, a concerned look as Harry cried out, kicking up the blanket. 'I haven't inherited the green fingers though, every plant pot in our house has died a death on my watch.'

'My mum loved the garden too,' Elsie said fondly, feeling a familiar ache in her chest. 'But you're too busy for all that,' she added kindly, watching as Scarlet fussed again over the pram.

The sentence was rewarded with a smile.

'Do you have kids?' Scarlet asked.

Elsie would normally have responded in a curt manner but today, she felt different. Today, she found herself simply shaking her head. 'I'm sad to say I do not.'

Scarlet's smooth forehead crinkled. 'Oh, I'm sorry, I didn't mean to pry.'

Elsie waved her concern away. 'It's alright. The chance of all that disappeared a long time ago.' She glanced across at Billy, who was zigzagging down the path ahead.

Scarlet's face relaxed and then Harry wailed again. 'I better get going or he'll only get worse,' she apologised. 'But you take care, Mrs Maple. I'll look forward to seeing you in the library soon.'

'It's Elsie,' Elsie said for the second time that day, feeling the tiniest glow inside her.

'Elsie,' Scarlet repeated as she moved away, and something about the way she said it made Elsie want to weep. Apart from Mr Porter the butcher, no one used her first name – she'd been Mrs Maple for twenty-eight years.

Chapter 14

BILLY

Mum was literally always working now. We were meant to have a day together, it was half term and she'd promised, but then stupid Dick had phoned and she hadn't even argued with him. She zipped up her skirt quickly, apologising, but this felt just like all the times Dad would tell me we could go to the trampoline centre, or go-karting, or bowling and then he'd spend the day smelling funny, lying on the sofa taking paracetamol. Mum had always kept her promises but now it was just her she was doing that a lot less, like bits of Dad had come with her.

Thinking about Dad still made me sad and sort of confused because sometimes other memories of him popped into my head that I didn't want. I'd stopped asking when he was coming, knowing that Mum had left him. She asked me if I missed him, and I did, and then she cried a little and said she was sorry and that she would sort something out and could I be patient and she'd explain. I hated Mum crying. I'd heard her once right in the middle of the night, like I used to sometimes in London, so I'd given her a hug and told her I was OK, even if I wasn't.

So, I was headed next door. Mrs Maple always said yes to looking after me – I don't think she really ever had any plans and I never heard anyone else in her house. I didn't mind going there as much now because

Mrs Maple was a little more chilled but I still had to be on my best behaviour and sometimes I'd do something that would upset her, like if I touched some of her china things or asked too many questions, and she'd get that hard look on her face and her mouth would go all small, like she was trying to stop from snapping at me.

Today was warmer and I wanted to wear shorts but my shorts are back in London and Mum said I'd have to wait because she couldn't go shopping and really, I knew it was because we didn't have a lot of money. She came back last week with a T-shirt that I knew was from the village charity shop because it had been in the window when I'd walked past. She pretended she'd just taken off the tags though and I looked at her 'like I wasn't born yesterday' as Mrs Maple would say.

I still can't really call her Elsie; she asks me to but it sounds all funny. Sometimes I call her 'Ells' because she looks really mad and then sort of laughs and it makes me chuckle. She can be so weird.

Today when we got to hers I could see her sat at her desk in the front room with a funny look on her face and she was holding her pen. She took a while to answer the door, purple ink still on her fingers.

'Billy,' her voice was faraway, as if she was still in the front room at her desk, not stood in front of us in her porch.

'I don't know how to repay you,' Mum started and Mrs Maple batted her words away with a hand and 'Don't be silly, you get on.'

'Thank you. Love you, Billy,' Mum said and I am glad it was only Mrs Maple watching it as I felt heat in the roots of my hair.

An hour later we were sat in the garden. Mrs Maple had planned to show me how to deadhead some spring bulbs but instead we were both sat on the chairs on the patio enjoying the sun.

'I've got an idea,' she said suddenly, and moved into the kitchen.

My heart sank as I realised she would probably return with a plate of custard creams. But she came back with a sheet of paper in her hands and I realised it was the map. 'Look,' she said, lifting it to me, 'we need to get going.'

I didn't ask questions – she never normally seemed to like the map, just followed her around her kitchen as she put various things in her basket, a glass bottle, a bag that rustled, and then moved to her porch, rooting around in the trunk until she pulled out a tartan rug.

'Come on, look lively!' She ushered me out the door. She sneezed. 'Hayfever,' she said, stepping onto the pavement. 'You always said my sneezes made you laugh!'

'Pardon?' I replied.

'Oh… oh, nothing…'

We headed down the high street, Mrs Maple marching ahead with an energy I wasn't used to. She seemed determined to lead us somewhere and I wondered where that was, trying to remember the spots on the map.

I was just about to ask when I heard a high-pitched whistle and turned my head in the direction of the noise. Daniel was stood on the other side of the road by the café, two fingers in his mouth, staring straight at me. I felt myself shrink back. Half a term of taunts, laughter and smirks had made sure no one else wanted to speak to me. I was stressed out every time he came near me.

Mrs Maple had stopped and I'd almost walked into her, watching in slow-motion horror as she handed me her basket, sneezing and searching for a tissue. So, there I was, holding the basket over one arm, accompanying an old lady to God knows where. Daniel was laughing, turning back to the café, calling to someone inside.

Get me away from here, I thought, wanting to throw the basket down and run back home.

'Come on, don't dawdle,' Mrs Maple said, taking her basket back.

Dragging my feet along the ground, I followed, my mind taken up with all the things I wished would happen to Daniel. None of them nice.

Mrs Maple looked over her shoulder at me, a small frown on her face. When she ushered me round the corner to a sleek brown building overlooking the meadow, I failed to react to her enthusiastic, 'Ta Da!' A bit hot and now very bothered, I just wanted to go home, get to my room, close the curtains and hide.

Mrs Maple walked over to the door of the building. 'You can rent boats,' she explained. 'We don't have to,' she added in a quick voice, 'you seem a little out of sorts.'

'Nah,' I replied, not wanting to explain it all, embarrassed it was that obvious. 'Boats,' I said, 'cool!'

Her whole body relaxed and I realised this was obviously a bit of a big deal for her. She handed over the money and we were led outside where boats and canoes were moored to the bank of the river, rocking gently side by side, clunking with every ripple, pools of water collected in the bottom.

Mrs Maple chose a rowing boat and the man in the polo shirt helped her in, placing her bag inside a waterproof sack that clipped under the seat. His hand was sandpaper as he helped me on and I wobbled as I sat down sharply on the hard, wooden plank. Passing me an oar, he gave us a gentle push and we floated backwards out onto the river.

'Right,' Mrs Maple was sat behind me calling instructions. 'You set the pace, Billy, and I'll follow you. Oops! Don't direct us into the reeds there, good boy.'

This was dragging me out of my glum mood – I'd never been in a boat before, or on the river. I'd walked over the Thames in London and watched speedboats and ferries move below but this was different. Everything was still and green and made my insides feel calm.

We steered the small white boat slowly down the river, trees dripping into the water either side, reeds clustered along the bank, a bright blue-chested bird flapping manically on the surface of the water before zipping away like a rocket.

'A hummingbird,' Mrs Maple said, her voice filled with wonder as she continued to point out the different sights. The river cut through fields, a forest of trees stretching into the distance, the few clouds reflected in the surface of the water that danced with sunlight.

'Aren't willow trees wonderful, Billy? You know this was the stretch of river that inspired *The Wind in the Willows*.'

I didn't reply, I'd not seen the movie.

'I imagine Mole and Ratty stretched out, chatting in the sunshine. Mother would ask me to make up their conversations.'

This wasn't the first time Mrs Maple had mentioned her mother. It was as if the map was reminding her of these things.

'You've read it of course, Billy,' she called from behind me.

I shook my head.

'That's a shame. I suppose it's all Harry Potter now. Scarlet once told me that was rather a success.'

Truth was, I wasn't much of a reader. I had to read for school and that was enough for me. Reading was boring, and most of the books didn't even have pictures. I didn't say anything to Mrs Maple though 'cos her house had a few bookshelves.

A narrowboat passed us, and a man in a navy blue peaked cap gave us a wave from the back, one hand on a pole. A family of ducks paddled by and we passed a tree, a piece of old rope hanging from a branch.

'That reminds me of a spot further along. We'd swing into the river and go swimming,' Mrs Maple said. She was a lot chattier in a boat. 'We used to swim in our underwear,' she called out, a giggle too.

Alarmed at that thought, I rowed a bit faster, my oar clashing with Mrs Maple's. It was warm but there was no way I was going to strip down to my pants and get in the river, that's gross. It's all greeny-brown and you can't see the bottom: there were probably crocodiles.

'It's time for lunch,' Mrs Maple called a moment later. 'Turn around and help me with the picnic.'

Not custard creams, I silently prayed. Twisting on my seat, the oars trailing in the water as the boat rocked to the side, I gripped the edge.

Mrs Maple struggled a bit to pull out the bag and I felt bad for gripping the side and not helping her. She reached inside, producing bananas, a box of raisins, fresh white rolls and custard creams wrapped up in tin foil. *I knew it.* We sat facing each other, my knees nudging Mrs Maple's as I ate, unable to shake off the bad mood inside me.

Mrs Maple turned to look at two swans and I made my move. 'Oh no, my biscuit!' I said, watching it slowly disappear into the murky water.

Mrs Maple looked back. 'Oh, what a shame, Billy.'

I gave her my most disappointed face.

'You've been very quiet today, Billy. Not seasick?' She tilted her head to the side.

There was barely a breeze as I tore along the edge of the box of raisins, littering the bottom of the boat with tiny pieces of cardboard. Maybe it was the way she was waiting, her eyes kind, or the feeling that we were totally alone that made me want to confess but I found myself opening my mouth, needing to get things off my chest.

'I saw a boy from school on the way,' I explained, 'Daniel.' His name, spat out. 'He's... he's...'

What was he? He was a bully, I thought, my mind full of all the nasty things he did. His names for me, his mimicking my accent, the rumours he spread about me so no one else wanted to talk to me – my mum was a prostitute, my dad was in jail, I had worms, I had nits, I wiped snot on everything, the clothes he made fun of, the feet he tripped.

'No one stands up to him. They all listen and I don't know... it's not going to ever stop. I hate him. And no one cares, the teachers don't even notice...' Now I was talking, I couldn't seem to stop. 'He's got these little mates and they make my life hell and it's not true, any of it, and I swear some of the other kids would hang out with me but they're too frightened. And there's a WhatsApp group apparently called "I hate Billy" and it's just full of them, swapping mean stuff about me. Javid showed me.'

'A What's what?'

I explained, chest heaving up and down: 'It's like texts, like loads of messages you send to a group. And they all just talk about me on it...'

Mrs Maple sat back, eyes going all round, as I went on and on.

'And they say stuff about Mum that isn't true. And I know Dad would want to beat them all up, but he isn't here and Mum says we can't see him even though that's so unfair because *she's* the one that left and he probably misses us loads and I just want to go home and not be in this stupid place and...' I hadn't noticed that the tears had started but there was no stopping them now. 'But you can't tell my mum because she'll hate me for talking about it because she keeps telling me to just let it go and she'll explain later, and she used to enjoy her job and now she works for that Dick so she's always in a bad mood and tired.'

A large bird flew overhead as I faded away, my face damp. Mrs Maple didn't do much, didn't even tell me off for swearing. She just sat there and I looked down, bringing my hands together in my lap, worried she'd be cross with me. Then she leant forward and placed her hand on my knee. 'Oh, Billy,' she said, 'oh dear!'

And there wasn't much more she could say really. It was a small thing but it did make things a tiny bit better. That I had finally said something to someone and she had just listened.

She thought for a moment, placing our rubbish back in the bag and clipping it under the seat again. 'You need something to cheer you up,' she said, and then, with barely any warning, she stood right up so that the boat rocked dangerously from side to side, my hands shooting out to clutch both sides.

And then she jumped, just like that, right over the side, her feet circling for a moment before she hit the water, an enormous splash as freezing-cold droplets sprayed me in the boat.

I leaned over the edge, the boat tilting as I watched her appear, hair flattened and soaked, mouth opening and closing, out of the water. 'So cold!' she gasped.

'You're mental,' I said, with a massive surprise laugh as I watched her breaststroke about the boat, and suddenly I was leaping off the side too and bombing the water, splashing her, and it was freezing and it made me gasp and paddle so fast.

'Oh my God!' I cried, barely able to feel my skin, regretting my jump the moment I was in. 'There's an eel or... something...' I was convinced something brushed my leg. 'Oh my God!'

Mrs Maple was laughing so hard she looked like she might go under.

'What lives in here?' I asked her, unable to get back on the boat now.

'Nothing. Just swim, you silly thing!' she called out. 'Enjoy it.'

We swam and swam, around the little boat, up and down under the willow trees, the water less cold the more I moved, Mrs Maple encouraging me. For a moment we were the only two people in the world and it was just the smooth, cool water, our tiny boat and our shouts of laughter.

Chapter 15

ELSIE

'He's over again later,' Elsie said as Scarlet perched on the edge of the table Elsie was sat at, a pile of books in her arms. She should be at home. She still needed to watch the second half of a movie she had started days ago. Her chalkboard wouldn't get checked. But Elsie didn't want to go. She'd decided to stay in the library today, to read at the desk and engage Scarlet in conversation when she passed by to restack the audiobooks or neaten the children's section. 'We'll be in the garden again.'

'I can see that's where you spend your time.' Scarlet smiled, turning to place one of the books back in its rightful slot. 'You've got a good glow already.'

'Skin damage, more like,' Elsie blushed.

Scarlet had greeted her warmly when she had appeared in the library, asking after Billy almost immediately. Since she had bumped into her by the pillbox Elsie felt that she now could talk more, asking after Harry, who was about to crawl any day now. 'He sort of drags himself along the ground a bit, like he's a man in a desert searching for water,' Scarlet said, pausing from tapping at the front-desk computer to laugh.

Elsie smiled, surprising herself, and then chuckled before telling Scarlet about their boat trip, her jumping in. How they had pushed the boat through the reeds to the bank, clambering up in their heavy, wet clothes to get back in, teeth chattering with cold, the man in the polo shirt staring at them as they stepped out dripping, moved through the village soaked, laughing and leaving a trail of wet footprints behind them.

'I wish I could do more though. It's been hard for him, he seems rather lonely.'

'Bless him! Well, he's lucky to have you looking out for him,' Scarlet said, reaching to pick up some books left on the returned shelf. 'Well, I don't want to disturb you if you're searching for your next read.' That was the moment Elsie decided to stay in the small space, read a chapter or two there.

Elsie watched Scarlet move to the back of the room, wondering why it had taken her so long to talk in a place she visited so often. She must have visited that library every week for the last twenty years. She had convinced herself it was a library, a place to be silent, but she knew this was an excuse. Plenty of people lowered their voices as they chatted with Scarlet or the other librarian, as they renewed their books or rented a DVD.

Feeling more relaxed than ever, she made sure to wave her goodbye when she left. At home, sat at her writing desk, Elsie filled a sheet of paper in her purple ink, the tone brighter than it had been in years, news coming more easily, the usual pang as she walked down the lane towards the postbox a little less painful.

Billy appeared after school, drawing up short when he saw she was not in her usual spot at the table. Elsie had thrown caution to the wind and was already in the garden, out of synch with her usual schedule.

'What about your tea?' Billy asked, clearly so used to Elsie's routines that it made her flush.

'I just felt like gardening,' Elsie said, realising what a slave she had become to her timings, the order of her day.

Today, she wanted them to sow some cosmos, a quick-germinating annual, and then trim the row of box balls next to the patio. She wouldn't allow him near the larger shears, too dangerous for a ten-year-old, but had set aside a small pair of hand shears.

Billy had his gloves and pink apron on before she had even fetched her own gloves.

'We must get you overalls,' she said, seeing him stood in the flowery item.

Billy shrugged. 'Feels like mine now. Anyway, it's only for getting covered in dirt.'

Elsie smiled at him. Such an amenable boy, he deserved friends, and lots of them, she thought as he walked down to the greenhouse and collected the tray of cosmos they were going to plant that day.

He was a great pupil. One of the borders in the garden had been completely transformed and he was constantly asking her questions, some she couldn't answer and had to look up in her ancient book on gardening. She had always done the same thing in the garden, honouring the memory of her mother, but Billy was keen to experiment, wanted to grow vegetables and more. She had been forced to line up some old clay guttering and bought Billy a packet of carrot seeds which were now taking hold.

He was less interested in tending to her clematis and her poppies, but was a huge help with the more physical jobs, removing the ladder or the large spade from her hands with a gentle sigh: 'Come on, Mrs Maple, let me.'

'It's Elsie,' she'd protest every time.

'Alright, Ells, alright, settle down.'

Which always made her laugh.

Watching him work – the atmosphere easy as he mentioned the things he'd done at school, the focus on his lessons and not the other pupils – filled her heart and she was forming a few ideas of her own. Some of the work was hard and boring and she offered him the chance to earn pocket money. 'Good for you to have your own,' she'd said, handing him coins for an hour of weeding or mowing the lawn.

'No, you're alright,' he'd replied, trying to give them back.

'Don't be silly, you're *saving* me money, Billy, I'd only have to hire a gardener,' she said, realising it was the truth, that some of these jobs were now beyond her. That thought made her stomach lurch for a second, but it didn't sting as much as it used to.

Sometimes she asked him about that nasty boy at his school, Daniel, and he would mumble a reply. It certainly didn't seem like things were getting better. She should have said more that day on the boat, offered more wisdom, but what could she really share? She had never been to school herself, there was only ever her mother and her so there were no playground politics, no peers, no friends. She didn't feel that she could help him aside from listen if he wanted to talk.

It started to spit with rain and they ran inside, eating pitta bread and dip, Billy ignoring the small sticks of celery and carrot. His eyes glanced across to the dresser and with no real warning, asked, 'So have you found out any more about what the tin means?'

'Oh,' she said, one hand cupping her neck, rubbing at it. 'Oh, I've hardly thought about it, really,' she said, fiddling now with the bottom of the tablecloth.

'I still don't get why your mum gave you the map of the village,' he said, his small face screwed up.

She answered his first question. 'A lot of the things, the boiled sweets and such,' Elsie said, feeling her insides squeeze, her voice rise a pitch, 'were just lovely memories we had together.' Why did it hurt so much to say that? She thought then of one place on the map, the place she was forever trying not to think about. Had her mother visited that place too? Had that meant the most to her? Was that why it hurt?

'And you never knew your dad?' Billy asked, something changing in his expression.

'No, I never did. My mother was seven months pregnant with me when he was in the motorcycle accident.'

Billy considered that fact. 'That's sad. I bet he was sick if he drove a motorbike.'

Elsie smiled sadly at that simple statement. 'My mother always spoke fondly of him,' she said, 'so yes, I think he probably was "sick".'

Billy always laughed when she used his language. 'What about the other stuff in the tin, the blanket and stuff? What does it all mean?'

Elsie stood up, pretending to need to wash the plate of pitta bread. 'I've no idea,' she said, the words high, strangled.

'Weird.'

'Shall we walk?' Elsie said, suddenly feeling the house was small and dark. 'It looks like the rain's stopped, and I wanted to show you something.' She was aware she was speaking too quickly.

Billy let her, shrugging and following her to the door, where she handed him a cagoule in his size and explained, 'I saw it in a charity shop, thought it might fit for rainy days.'

'Thanks, Mrs M,' Billy replied, taking the navy cagoule and throwing it over himself, tightening the string in the hooded part and grinning at her.

Elsie felt the tension lessen. Billy had already moved on.

Elsie set off, Billy behind her, the narrow alleys between familiar roads soggy underfoot, raindrops clinging to the nettles and grass. Billy excitedly pointed out all the places they had seen drawn on the map. 'That's the church,' he said as they passed, 'and this is the path behind the old fire station.' They wound their way through, the sky a strange mix of colours, a cool blue line on the horizon, fat, grey clouds pushing down on it. Up ahead were the allotments, practically empty, people sheltering from the recent rainfall inside.

'I wanted to bring you here,' Elsie admitted, pushing on the gate and turning immediately right, walking on the narrow space between two flower beds, past a water butt, a compost heap, towards the corner of the allotments. She stopped in front of a large rectangular patch, the soil pockmarked with watery spots and a shed, its planks rotting, to the side.

'What's this?' Billy asked as Elsie turned to him.

'It used to be ours: Mother's and mine.' Elsie gazed around at the sorry state of the patch.

Billy's eyes widened. 'You own this?' he asked, eyes drinking in the size of it.

'No, I don't own it, we rented it. Everyone rents their patch.'

'You mean you can pay for one of these?' Billy asked, his forehead wrinkling in confusion.

Elsie nodded, 'They renew every year.'

'Cool!' Billy glanced at the space. 'Bet it costs a lot.'

'Well, it was about two pounds back in the day so I doubt it.'

'Two pounds! What, a day?' Billy asked, moving across to the shed, entirely empty, cobwebs clinging to the corners, weeds poking through the slats of the stairs.

'A year.'

'A year?' Billy stopped dead, his palm on the wood.

'Well, it's probably more now. Twenty perhaps.'

'Twenty quid! For the year. The whole year?' Billy looked as if he might fall down with the shock of it. 'In London once someone sold their garage for a hundred grand. Dad told me. Twenty quid!' he repeated, looking back at the patch.

'I thought walking around here we could get some ideas for the garden,' Elsie said, one arm taking in the different rectangle patches, some lined with flowers, others vegetables, some derelict, some manicured to perfection.

They moved between them, winding their way round, taking in thin leeks, neat rows of potatoes, an overflowing barrel, flies spread-eagled on the surface of the water, small, polite signs pinned to a board about a nearby garden centre, a market on a Friday and one that forced Elsie to stop and stare. Discreetly, she pulled the sheet from its pin and put it in her pocket, the paper damp from the recent rain, the ink running. She had no idea that June was the answer to it all, but it would be worth it, she thought.

They retraced their steps back to Elsie's house, swapping ideas, making plans for the beds in Elsie's garden, Billy keen to make a start. They sat in the front room, Billy on the sofa with a notepad and pen. Seeing him there, bent over a sheet of paper thinking up more ideas for the garden, the wallpaper busy with flowers behind him, the higgledy-piggledy paintings and prints of her mother, it occurred to her how dated the room must seem to him, this modern boy.

He was still working as Elsie brought him pizza on a chopping board, delighted by his response. Sausages, pizza... these were not things she normally cooked but she didn't feel her haddock chowder would go down as well. He was still there as the sky darkened and Samantha appeared, weary from a long shift, a ladder in her tights, a red mark on the bottom of her white shirt, her make-up mostly rubbed away.

'Come in, come in,' Elsie said to her, shocked to see how much weight this woman had lost in such a short period of time, her curves now sharp jutting bones, her face pale.

Billy came running over, already talking before his mother sat down. Elsie offered her a slice of pizza, which she waved away: 'I ate at the restaurant.' Elsie didn't know her well enough to expose the lie. Samantha didn't look like she'd had a good meal in weeks.

'Hey Billy, we better get home now, eh? Leave Mrs Maple to her evening.'

The thought of the empty house momentarily robbed Elsie of words: how quiet, how lonely it would suddenly seem. She realised all these snatched afternoons or mornings or evenings with Billy were making her used to the noise of another person in the house again. She hadn't realised how much she had craved it.

'Just you and me again,' she said aloud.

Samantha was about to say something and then looked across at Billy.

'What's that, Billy?' Samantha asked, her face alarmed as Billy pocketed the five-pound note Elsie had given him earlier that day for mowing the lawn.

Billy looked sharply across at Elsie, worried he was in trouble. 'Elsie gave me it,' he said quietly, a rare use of her name.

'Billy, go and wash your hands before we go,' Samantha replied and Billy didn't need to be told twice, throwing one concerned look back at Elsie as he headed to the downstairs loo.

'I hope you don't mind,' Elsie explained. 'I did give it to him. A bit of pocket money for when he does some jobs for me, that's all.'

Samantha wrung her hands, looking back at Elsie. 'But I should be paying *you* for looking after him,' she said, raking a hand through her hair that needed a trim more than ever, her fringe now totally grown out.

'Honestly, he deserves it,' Elsie insisted. 'I need the help and he's giving it to me in spades, quite literally. He has a real talent for the garden. I'd only have to pay a gardener to come in.'

'But…'

'No buts, I want to,' Elsie said firmly.

Samantha sat in her chair looking defeated, too many other things weighing on her to put up more of a fight.

'I want to do it for him,' Elsie said, reassuring. 'And that reminds me…'

Pulling out the sheet of paper from her coat pocket she had stolen from the allotment, she told Samantha about her idea.

*

Sulham Woods is always stunning in autumn and I remember one day in November we walked around the fields at the back of the village, out past the empty allotments, a few brave chickens pecking at the hard earth, over the stile and into the lane to delve into the woods. Blazing orange and red leaves stretched over our heads and under our feet as if we were walking through a tunnel of fire. Walking quickly to stay warm, thick coats keeping the cold at bay, our faces were mostly obscured, flushed cheeks and pink noses.

We'd stopped on a tree trunk, huddled together, grateful for the other large tree to keep the wind from biting at us. You had produced a Marathon chocolate bar from your pocket, breaking one in two and passing me the larger half. Always comfortable together. We sat in the chittering quiet of the forest, the rustle above, the smell of a distant bonfire in the air. Our breaths formed clouds of smoke as we talked, swapping silly stories to make the other one laugh. A game we played.

My hands were cold and I told you I'd forgotten my gloves. You clasped my hands in both of yours to warm them and then transferred your own pair to me. I thought then you'd offer me anything, even if it meant you were put out. You said it was nothing, batted the gesture off with a dismissive hand. But I knew that was what love looked like: I knew it was everything.

Chapter 16

BILLY

I was hanging out at Elsie's house a lot. Dick was making Mum work extra hours because the new girl – Kia – had gone to work in the pub so Mum had to do her shifts. In London, Mum had worked at home making bracelets, necklaces, hair braid things for girls, with pots of beads in every colour on our tiny kitchen table, Dad annoyed if she left them all out. She sold the finished jewellery at Brixton market and I helped her sometimes when she had to take me too. She stayed up late working on them after I went to bed but she always said she liked doing it because it was better than a real job. I think waitressing is a real job. She didn't bring any of her beads and wires and little clipper things with her from London anyway.

Elsie and I had visited loads of places on the map and today we were going to a big house thing that was apparently part of something called the National Trust, which meant it wasn't owned by one wealthy person.

Mum had called for me as she had to leave but when I got to the bottom of the stairs it didn't look like she was going into work. She wasn't wearing her white top and black skirt, she was wearing jeans and a pale blue shirt and her hair was neat with one of those headbands the girls in my school wear to keep their hair tidy.

'I need to go into Reading for something, something to do with your dad,' she'd said. Whenever she talked about him she scratched at her arm or fiddled with her hair, ready for the questions, the anger. But today I didn't feel like getting angry or asking anything at all. She'd made me pancakes with stewed apple that morning and we'd dragged our chairs outside and eaten in the sunshine and I was going to the National Trust house.

My eyes fell on her handbag, where a big brown envelope was sticking out. She'd been filling out forms the night before and having quiet conversations on the phone every now and again with all of the pieces of paper fanned out in front of her as she chewed on a pen and a little bit of me felt quite sick inside because I knew what the forms meant. Dad wouldn't like it and I wondered what he'd do.

She'd made me promise before not to tell people at school I used to be called something different and I wasn't sure why and didn't bother pointing out that I had no one to tell. When we'd arrived in the village she'd put down her own surname, the one before she married Dad, so that at school I was William Greenwood on the register, not Billy Skinner. For the millionth time I wished I could talk to Liam about it all, or anyone.

'Come on,' she'd said, bustling me out the door.

Elsie was waiting for me, sat on the edge of her sofa talking to the walls again. 'And we're off!' she called out as if she was saying goodbye to somebody.

I looked around. 'Alright, Elsie?'

She had stood up and was rearranging the thousand billion cushions on her sofa: one pink one with diagonal orange squares, one with the newt embroidered into it. I was sure she'd heard me. I could see a half-finished letter on the desk in the front room, with lots of purple ink in neat lines, and I almost asked her who she wrote to as she never really mentioned any friends, and there weren't really photos of other people except her mum on the wall. I didn't ask though because she didn't like questions like that, like when I found the tin.

We had to get a taxi there and when the man pulled up outside, I opened the door for Elsie and she beamed at me, telling me I was a good boy, which made me feel a bit like I was an inch taller.

I got in and rested my head back on the seat, a flash of memory at the last time I had been in a taxi, the man who had driven us in the early hours of the morning to the coach station while I held a banana, the funny feeling in my tummy as we'd pulled away from the block of flats where we'd lived, Dad asleep in the bedroom back at our place. We had left him there.

I wondered then what he'd thought when he'd woken. He got up pretty late when he wasn't working on a job, and in the months before we'd left he hadn't worked a lot and he was angry about one old man who had wanted to take him to court over an extension he'd done on his house that I don't think he'd finished but it hadn't been his fault and the old man was the rude word Grandma was. He'd broken the table lamp when he'd been telling the story because he'd got so mad. I didn't really want to think about that now.

I wonder if he had realised straight away that we'd gone, not just out for milk or to the shops. I wonder what he'd thought. I wonder when or if he started to miss me.

I coughed as I felt tears building like they always did these days, the taxi now over the mini roundabouts in the village and turning right past the estate agent and the launderette, the garage with its flash cars all sat waiting for customers, and under the railway tunnel and past the restaurant overlooking the weir. The river sparkled in the sunshine, twisting out of the village and into green hills and trees in the distance. We drove along, a crumbling old wall to our left, large gateways and houses on our right.

'This is it,' Elsie said after a while, pointing to a large entrance and driveway sweeping out of view. It was like where the queen would live if she had a place near us. Elsie paid the taxi driver and we stepped out onto gravel, a large fountain in the centre, water spilling out of the lips of what looked to be a man with a fish tail.

'They open their gardens at this time of year so I thought we could walk around the grounds?' Elsie said, setting off past the fountain to some steps. I followed her, trying to look enthusiastic but I hoped the walk didn't take long. I wasn't sure about walks. What was the point of them? We weren't even taking a ball. Then I looked down and saw the biggest garden in the world. My mouth fell open.

'My mother used to bring me here, for inspiration for the garden,' Elsie explained, stopping at a sign, a beautiful border bursting with large flowers of every colour: deep purples, bright oranges. 'Look,' she said, pointing to some of the flowers as we passed: spiky leaves, clusters of petals, long grasses, neat rose bushes. My eyes were round as Elsie told me about the flowers and plants, her normal voice different when she was talking about the garden: higher, more excited.

'It's sick,' I said, and I was being honest. It *was* sick. It was just massive and crammed with so much to look at, and I was pretty sure there was a maze and everything. We were heading down a pebbled path, new trees lining our route, a sparkling circle of lake at the bottom.

'My mother loved the lake,' Elsie said, no more quick chatter about the new saplings, the different species of tree.

'What was your mum like?' I asked, wanting to get the excited Elsie back.

Her face changed again, a soft bite of her lip before she spoke. 'She was—' Elsie stopped right in the middle of the path. 'Everything. It was just… us,' she said.

'Like me and Mum,' I nodded, but something in the way she nodded didn't make me feel it was the same.

She didn't say anything else and didn't talk more about the signs or the plants.

We walked around the lake. I was distracted by smiling people passing us, saying hello even though we didn't know them. That was so weird, it never happened in London. If I'd gone out saying hello to everyone in Brixton they'd think I was going to take their wallet.

We spent a while exploring the paths down by the lake, Elsie writing down a few of the names on the signs in a little notebook she pulled out. I liked the fact she asked me which flowers I liked and made a note of them. Then we went inside the maze, which was so cool and you had to keep remembering which way you'd turned to check you could get out.

We were in there a while and once out, we followed the path back towards the house, which was this enormous palace-type place with thick white-grey stone and floor-to-ceiling windows and scaffolding on one side where they were fixing a turret, a window in the top like in *Sleeping Beauty*.

She was about to order us a taxi back but changed her mind. 'How about a cream tea?'

My stomach rumbled, the pancakes seemed forever ago now. I followed her past a sign with an arrow and into a massive dining room, which had a chandelier and a maroon carpet with thick gold swirls. I felt a bit embarrassed I was wearing a bright orange T-shirt but Elsie didn't seem to care. I wished I was wearing one of my new ones. She'd given me a couple of long-sleeved tops. She'd said they'd been lying around in her house but it was like the worst lie and I'd found the price tags on them. She was weird, but nice.

The afternoon tea was brilliant because it wasn't really tea but scones with thick clotted cream and scoops of strawberry jam with enormous chunks of actual strawberry inside and I was allowed a vanilla milkshake instead of the pot of Earl Grey that Elsie ordered. By the end I was totally stuffed and sat back in my chair, staring up at the cream ceiling which was full of a hundred different-sized swirls.

'This place is amazing,' I said and Elsie gave me a wide smile, dabbing at the corners of her mouth.

'I'm so glad. I hoped you would like it. I haven't been back here in years... I didn't think I'd...' Elsie trailed off, and I think she was back in the past, a small, sad smile on her face. I think she was thinking about her mum.

A man in a smart suit came over and interrupted and Elsie asked for the bill. She giggled when I'd put on my poshest voice to thank the man in the suit for my 'delightful tea'.

'Delightful,' she teased as he walked away.

'I panicked!'

Elsie paid and we left the room. Elsie went off to find where to book a taxi and I felt a bit sad to be leaving. There were big double doors opposite and a sign outside said, 'LINE DRAWING: AN INTRO-DUCTORY CLASS'. A man in his twenties with shoulder-length hair appeared and suddenly he was ushering me inside and telling me which table to join.

Elsie appeared behind me and the man greeted her too, 'Oh, wonderful! I really hoped there'd be more take up, so good of you to support us. It's just a donation at the end, for repairs to the house, they're fixing the roof again...'

'Oh, we…'

I knew Elsie was trying to get us out of it and my mouth was wobbling, wanting to break out laughing. I also really wanted the day to keep going.

'Come on, Ells, let's learn how to draw,' I said, giggling when she glared at me.

'I haven't drawn in years,' she said, her eyes round.

'It will return,' the man told her, tucking his hair behind his ears, and I nodded, patting Elsie's arm as I went and stood behind a table, all the materials laid out on the surface, pencils of every shape and size, a rubber, some paper.

'Come on,' I said, her expression making me laugh. I liked to draw and this would definitely be more fun than heading back to sit waiting for Mum to return from her shift. We still had no television and Elsie never watched it. I couldn't imagine owning a TV and choosing not to turn it on. She could be so weird.

She moved to the table next door, looking really frightened now, holding her pencil the wrong way round. I gave her a thumbs up. The man was very keen and he moved around the room making encouraging noises at the things we were trying to draw.

'Why don't you draw me?' I suggested to Elsie, who was still holding the pencil upside down and looking dumbly at the blank page in front of her. 'You draw me and I'll draw you,' I said. 'It'll be fun.'

Picking up one of the pencils, I started to sketch, trying to get her straight grey hair right, the parting in the middle, the shape of the nose, the tiniest scar on the left side I'd never noticed. Her eyes, light blue looking at me desperately, still not sure where to begin.

'Come on,' I said. 'Just make me better-looking,' I suggested, giving her a stupid wide grin, which made her relax a little.

The man leapt across and started to help her, guiding her hand across the page, which started to make her blush. 'Thank you,' she said to him as he complimented her on the shape of my jawline. 'You've captured his essence already,' the man said, and Elsie went all twittery, flapping her hand in front of her face. 'Oh, I don't know about that,' she blushed.

'Someone's got a crush,' I whispered as the man turned away to help the woman behind us.

'Nonsense!' Elsie said, eyes down on her page, her cheeks going pinker. 'Now be quiet or I'll give you an extra-large nose.'

The hour zipped past, Elsie seemed totally relaxed now. I learnt about shading, the man showing me how to use the different pencils, how to get the twinkle in Elsie's eye.

'I don't twinkle,' she twinkled, with the high voice again, the one that made me want to crease up.

Her own picture was pretty good. She'd spent a long time on my short hair, making the haircut look less worse than it was, and she'd done a good job of making it look a bit like me.

When I spun mine round to her I felt a small thrill at the look on her face. 'Billy,' she said, her voice filled with wonder, 'that is really, really good, you have such a talent.'

Our teacher had clearly overheard and came over to inspect our work. I sat straighter in my chair as he bent over to study the pictures.

'You have a careful hand,' he said to Elsie, 'and you listened when I explained the contouring in that section.' He beamed. Elsie looked pleased, biting her lip as he stared at my picture.

'Young man,' he said, 'this is excellent, she is quite right. You have captured the expression on her face perfectly and played with light in an extraordinary way. You should be impossibly proud of your efforts. Well done!'

It was my turn to blush. The man turned, called away to another part of the room.

'Someone's got a crush,' Elsie whispered to me, leaning across her table to mine.

I couldn't help the shout of laughter that made everyone turn our way.

Chapter 17

ELSIE

This morning Elsie felt nervous. She and Billy had explored almost all the places on the map over the last few weeks and today they were headed somewhere that always reminded her of her mother, somewhere she hadn't visited in almost thirty years.

Elsie walked down to see her mother early that morning, as she always did on a Friday, sometimes visiting on a birthday or anniversary, and sometimes when she felt unbearably alone and needed to talk. Walking past the shops, their 'CLOSED' signs hanging in the window, there were no pedestrians, only the occasional car inching by. The day would be warm, the sky a milky blue, the air still.

The graveyard was empty as Elsie moved under the lychgate framed with creepers, her fist tight on the pale pink flowers she had picked that morning, her bare feet on the dew of the lawn as she made her selection. Her mother's favourites.

She replaced the old with the new, a small bottle of water used to top up the vase, a few large stones in the base so it remained standing even in the most adverse weather conditions.

'Hello, Mother,' she began softly.

She stood in front of the gravestone, the familiar dates a blur as a hundred memories flooded her. Remembering the day, aged thirty-four, when she had stood at this very spot watching her mother's coffin lowered into the ground, surrounded by a handful of locals, heads bowed, Mr Porter giving her a sad nod as he caught her eye. She had watched as the first fistful of earth was thrown and more to follow. It hadn't been a long illness, the cancer had already spread to her lymph nodes by the time they caught it. An elderly couple she didn't recognise had been hovering by the lychgate and a card had been sent a few days later: her grandparents.

She knew now why she didn't have holidays with her grandparents, why her mother had been estranged.

She never wrote back.

Elsie had been back here a hundred times, some days disbelieving – was she really gone? Re-reading the name of the stone over and over as if it might sink in: Rosa Maple. It had always been just the two of them and it seemed impossible her mother had left her alone in this way. She had been Elsie's everything and Elsie had been her world.

Her mum's belongings were still in her bedroom, her tri-mirror reflecting the combs and bottles on her dressing table. In the wardrobe were her dresses, full skirts, her blouses, her cardigans, kept in clothes bags, away from the moths that would eat away at them. Her queen-size bed was still made, the pink and grey quilt she so loved folded neatly over the foot of it.

Elsie still slept in the bedroom on the landing opposite, the smaller room, remembering the times her mother would sit propped up next to her in the small single bed and read fairy tales in the lamplight, Elsie snuggled into the crook of her arm, laughing as her softly-spoken, shy mother attempted all the voices. She knew she would never move. Those things were what was left and she wouldn't ever let them go.

She left the graveyard, the high street a little busier: an elderly man and his dog; the lone customer in the small supermarket; the general store manager dragging the pots, spades, buckets of balls under their blue, striped awning; the butcher, Mr Porter, placing the chilled trays out on display, a hand raised as he saw her. Elsie nodded, giving him a small smile of acknowledgement.

The chemist was pretty empty, a man with a tartan, wheeled shopper rattling vitamin bottles. June stood behind the counter, arms folded, watching him through narrowed eyes.

'Elsie,' she said, uncrossing them as Elsie approached, her eyes still on the man shaking the bottles. 'They're multivitamins,' she called out and he hurriedly put them back. 'People, Elsie, people!'

'Um, yes, quite.'

'As if I don't have better things to do, Elsie, than rearrange the shelves…'

'Right,' Elsie said, thinking that sounded like a fundamental part of June's job.

'It takes me an age to get the labels all facing out. But do people appreciate it? No, Elsie, no, they don't…'

She was about to launch into another complaint, the pharmacist busily moving up and down the shelves behind her.

'I was hoping to see you,' Elsie started.

June's magenta lips puckered. 'Me?' She leant conspiratorially across the counter, a glance back at the pharmacist still busy checking the shelves. 'Is it a female issue, Elsie? There's a side room if you want privacy? And,' she stepped back to indicate the shelves behind her, 'we keep the creams for delicate areas on the bottom shel—'

'No,' Elsie interrupted, her face flaring with heat, the man with the tartan shopper approaching, clutching a bottle of vitamins. 'No, nothing like that. It was, well, I saw a sign…' she began and explained what she needed.

She eventually left, the man with the vitamins handing over his bottle to June with a frightened expression. Elsie felt a bubble of excitement at what she had begun, and a tiny surprise that June had been so amenable.

At home, she moved around, ticking her chalkboard, racing through her usual jobs, skipping others. They could wait. Then, once he was due to arrive, she dressed in cropped trousers and a loose-fitting top with a scalloped neckline. She had seen it in the window of the boutique of the high street and, on a whim, had purchased it. A little different from her normal clothes. Combing her hair, she stood back, staring at herself in the small mirror in her bedroom. 'What do you think? Presentable?' A knock on the door and she descended the stairs to answer it.

Billy appeared, in shorts and the familiar orange T-shirt. He wore about three on a loop; she really must take the boy shopping or work out how to get him some more new clothes without embarrassing him. She'd given him two tops the other day but he needed more. Perhaps she could ask Scarlet in the library to help her with some 'online shopping' – she had read an article that said lots of people were doing that.

'I've packed a picnic,' she said as he followed her into the kitchen, a small basket covered in a tea towel on the side.

'Do you need to do anything before we go?' Billy asked, used to her routines and timings, knowing she had a plan for her day. He asked it with a half-smile on his face.

'No, Billy Greenwood, I am at your disposal.'

He frowned. 'What does that mean?'

Elsie laughed. 'It means we can leave. You carry the basket, I'll take the rug.'

Billy hooked the basket over his arm and headed to the front door.

For a moment Elsie was taken over with panic. Perhaps she could make up some excuse? Perhaps they could picnic elsewhere? Perhaps…

Billy turned, interrupting her inner monologue.

'Coming?'

Elsie took a breath and nodded, 'I am.'

The hedgerows needing cutting, the grass on the verges spilling over the tarmac as they meandered down the lane, speckled with shadows from the trees above. Elsie stopped at the gap in the hedge, a small turnstile taking them through two fields. Billy offered her a hand as he hopped down on the other side.

'I'm not that old,' she said, laughing and joining him.

Billy shrugged. 'Just being a gent, Mrs M,' he said, whistling and strolling off. Her heart bloomed for this boy, the moments where he relaxed and joked with her revealing a confident young person.

'And how are you getting on, Billy? At school, I mean? Have you made any new friends?'

Billy raised an eyebrow. 'New?'

Elsie flushed; he really could get to the heart of things.

'Nah, it's alright,' he said, batting a hand at her. 'There's a girl, Becky, she sort of smiles at me but I think she's quite shy and all the girls move everywhere together, and I was paired up with Ben in maths last week and we got on because we both like video games and he said I should play his PlayStation with him, but then some of the other boys had a word and he hasn't asked again…'

'That's a shame. Perhaps you could arrange to see him after school one day, away from the others.'

Billy shrugged, kicking the long grass. 'Mum won't let me get a mobile and they all talk to each other on them, which sucks.'

They burst through the trees, pine needles blanketing the ground, the air cooler in amongst the soaring trunks. Billy stared around at the blanket of purple. As far as the eye could see, the bluebells stretched into the distance, enormous clumps in between the trees so that the ground was awash with them. The scent was overpowering, her mother's favourite perfume, and for a second Elsie's head spun with it.

'My mother,' she tried to steady her voice, 'my mother loved to visit the woods, do the bluebell walk. We would visit every year and she would lie in amongst them, delighting in their colour and smell.'

She was back there with her for a moment. Her mother, never usually one for theatrics, her laughter louder and brighter as she unfurled the blanket they'd sit on, 'Isn't it beautiful, my darling girl.' She was brighter in this place.

'There's millions,' Billy said, eyes stretched in wonder, walking alongside Elsie as she navigated long-forgotten paths, every so often glimpsing the fields through the trees, the working farm below, the lane hidden at the bottom of the valley as they climbed higher.

A grey squirrel scampered up a tree as they approached, the chatter of insects accompanied the sound of their footsteps as they moved. The day grew warmer and Elsie looked around for a shady spot, laying the tartan rug on the ground, instructing Billy to remove the things from the basket.

He took out two glass tumblers – 'No wonder this thing weighed a ton' – and set them on the rug next to the cans of ginger beer Elsie had bought the day before.

'Pear squash?'

'Not this time!' Elsie laughed. 'It's ginger beer, like we are in an Enid Blyton book,' she announced, pulling off the tab.

Billy looked at her blankly and Elsie laughed again. 'Another book you haven't read?'

He accepted the fizzy drink, adding, 'Is this *Windy Willows* all over again? You're still not over it?'

'*The Wind in the Willows*,' Elsie stressed, laughing. 'It's a classic, Billy.'

'If you say so. I'm more into films.'

Elsie rolled her eyes in mock exasperation, and then remembered that first trip to the cinema. It had only been a few weeks ago but it seemed a lifetime; this boy had become such an important part of her week. The thought jolted her: what if something happened to him? She reached for her own glass, trying not to feel the panic, the worry of losing yet another person in her life.

Billy hadn't noticed her serious expression, the shake of her hand as she poured the ginger beer.

'So,' Billy said, after polishing off his ham sandwiches, so full he hadn't been able to finish his custard cream, 'what next?'

'What do you mean?' Elsie asked, resting back on the palms of her hands, her head tilted towards the sky, the sun dappled on her face, the leaves a canopy above them.

'Well, we've explored most of the map, apart from that house in that village, Goring.' He pronounced it 'Go Ring'.

'Goring,' Elsie corrected.

'Yeah, Goring. We should go there…'

Elsie sat up straighter, the start of a pulse in her neck.

'It's like one of the only places outside the village on the map. Is it a museum or somewhere you went with your mum?'

'I…' Elsie licked her lips, tried to buy herself some time as she thought. 'It's nothing, it's… No, we never…' How could she explain she had never visited with her mother? How could she explain that she hadn't known the importance of the place until that day all those years ago?

She thought back to that afternoon, her confusion as she stood outside the house, triple-checking its location on the map, her brow pulled together as the enormity of what she was seeing, what she was discovering, sunk in. She had left as quickly as she'd arrived, wandering back along the river in a daze, tears pricking her eyes, all the way down the Thames path, not taking in the sights – the river meandering, the swans, the boats idling – not noticing the rain as it had started to fall, bouncing on the surface of the water, wetting her hair, dripping down her collar. Not realising she had returned home until she was stood back in her kitchen, staring round at the familiar room, the house she had shared with her mother, knowing everything had irreversibly changed.

She remembered seeing the tin on the dresser, the bold red snapping her out of her catatonic state. She had dug the hole that night, the rain still falling, a light mist clinging to her skin, growing heavier as she raked at the soil with her bare hands.

She had lowered the tin into the damp soil, needing to see it gone but unable to throw it away. Under the ground it had gone, deep, but she fetched one thing from it first, the sheet of paper that had caused her to head out that morning, placing it in the waistband of her trousers. She had pushed the soil over the tin until the red had disappeared completely, smoothing and patting as she cried so many tears: confused, frightened, angry.

No one had seen her in the darkness, knelt in the mud, weeping as she buried that tin forever, not realising then that it would be found twenty-eight years later when Billy would uncover it, lift it out and threaten to expose her biggest secret.

'…Mum's working Saturday again, we could head there then?' Billy was still talking as Elsie was lost, back there in the dark, in the cold, alone. 'Mrs M? Elsie?' he nudged her.

'No,' she snapped, barely back in the present, the same emotions surging in her as if she was still kneeling in the soil after her discovery, clawing desperately at the earth, mud clumped under nails, her world crashing down around her. 'Leave it, it's nothing,' she said, her anger causing Billy to recoil.

He looked down, only the top of his head visible as he stared at the rug, the day ruined. She couldn't fix it, wasn't able to. She simply watched as he got up silently and she just let him go.

*

One of my favourite days was the day you borrowed the tandem bike. We'd pushed it off the pavement, wobbly and screeching, and wheeled it slowly down the high street. People stared as we passed, shouting and cackling when the pedals spun away from us as we lost the rhythm of it. June had glared at us, too much joy, too much show. We were making a spectacle of ourselves. And for a second I worried people were watching – I wasn't used to people caring what I did – and then you twisted in your seat at the front and poked your tongue out at me.

I hadn't cared then, the whole world could go to hell in a handcart because I was happy, the two of us against the world.

We'd got the hang of it, calling to each other, pointing out sights: a red kite diving, a flash of sunlight on the river, a pub sign…

Stopping in, we had propped up the bike, ordered drinks, the cider sticky and sweet, and moved through to the terrace at the back. As we rested back in our chairs, we listened to the roar as the water tumbled over the weir below us, sipping cold drinks, droplets slipping down the outside of the glass, our legs aching from the earlier exertion. We had clinked glasses, our contented expressions mirroring each other.

Would it always be like this, I had wondered as I watched you get up, stand next to the railing, arms folded on the top as you watched boats idling past. Your profile so familiar to me, your voice the one I always recalled. I couldn't imagine a world without you in it. I didn't want to live in that world.

Chapter 18

BILLY

She'd been pretty chilled recently and I started to like going round there. Big mistake. Our new house was boring because Mum was always tired or working and we still had no TV anyway and I hadn't been able to bring my BMX from London, so I spent a lot of time kicking the football against the fence, which Mum said got on her nerves. Then she'd get stressed because I'd want to talk about Dad and ask if we were ever going to see him, even when I was an adult, and he'd said we could go to Florida when I was eleven and I didn't understand why she was stopping me.

Mrs Maple had started to do nice things, like she wouldn't always make me wait while she did stuff like clean the oven or hoover the front room or polish all her weird figurines but when I appeared she'd have something for us to do. And she talked to the walls less and less.

We worked in the garden a lot and she showed me loads of cool things. It was brilliant watching it all grow right in front of my eyes and she paid me money too. She got me my own jigsaw, which was way easier than her crazy blue-sky one; she'd said it was an old one but she'd left the price tag on again. Same with the paints she'd got that we spent an afternoon with. It was nice of her. She told me I could take them home with me: 'What would I do with them?' she fussed, shushing me out the door, which she always did when she was a bit embarrassed.

She left me out this form on her table for the allotments with a ten-pound note to start me off and I knew she had gone to see that woman called June, who worked part-time in the chemist but also ran the allotments in the village, even though I knew she didn't like June because she'd 'stepped out with the butcher', whatever that means, and she'd then left him and he'd been sad.

'Something to save for,' she'd written on a note stuck to it.

My own allotment. I thought of that big patch and all the things I would need to do and a little part of me froze: I wasn't good enough to do it.

And then she ruined everything by getting all angry about things; sometimes you never knew what would set her off. Like one time I pointed out the crack in her teapot was getting bigger and she better buy a new one soon and she raised her voice at me that she wouldn't and I didn't even really care, and then the other day we were having a picnic and she was so rude when I asked her about seeing the house on the map. Loads of the places on the map are nice so I don't know why she got so funny about it. She did apologise for being nasty, but only because Mum saw that she had let me walk back along the lane alone and had been a bit frosty about it with her.

I was meant to be round there today but Mum left for work already and I suddenly felt like doing something on my own. It was really hot and I didn't want to work in the garden anyway. I wanted to check out that place on the map. I decided to get the train to Goring and I reckoned no one would even check my ticket as it's like two seconds away.

There was literally no one on the train when I got on and I sat with my feet up on the seat opposite feeling a bit nervous, as if Mum would

appear and get all worried but really, it's not like London, where there
is loads of danger. Out here you hardly see anyone some days, not like
Brixton, which was always rammed.

When I got off the train Goring was pretty, terraced houses lining
the road, small shops with bright flowerboxes and the widest stretch
of river running under the bridge. I leant over, dropping a pebble into
the water as it flowed underneath, seeing my wobbly reflection as I
stared down into it. I remembered the day out on the rowing boat
when Elsie had just jumped in, how we'd walked back to her house
completely drenched. That thought gave me a bit of a lump in my
throat. I hoped she wouldn't be cross I'd come here. I just wanted to
see what it was and then head back.

I moved on, up the road, past a pub that was on the map so I knew
I was close. A right-hand turn and the road forked. Taking the left,
I moved slowly down, hearing a tinny clink – a brown sign pointing
to a golf course on the other side. It was well posh: I saw four cars in
someone's drive and one of them was a Porsche! And I couldn't see into
other houses because they had electric gates that completely blocked
the view, some with little black CCTV cameras at the top – to put off
robbers maybe? Daniel would say I'd know.

I hoped there wouldn't be gates where I was headed. Remembering
the small field on the map, a park in the corner, I felt excited when I
saw some swings. I was definitely close. The house was set back from
the road, down its own small lane, which was all dusty with big pebbles
that were kicked in every direction as I walked. There were two stone
pillars and a big circular drive around a small green circle of grass that
had definitely been mowed recently and the house was painted white
and had big windows in the front and creamy roses winding round
them. I followed a low wall around the edge, peeking through the

bushes to see more of the house, an entrance on the side, a garden at the back that sloped down, a hint of blue water beyond, the top of some wire fencing. It was massive. But it wasn't like the National Trust place or a museum or anything like that – it looked like somebody's actual house, just ten times as big as normal.

There was no way I was walking up the gravel drive to knock on the door; there was an enormous brass knocker in the middle which gleamed even from this far away. They probably had a butler to answer it.

I wondered why it was drawn on the map. Maybe it wasn't this house at all, this looked like the home of a really, really rich family – what had that got to do with Mrs Maple? But there was no other house around. The wood to the right looked like it was connected to the house.

It was so quiet, suddenly it seemed like I was in the middle of nowhere. I knew the river was somewhere off to the right, not far from where I was stood, but I couldn't imagine living in a house far away from another human being – it was the opposite of our old block of flats, one of four in a space about as big as this place.

I wondered if I'd imagined it but suddenly I heard a shout and saw a flash of bright pink through the trees, in the garden. I ducked down, worried someone had seen me and would appear with a big gun and tell me to go away. But no one came and I popped my head back up through the bush.

'Hello,' said a girl standing the other side.

I screamed in an embarrassing high-pitched way, one hand flying to my chest as she started giggling.

'Sorry, I TOLD Rory I'd seen someone and he was too scared to come and look, and he's gone inside to tell everyone that I might be being KIDNAPPED!'

'I…' My whole body was still too shocked that she'd just popped up and I couldn't seem to form any words. Also, she spoke really quickly.

'You're not going to kidnap me, are you? You don't look like a kidnapper. I imagine they are older and a lot more horrid but you look nice, well, scared, because I just frightened you, but you have kind eyes. My grandma says that about people…'

'Sorry,' I muttered, backing away, 'I didn't mean to get seen… I was… I'll go.' I was at the wrong place, there was no way this big house, and this strange talking girl, had anything to do with Mrs Maple and her quiet, ordered life.

'Oh God, don't go! I am soooo bored. It's so hot and I wanted to play tennis but Rory keeps wanting to play with his stupid *Star Wars* stuff and you can't play on your own. Well, not really, you can practise serving and stuff, but it gets really dull, really quickly…'

'I play tennis,' I said, wondering why I opened my stupid mouth. I thought then of the terrible practices at school, Mr Williams shouting instructions at me as I scuttled back and forward. I'd got a little better but I wasn't exactly any good.

The girl clapped her hands together once. 'Oh my God, do you? Are you any good? I'm rubbish but I really like it and I've invented a new way of playing where you can hit the ball after two bounces, which is so much better although Rory moans that it's not the proper rules like at Wimbledon but I don't want to be Serena Williams, I just want to play tennis, you know?'

'Yeah, I…' I scuffed a toe along the ground, awkward in front of this confident girl who was probably my age, maybe a tiny bit older. She was the same height, that was for sure.

'I'm Ottilie, by the way, Tilly for short.' She stopped and looked at me funny.

'Oh, I'm Billy,' I said, realising she might have been waiting for me to introduce myself. 'Well, William, but no one ever calls me that.'

'Yes, you don't want to be Willy either, do you? I like Billy,' she said and I didn't know what to do with myself because she'd just talked about willies.

'So, do you want to play tennis? We've got rackets and stuff.'

'Well, I'm, I'm not sure. I…'

'Follow me round here and we can talk, it's odd talking to you through a bush.' She disappeared as suddenly as she had appeared, a streak of pink through the gaps in the bush.

I found myself following, round the wall, towards the bottom of the driveway, palms slippery with this strange new situation. I should've said I needed to go, needed to get back, but it felt so nice to meet someone my age, someone who didn't want to trip me up or make fun of my accent: someone nice.

'That's what you look like then,' she said when I appeared in the gap between the pillars. 'I could only see your head and shoulders. I like your trainers. I have some kind of like that, but I'm not wearing them today. So, do you really want to play tennis?'

Feeling awkward and embarrassed, I bit my lip. 'Well, no, I just…' Did I want to play tennis? Actually, I did. I wanted to run around and play and not have to head over to Mrs Maple's or home to a silent house and a sad microwaved pizza.

'Rory will be sooooo cross I've found a friend and don't need him!' Tilly said, spinning on her heel, brown ponytail snapping round as she moved.

The sudden mention of the word 'friend' did something to me, a small glow in my stomach. It had been so long since anyone had thought of me as a friend that I so desperately wanted to follow this girl onto the drive and out to the tennis courts.

She spun back around, hands up, 'Rory's my brother, by the way. Not my boyfriend or anything.'

'Right,' I said, feeling my cheeks flame.

'I don't have a boyfriend. Mum says I am waaaayyy too young but loads of my friends have them. How old are you? I'm eleven – well, eleven and a half.'

'I'm ten,' I muttered.

'Definitely too young then.'

'I…' Why couldn't I be like her? I wasn't normally so tongue-tied and slow-sounding but this all felt so strange.

Up ahead, a boy maybe a year or two younger than me burst out of a side door of the house and pointed in our direction.

'It's OK,' Ottilie shouted over her shoulder, ponytail whipping round again, 'he's not going to kidnap me.'

The boy, Rory, raced straight back inside.

'Ha ha! Come on, let's go and say hi or Mummy will worry I really have been kidnapped, not that anything that exciting could happen at Grandma's.'

And just like that she raced off, spitting up gravel stones as she did, past a double garage, a cluster of pots filled with lavender – I remembered Mrs Maple telling me about them – along the side of the enormous house before she disappeared round the corner.

I stopped for a second. Should I be here? I knew perhaps I shouldn't, that Mum and Mrs Maple might not like it, but in that moment, I felt a surge of relief to have met Tilly. Something about her dimpled smile and her easy way of talking filled me with confidence. This place couldn't be bad if it had been on Mrs Maple's map, only good things were on the map. And with that thought, I chased after her.

Chapter 19

ELSIE

Billy appeared, panting on her doorstep, his cheeks flushed pink, his dark brown hair sticking up, in need of another cut soon, the hair damp at the temples.

'Thank goodness, I was worried sick,' she said, ushering him inside. 'Your mother had told me you'd be here hours ago. I didn't know what to do, didn't want to disturb her at work, make her worry and of course I didn't know how to get hold of you and what if…?'

Elsie had worked herself into a panic, her skin prickling with worry as the allotted arrival time had come and gone. The teapot had grown cold, the plates of custard creams abandoned as she had walked out of her house to next door, giving a tentative knock followed by silence, a deep breath and then a louder knock, two pushes on the doorbell.

'Billy,' she'd called out to an upstairs window.

The last time she had seen him hadn't ended well, the bluebell walk a complete disaster after she'd barked at him. What if he was angry, punishing her? She'd pushed the doorbell for a third time long and hard, cupping her face and pressing it against the window, shocked as ever by the sparse front room. There was a new rug in dark grey that hadn't been there before: she must offer some things to Samantha to make the place more of a home.

'Billy,' she'd repeated, her breath clouding the glass.

She'd returned to her own house, her heart tight with panic, pacing the living room. If she interrupted Samantha at work, she would frighten the woman. She couldn't very well call the police, he was only an hour late.

She had sat down and then stood up again, biting her lip. Moving to the table with the telephone, she had lifted the receiver, the sound of the dial tone foreign, months since she had made a call. The last time had been renewing her house insurance. *Who would she phone?* she had thought as she dithered over the buttons before replacing it.

'I forgot, I'm sorry,' Billy said, racing past her through the house towards the kitchen. 'Do you want me to put the kettle on, get the teapot?'

'Don't change the subject, young man,' Elsie said in her most stern voice as she followed him into the room, watched him reach to fill the kettle.

'I'm sorry,' Billy said, approaching her, suddenly leaning in to place one arm around her waist, a quick one-armed hug of apology. The movement so surprised Elsie she froze, unable to remember anyone wanting to hold her like that, touch her to reassure.

'I…' How could she stay angry after that?

'We can have tea,' Billy called, moving across to the dresser to fetch the polka-dot teapot as if he owned the place.

'Billy Greenwood,' Elsie said, following him into her kitchen, watching this energetic boy fly around the room, fetching the familiar items. What had come over him? He had a smile on his face, a spring in his step. Her fears had melted away and now she was curious. She realised then how serious and quiet he could often be, wondered what had brought on this change.

'I met this cool girl, right?' Billy said, filling the kettle from the sink, 'Tilly. Well, it is something like Ottamilly or something, but Tilly for short...'

'You let me do that, I don't want you setting fire to yourself.' Elsie took the kettle from him, lighting the hob with a match. 'So, a girl...?' She gave him a raised eyebrow.

'No,' he flushed, 'not like that.'

'Like what?' Elsie frowned, genuinely baffled.

'She was just cool and she let me play tennis with her and she was pretty bad too but we both got better, and then she showed me this treehouse that was, like, bigger than my bedroom and it had furniture in it and stuff and a lookout point over a wood, and her brother Rory was nice too and we ate lemon drizzle cake...'

Elsie couldn't believe that Billy had finally made a friend, delighted that he was sharing these stories. She had felt so helpless hearing his problems from school, wanting to march into that playground herself and have it out with this Daniel.

She noticed Billy looking at something, plunging the item back in his pocket as she moved past him to fetch the plate for the custard creams.

'All OK?' she asked, wondering if he would share what he was hiding.

'Yeah, I'll get the rest,' he said quickly.

People were allowed their little secrets, she thought.

Billy reached for the teacups and saucers, Elsie smiling for a moment at their ritual that had become so important to her. How wonderful to have him feeling more at home, more at ease. This new friend had clearly contributed to that.

'So where is this delightful creature from? What a time you've had!'

Billy fell quiet, his eyes darting quickly around the room, not resting. 'OK,' he said slowly, 'so don't get angry...'

Elsie frowned, the kettle whistling impatiently, making them both jump. 'Why would I get angry?' she asked, a smile in her voice as she twisted the dial of the hob.

'Well...' Billy was scuffing the kitchen floor with a shoe, 'I met her at the house.'

Elsie didn't follow his drift, her smile fading as she tried to decipher the meaning.

'The house on the map,' Billy clarified.

Elsie's eyes widened in sudden, sheer panic. 'You, what the...? Why...?' She felt as if someone had pushed her from a great height, the shock of pedalling in the wind, the ground disappearing beneath her before she fell.

Billy had both his hands up, alarmed by her reaction, 'She's nice, and really, it's fine. It's amazing actually because you will *never* guess what I found out...'

Elsie was too shocked to interrupt, so many thoughts crowding into her head that she barely heard Billy talking.

He turned then and raced across to the dresser, 'I know!' he announced triumphantly, reaching to lift the familiar red tin down, plucking the blanket from the top. 'I know whose blanket this is... well, I *think* I know...' he said, holding it aloft and waiting for Elsie to respond. 'It's Tilly's grandma's blanket!' he finished, his face expectant.

Elsie felt nausea swirl, her legs jelly. 'I...'

'Isn't that insane? She asked me how I knew about the house and I told her about the map and the tin and the stuff inside, and Tilly said that her grandma has the same birthday as the baby in the photo...'

He was speaking absurdly fast, Elsie's whole brain spinning with the words, '*So* weird!'

'That's, she's…' Elsie could barely find the words, was struggling to breathe.

'Elsie?' Billy's face loomed, concern etched on his young features. 'Are you OK? You're not angry? Isn't that cool, that she might be the baby? Tilly thought it was amazing that we found this old thing from so long ago…'

'You don't understand,' Elsie said, swatting her hand, feeling choked by the truth, the thing she had been denying for so long, the secret that had caused her so much pain.

'They've invited me back, anytime, they said. They have a tennis court and it's so cool there, massive but not posh, they don't make you take off your shoes inside or anything…'

Elsie looked up, horrified. 'You can't go back there,' she spluttered in alarm.

You can't, I refuse.

'But they invited me,' Billy replied, his face filled with hurt. 'It's nothing to do with you,' he said, chin lifted in defiance, 'she's *my* friend.'

'It's *everything* to do with me and you will not go back there.' Elsie's voice was steel. 'How *dare* you meddle. I told you not to, I *told* you,' she hissed through tight lips, tears brimming, fists clenched, her knuckles white. 'That tin… That tin should have stayed in the ground.'

It was Billy's turn to look confused, his face moving from excitement to bafflement in mere seconds, his mouth moving up and down as if he couldn't select the right words. 'But? Wha-what do you mean?'

She stood up, suddenly. 'You weren't meant to find it. It was never *meant* to be found.'

'I don't understand...' Billy's brain was working, head tilted to one side, eyes narrowed. 'Did you *know* it was there?' he asked, his face serious.

Elsie said nothing at first, everything roaring within her so that she wasn't really in the room any more but caught up in her own red-hot brain.

'Of course I knew...' Elsie turned so suddenly, she jogged the table. 'I buried it,' she half-shouted.

The teapot Billy had been holding left his grip, his eyes wide in surprise at Elsie's raised voice. They watched it as it fell, turning in the air, the polka dots blurring until it hit the tiles of the kitchen floor and smashed, pieces scattering to every corner of the room.

Billy looked in horror at his feet, at Elsie, everything collapsing in front of him.

'Get out,' Elsie said, her eyes filling with tears: the anger, hurt, sadness scalding her. The teapot, her mother's favourite teapot. The memory box. The blanket. The baby.

'I'm sorry...' Billy held both hands up, took a step forward, pottery crunching beneath his foot.

The noise caused Elsie to make a keening sound. 'Get OUT!'

Billy looked as if he'd been physically slapped; another crunch as he scrambled backwards to get out of the kitchen, out of her presence. Elsie's chest moved up and down as she struggled to breathe through the mad swirl of her thoughts. What had he done? How dare he go there? *How dare he?*

She barely heard the door slam behind him, couldn't follow if she wanted, floored by the tsunami of feeling. With a shaking hand, she reached for the blanket, sinking slowly into the chair, the floor still devastated by jagged pottery.

She sat there, gripping the blanket. 'You've done this,' she said aloud, twisting the blanket in her hands, 'don't you see? This is what your secrets do. Bring me misery…'

Elsie had found the tin shortly after her mother had died. The breast cancer had spread quickly and the illness was brief and painful. Elsie imagined her mother moving slowly to place the things inside the red tin, the jigsaw of her secrets.

Elsie had spent hours at her bed before she died, falling asleep in a chair pushed up to the duvet, holding her hand, and yet her mother hadn't said a word. It was only afterwards, when Elsie had been searching for the pale blue silk scarf, a favourite of her mother's, something inconsequential to stop herself unravelling on the morning of the funeral, that she had discovered the tin and what was inside.

It had changed everything.

'Two peas in a pod… but… but we *weren't*, were we, Mother?'

She barely remembered the funeral, going over the items in the tin in her head, the letter her mother had left her. It felt like everything her mother had ever told her was built on sand and gradually all the granules were slipping through her fingers.

She recalled her own visit to the house on the map all those years ago. She recalled standing next to those grand pillars, heart hammering, stealthily creeping around the low wall to peer into a side window. She recalled seeing her there, a smile on her face as she gazed out of the window, scrubbing at something in the sink. Elsie recalled her stomach flipping at the sight. She recalled stepping forward to take a closer look.

Her sister.

Chapter 20

BILLY

God, I hadn't meant to drop it. Her face… I'd just turned and legged it out of her house and down the high street, quickly peering into the window of the restaurant so Mum wouldn't see me pass. She wasn't there, maybe she was in the kitchen at the back. I ran faster. She'd be so mad if she knew I'd left Mrs Maple's house, gone on a train on my own.

I didn't want to get yelled at again.

The corner shop sold SIM cards, a flashing rectangular sign in the bottom corner of the glass telling me so. I got out the money Elsie had given me for all the gardening and slid it across the counter. This was more important than saving for other things. I thought of the form for the allotments – I'd really wanted to get to the village hall and hand it in. That idea disappeared with the memory of Elsie shouting at me. Gardening was our thing and now I wasn't sure I wanted anything to do with her.

I pulled out the object from my back pocket. It had been Tilly's idea. It was an old handset of hers, an iPhone, unlocked but still way more expensive than anything I'd be able to get. Slipping the SIM card inside, I clicked the back closed and waited as the screen came to life: 29 per cent battery, I had time.

I moved faster back down the road to the cafe, my heart beating fast as I saw the free Wi-Fi password on the board. Within minutes I'd downloaded the apps I needed. Tilly had typed in her number: 'Everyone's got one and some kids at my school have got two because their parents take them off them at night. I had this one forever ago. I'll message you, yeah?'

I tapped out a text. A simple *Hey* and waited, staring at the screen, hungry for a ping, a buzz.

There was something else I needed to do. Opening Facebook, I went to my account. Liam and I had set them up even though we weren't old enough. I was surprised to see a couple of friend requests from three kids in my class. I didn't have much time so I accepted them and sent my new mobile number in messages to them. Becky sent me a smiley face back, which almost distracted me from what I was doing.

Typing in a name, I scrolled the tiny thumbnails until I found the one I wanted. The message was short and I hovered over the send button, feeling a short stab of worry. Mum wouldn't like it and I trusted her. I bit my lip. But lately she'd been so full of secrets, avoiding my questions, getting cross with me for asking them. And what harm could it do?

As I'd seen with Mrs Maple, who could I really trust?

I couldn't believe she'd known about that tin, had let me believe I'd discovered it. I needed to do something for myself. I was almost a grown-up now, almost a teenager – sort of. I felt some of Tilly's earlier confidence rub off on me.

I pressed 'Send'.

I just felt in the dark about everything. Mum never talked about anything and Mrs Maple was always making out she knew nothing.

Who buries a tin in their own garden full of junk? Why'd she been so angry? I felt tears build in my throat. We'd followed that map, done a whole load of fun things, and all the time she'd said nothing, let me believe she'd never laid eyes on it before. It didn't make any sense.

And I couldn't work out how Tilly fitted into it all. Why would Elsie bury a tin with a photo of Tilly's grandma? Maybe it was a different baby, maybe the date was just an odd coincidence? Then I thought back to earlier that day.

Tilly had dragged me inside after her grandma had called from the stone terrace at the back of their massive house. We'd been in the treehouse, Rory joining us, agreeing to be held hostage as Tilly and me tied twine around his ankles to a chair.

'He's a good sport, aren't you, Rory? You don't mind. He likes to be the prisoner,' Tilly told me. Looking at Rory's face, I wasn't absolutely sure.

Then Rory had begged us both to play Swingball, which was a pole with a ball attached, and only stopped asking when Tilly threatened to tell their mum that he'd thrown out his shorts after he'd peed himself when she'd been tickling him.

'Oh my God, Tilly, shut up!' he said, cheeks burning red. I'd coughed and looked away. I wasn't used to seeing brothers and sisters together and it was sort of weird but cool.

Tilly laughed. 'Billy doesn't care, he can keep a secret. He found us on a map.'

Her grandma had called and Tilly had started climbing down the ladder, head disappearing as she called, 'Come on, Billy!'

Rory was still struggling with the twine.

Tilly's grandma was shielding her eyes from the sun as she watched us streak up the lawn. The grass looked like a big green zebra crossing, dark and light, cut in perfect stripes, the stone terrace edged with a border of purple and magenta dahlias, big pink oriental poppies that

I knew Elsie loved. For a second I was distracted, almost tripping as I stared at all the colours, couldn't believe I knew all the fancy names.

'And who is this?' her voice was teasing as she tipped her head to one side.

'This is Billy. Billy, Grandma,' Tilly said, motioning between us.

'Nice to meet you,' I mumbled, cold terror making me shy. What if Tilly told her how we'd met? That I'd been watching their house? What would this lady with her large gold button-type earrings and clanking bracelets think? Daniel had called me a robber and I suddenly thought of my London accent and crap clothes and how it might look.

The lady didn't seem suspicious though and she seemed really familiar and I couldn't stop myself smiling at her. Her voice was clipped but friendly, like I'd imagine the Queen to speak: 'You too, Billy.'

She was wearing a bright turquoise shirt and cream trousers and held out her hand to me. No one ever really shook my hand and I wasn't sure I did a very good job of it, my palms sticky with nerves.

'Are you a school friend of Tilly's here?'

'I'm...' I was already looking around for some inspiration. What was I? How had I ended up at this house?

Tilly diverted attention away from my reply. 'Gran, can we have some Sprite and a biscuit? I'm starving,' she said dramatically, giving a toothy grin.

The woman waved her away with an indulgent smile. 'Go on then, show Billy where to go and watch how you go, your mum is painting the hallway.'

It was over lemonade and biscuits covered in chocolate (no custard creams!) that I finally admitted to Tilly's grandma what had brought me to the house. I talked about the tin, the map, the house the only place we hadn't visited.

'And Elsie, she doesn't know you're here?'

I shook my head. 'The tin was full of other stuff too, like a pearl necklace and a picture of a man and this baby with the date 2nd March... Although I wanted it to be treasure.'

I hadn't noticed that Tilly's grandma had fallen silent at the date, her face white as she looked at me.

'Sorry, could you describe the things inside the tin again?' she asked in a slow, careful voice as Tilly piped up, 'Your birthday is March too!'

Something changed in the air.

I'd told her about the photos, the brush, the blanket, the boiled sweets and she had just nodded, quietly leaning back, her own glass of lemonade abandoned as if she was in a daze.

I'd been walking across the gravel on my way home when she'd rushed up to me, gripping my arm and looking over her shoulder back at the house.

'Will you tell her... tell her I... I think, I think... I'm the baby,' she had said, glancing over her shoulder again. 'Tell her to come.'

I frowned, not fully understanding. Her hand was firm on my arm, her voice different to earlier: faster, lower. I opened my mouth, not sure how to reply. Tilly was in the house, waving at me from a top window. 'I...'

'Tell her,' the woman had repeated urgently and I nodded, something in her face making me agree, some deep feeling that I somehow knew this old lady, I trusted her. 'Tell her to come and see me.'

So, I had told Elsie about the baby but I hadn't been able to tell her what Tilly's grandma had said to me on the driveway because she got too angry to hear any more. Look at how it had ended. I was confused and fed up, but I didn't regret going to that house.

Tilly wrote back when I was walking home, the new phone vibrating in my pocket. I looked around as I pulled it out, staring at the screen, at the simple smiley face reply that gave me more joy than I'd felt since I turned up in this stupid village on the coach. I hadn't realised how much I'd missed having friends, having a normal life. Now I had this phone, I came up with a plan.

Chapter 21

ELSIE

She hadn't moved from that chair at the kitchen table for hours, the sky outside streaked with pinks and blues, the orange ball of sun finally sinking beneath the treeline, lengthening the shadows until she was sat in darkness, her dresser, counters, oven mere outlines in the room as she blinked and came to.

What a terrible mess, she thought as she switched the light on, the harsh yellow making her blink.

'I'm sorry,' she said aloud, walking across the tiled floor. The soft crunch of pottery underfoot, the pieces of the polka-dot teapot. 'I'm—' She cut the apology short, a wave of anger gripping her. 'What a mess!' She wasn't just talking about Billy.

She crouched on the floor, picking up the larger parts of the teapot, muttering as she came across yet more broken pieces. She thought of the hundreds of cups of tea poured from that pot, her mother covering it lovingly with a caddy, setting it down in the centre of the table, cleaning it ever so carefully. And now it was broken: ruined, like so many other things.

She sat at the table, desperate to fix it, fetching the superglue she kept in a drawer. With trembling hands, she tried to piece it back together.

It wasn't impossible, surely? The spout was still intact and maybe once the big pieces were held together the smaller bits would follow. It was like a complicated jigsaw, she tried to convince herself, her fingertips sticky with the glue, tiny china dust clinging to them like powder.

But it was impossible, she knew, her eyes straining with the effort, her heart sinking with every attempt. She fetched the dustpan and brush from beneath the sink and with a choke, scraped the whole lot into the bin.

The bell rang, a sharp, decisive noise in the still of the house, and Elsie frowned, weary from the day, wanting to get upstairs, run a bath, sink into the water and try to order her thoughts. So much had been stirred up, things that she hadn't dared consider for over two decades. The bell went again, longer, insistent, as if someone was leaning on the button.

Elsie moved tentatively through the house, seeing an outline through the glass of the door. She took a breath, knew she must be strong.

Opening the door, she found her arms crossing, a defensive gesture of old, immediately glad to have done so in the face of Samantha's obvious anger.

'He might act all grown-up, but he's just a boy,' Samantha began, as if Elsie had interrupted her already ranting, 'and I found him at home, on his own, because you kicked him out!'

Elsie said nothing, bone-tired, her emotions spent. It was all true too: she had told him to leave.

'I trusted you,' Samantha said, her face breaking. 'You seemed to understand,' she added, her voice catching on the words before she composed herself, lifted her chin.

Elsie almost broke at that. She had understood, she knew what it was like to have no one. More than anyone, she knew that.

'Well, we won't be troubling you in the future, that's for sure.'

Elsie nodded, capitulating immediately, just wanting to shut the door on this tirade.

But Samantha hadn't finished, her eyes welling as she swiped at her face. 'What's wrong in your life that you think shouting at a little boy is OK? I thought you cared about him, I thought he meant something to you. Is that just how you treat people?'

Was that how she treated people? Elsie wondered. She thought about all the times she had let her own anger and frustrations out on people in the village. June irritated her but was she really all that bad? Did gentle Scarlet deserve more from her? The number of times she had shut down the start of a conversation. And why did she always give Mr Porter the butcher, always kind, such short shrift?

But this was so much worse. Billy had meant something to her: she had liked him, and he had needed someone. She felt shame fill her up, didn't relish the feeling, it made her even sharper.

'He meddled.' She glared, trying to convince herself perhaps?

He had expressly ignored her after she had told him not to go to that house. He had brought this all down on them. He had, quite literally, dug up her past. Elsie breathed loudly through her nostrils, reminding herself that she had just spent the last few moments sweeping up the mess.

'He broke my teapot, he ignored my inst—'

'I'll pay you back for your damn teapot!' Samantha interrupted, her eyebrows shooting upwards in amazement. 'God, is that what all this is about?'

'I don't want money,' Elsie bristled. 'He was careless and he doesn't listen...'

'He's just a young boy.'

Elsie stopped, head bowed, a swell of shame in her stomach.

'I lived with someone who spoke to me any which way he could and I won't have my boy fall into the same trap of loving someone with the same traits,' Samantha continued, her voice wobbling.

Elsie flinched at the word love. Was that what she had been feeling these last few weeks for that small boy? She thought then of the times she had looked over at him in the garden, earnestly following her instructions, at his excitement at seeing things in the village, his joy as he leapt into the river, his babbling excitement at making a new friend…

'I've told him not to come over here. Do you know he wanted to apologise? He said the teapot was important to you. Well, it shouldn't be as bloody important to you as a person!'

Elsie deserved this: she had shouted at him, she had let him go, she hadn't followed him, hadn't cared where he had ended up. She had been irresponsible, selfish and cruel. Samantha was right.

'What about the restaurant?' Elsie asked in a quiet voice, needing to fix things, panicking for a moment that she had ruined everything.

'I'll ask Polly from work to watch him, she needs money for travelling.'

Elsie didn't point out that Samantha barely had enough money for rent. She couldn't summon any words. She should have stayed away in the first place, not got caught up in it all. She had always stayed out of other people's business, never getting involved in their lives. After so many years, what had possessed her to think she could have helped? She had only brought misery on the boy and herself. She needed to close this door, draw the curtains, stick to the routines she knew; no one to mess them up, no one to hurt.

Samantha had dried up, distracted by a light shining from her own house. 'I need to get back to him, I told him I was getting milk.'

She started to walk away, turned back to say one last thing, her face highlighted in the glow of the outdoor light. 'He told me not to come here,' she added, a bruised look on her face, 'was worried he'd make it worse. See who the adult is in this scenario?'

Elsie pressed her lips together, choking down the emotion.

Samantha left, leaving the gate swinging open, and Elsie watched, an ache in her chest for all the things said, all the things she couldn't defend.

'I always mess things up,' Elsie said aloud.

She had always been unlovable. She had known that since the day she opened that tin, a memory box of items, twenty-eight years ago. Since the day the world she had known, the person she was, the person she thought her mother had been, came crashing down around her ears.

*

I told you once that when I was a teenager I snuck out in the middle of the night, with a small bag, my torch, a sweater, some food. I had loaded up the bag, creeping around the kitchen: taking bread from its spot under the chalkboard, biscuits from the red tin, a carton of orange juice.

I was meeting a boy, someone I had met in the library a few days before. I had been returning a book, a saga about a family in Tennessee.

'Was it any good?' he had asked, taking a step towards me.

I hadn't seen him before, my forearms breaking into goosebumps at the proximity. I could feel my face working away – speak, Elsie, speak – but all those years without peers, it felt so strange to talk to someone my own age. I just didn't know how to do it.

His blue eyes were mischievous as if he was on the edge of a great joke.

'Awful,' I said and he threw his head back and my eyes rounded in amazement as I heard his laugh, throaty and loud, earning a fierce glare from the librarian behind the counter.

He walked me home and asked me questions and I found myself flicking my hair over one shoulder, speaking in a lighter voice. I brushed his arm when he said something amusing, amazed at my new, confident persona.

'Where do you go to school then?'

'I don't,' I admitted.

'Cool!'

I realised he thought that meant I was older than I was, not that I had never been, and I didn't correct him. I wanted to pretend I was this entirely different person, this older girl who had opinions about books she read, who tinkled with abandon, and could make good-looking boys laugh in libraries. I liked her.

We arranged to meet after his shift in a local pub – if he thought it was a strange time to meet, he didn't say anything.

'The meadow,' he said, one eyebrow raised in a question.

I'd nodded and told him to be there.

The high street had been deadly still, familiar places now foreign shapes in the dark. There had barely been any moon and I had walked underneath the railway bridge, heart hammering, my hands gripping the handles of my bag.

He never showed.

And I cried. I cried self-pitying tears. I didn't want to walk home with my bag of food and my cartons of juice. I didn't want to go home at all. I sat in the dark on the bench that overlooked the bridge as the tears fell. I'd just wanted a night and someone to share it with.

Because it was too much. It got too much at times. In the house. Just us. Always.

Chapter 22

BILLY

The forms were handed out right at the end of the day, the accompanying slips of paper with our groups typed on them. I knew the moment I saw it, I'd have to get out of it.

The whole class was going to the New Forest for the end-of-term camping trip and I'd been put in a walking group with three other boys: Daniel, Javid and Max. You couldn't make it up. Me and the boys who hated me most walking through a forest together, no teachers for a million miles as we trekked to some horrible campsite to eat stuff out of packets and sleep in tents. It was like the teachers could see inside my head and extract my worst-ever idea.

It was obvious Daniel was well up for the chance to make my life hell and he was there at the gate when school finished, Javid standing next to him as if he was glued to him. I hated them, their stupid smirking faces. Why couldn't they get bored and pick on someone else? Feeling my skin prickle, I knew I couldn't avoid them now they'd seen me.

Daniel was holding the form for the trip in his left hand, sneering at me. 'You'll be carrying my rucksack, obviously,' he said, waving it at me. 'You need to get the practice in…'

'Why's that?' I asked, trying to look bold enough to answer back, just wanting to get through the gate and home. I hated him.

'Only thing you'll be doing in the future, isn't it? "Sir, sir, can I take your bag?",' he mimicked my cockney accent again, bowing and making Javid laugh.

I ignored him, stepping around him to get through the gate.

He spat on the ground in front of me, flecks hitting my shoe, turning my stomach. 'Oops, fly in my mouth!' He smiled, his teeth stained yellow in the front, breath all meaty. 'Stay and talk, Billy-Boy.'

I mumbled something, not brave enough to tell him where to go. Was anyone seeing this? Would anyone help me? Becky was with another girl up ahead. It looked like she was hanging back, looking back at me over her shoulder: was it kindness or pity?

Daniel pulled out his mobile, scrolled to his photos, playing a short video clip. Confused, I forgot Becky as I listened to echoing laughter and chatter. The images were wobbly: plain white walls, everything at a strange angle as if a phone was resting on the floor, the close-up of someone, pink flesh. 'You love to show off *all* your body when you change for PE, don't you?'

Feeling my cheeks go red, my hands curl tight, I stood there. Had he videoed me when I'd used the PE changing rooms? The thought made me feel sick. The clip had been too quick but I saw naked bits… What had he filmed? Was it definitely me?

Daniel was examining it now and I could hear the distinctive sounds of the concrete rooms we all showered and dressed in. 'You're not very big down there, are you, Billy?' Max and Javid twitching before barks of nervous laughter.

Oh my God! I needed to see it again, how much had he filmed? He must have hidden the phone under the slatted benches. I felt my stomach flip.

'Before you ask, yep, I'm thinking of sending it to the whole class so they can rate your body, so keep an eye out. Oh, wait, you're not even on the group chat.' He followed the line with a long grunt, his face screwed up. Javid paused for a second, eyes flicking worriedly over my shoulder and back to Daniel before laughing. Daniel had noticed too, narrowing his eyes at his little minion. Javid shrank backwards. Daniel really did have everyone in his pocket.

'Plenty of time to catch you again when you're dropping your trousers to shit into a hole in the woods,' he laughed, sliding the phone back into his pocket, then grunted again.

He stepped backwards, one arm out as if giving me permission to leave, and, miserably, head drooping, I did just that, pushing at the sticky wooden gate, walking out of the school grounds. The thought of me stood oblivious in the changing room with its dark wooden benches, its wobbly biro graffiti on the grey walls as I was filmed, made me want to cry.

I got home quickly, finding a note from Mum telling me she'd be back in ten minutes. Blinking, wanting a hug, wishing I could tell her what was going on, I raced up to my room and slammed the door. I pressed my whole body against the wood and pulled out my own phone, saw the pathetically short list of contacts. Who could I call? I couldn't even tell Liam, it was too embarrassing to write the words down. Tilly? There was no way I could tell her about a naked video – I didn't want to lose my only friend.

Hot with shame and the most alone I had ever felt, I sat on the edge of my bed, knowing no one could really help. For a second I thought of heading next door. Mrs Maple had been good at listening in the past, knew how Daniel made me feel. Maybe if I told her what he'd done, I'd feel better. Peeking out of the window, craning to see over the fence into her garden, so much of it hidden from view, I wondered if she was down there on her knees in the soil. Did she need someone to drag that ladder over to the gutters for her?

Then I remembered how she had glared at me, shouted at me, her eyes cold, and my heart hardened again.

The door went and Mum called out. Hiding the phone as quickly as I could under the mattress, I headed downstairs.

I didn't hand over the form, had stuffed it deep in my bag hoping it would just disappear. But, just my luck, it seemed that Mum, for about the first time in forever, had spoken to another parent. 'Poppy's mum told me there was some end-of-term trip announced today?' she said, twisting her hair up and clipping it, her fringe tucked behind her ears.

'Yeah,' I grunted, panicking as to how I could downplay it.

'Apparently there's a few things we might need for it: walking boots and the like.' She worried at a nail. I wasn't a rocket scientist but even I had worked that we didn't have any money, there's only so much carrot soup she could make.

I saw my way in. 'That's OK. If we don't have any money, I don't have to go.'

Mum looked horrified. 'Oh, don't be silly, of course we'll find a way! I won't have you missing out because of something stupid like money. Someone will have some second-hand,' she said. 'Poppy's mum was going to ask around for me.' She ruffled my hair and moved to collapse on the sofa.

I wrinkled my nose, already picturing a stinky pair of used boots full of another boy's sweat, plastered in mud. Great. No doubt the other boys would all turn up with new gear, some special camping fashion I couldn't even begin to compete with.

'I've never even stayed away from home,' I began, moving across to her with puppy-dog eyes. Mum was a sucker for that kind of thing, always calling me her 'baby' even though I squirmed and wriggled out of her hugs. This time I sat and snuggled in closer, smelling her shampoo with a hint of garlic from the restaurant as I nestled there, like I was a toddler all over again.

She stroked my hair. 'Hmm…' She didn't seem convinced. 'That's nice, but it's the whole class, Billy. This is exactly the kind of time to do it, it's perfect. Everyone will feel the same.'

It didn't take long for me to drop the snuggly toddler act and move straight to another tack, standing up and moving angrily through to the kitchen. 'It sounds rubbish! We have to stay in tents, it'll probably rain.' I slammed a cupboard door open, not shocked to see a few tins and barely anything else. I missed London with the crisps and snack-size chocolate bars Mum always hid but badly enough I could sniff them out. A rotting banana rested on its side and I sighed and picked it up.

'That's not like you,' Mum said, appearing in the door. 'You've become positively outdoorsy,' she added, a smile on her face. 'I can't believe you leapt in the river.'

'Just once,' I snapped.

Her smile slid from her face.

I'd have to be ill. All I knew was that I wasn't getting on that coach in that last week of term. No way!

'I've got homework,' I said, pushing past her in the doorway. I shut my eyes as she simply said a quiet OK.

Upstairs, throwing myself on my bed, I couldn't be bothered to reach for my bag. Homework could wait. I pulled out the mobile again, but I didn't want to message Liam, not to just moan. It was different: if he was here, I could talk to him. I was about to throw the mobile back down again when I saw it, the notification on Facebook messenger, realising with a jolt of surprise who it was before I even clicked on it.

My finger lingered over it before I pressed down to read it.

Where are you?

I could just tell him, could type the letters, I thought. My dad could have been here with me in less than a couple of hours. But something stopped me answering, an uneasy feeling in my stomach.

I knew Mum wouldn't like it, her voice tense every time I asked her about him. The questions she avoided. How stressed she sounded when she told me not to get in touch. My guilt that I'd found him on Facebook, had hidden that fact from her.

So why didn't I tell him now? I did want to see him, missed him, and at the moment I needed people around, needed someone to notice what the hell was going on – to help. Dad had an edge. If he knew about Daniel, I was pretty sure he'd be angry, wouldn't let him get away with it.

But a memory, a memory I hadn't thought about for a while and had deliberately pushed deep down so I didn't have to, slunk in. It was a couple of years ago, stood in the doorway of my room in our flat in London, late.

I'd been woken by a noise, imagining monsters in the dark, the outline of my dressing gown making my heart beat fast as I scrabbled up in bed as things came into focus, the nightmare vanishing.

Hushed voices, a strange, strangled noise. Coming from inside the flat, definitely not outside.

They were stood in the corridor, Mum in her tracksuit bottoms and T-shirt, the material bunched in Dad's hand, her stomach visible. I'd looked away, not wanting to see her like that, see the bottom of her bra. Were they hugging?

Then I saw the expression on her face, her eyes white and round as Dad held her against the wall, his big arm across her small body, resting on her neck, her feet on tiptoes. Something I didn't quite understand. Other smaller memories starting to form a pattern I didn't want to complete.

It didn't look like a hug.

I'd stepped backwards, creeping quickly back to my bed, curled right up tight, face to the wall, felt the smallest creak of my door as someone pushed at it, light leaking into the room from the hallway.

I'd held my breath, squeezed my eyes tight. I was asleep: I hadn't seen anything, it had just been a bad dream.

The next morning I'd woken up and convinced myself it had been just that. Dad was sat at the table smiling at me, asking me about football practice, making a joke at Mum, who stood round-shouldered at the oven. It was fine, I'd thought, my answer sticking in my throat. It was fine, this was normal.

I tried to ignore Mum's face as she placed my cornflakes in front of me, pretended not to notice the bloodshot eyes or the purple mark that peeked out of the top of her trousers when she bent down to pick something up. It was fine, it was normal. I had forced myself to eat the whole bowl, feeling the cornflakes bubble in my stomach.

In the middle of nowhere! I finally wrote back on Facebook, as if I were joking. As if I didn't know what Dad was really asking.

I watched the little message send, shutting off the phone quickly, this time not wanting a reply, sticking the phone back where it belonged.

I could hear Mum downstairs fixing us something for dinner – baked beans again, probably – and bit my lip. I knew my dad, knew he wouldn't give up. And it was my fault: I had started this.

Chapter 23

ELSIE

The next few days were a mess of missed timings, lost hours, afternoons spent in the garden, her neck burning as she bent over, barely touching the soil. Jobs mounted up, weeds grew: the garden was becoming out of control once more.

The worst thing about it was that Elsie didn't care. The garden was no longer a comfort, no longer a place she could go to be with her memories of the past, the happy ones she chose to recall. Now all she saw was the spot under the tree where the soil had been disturbed, where the tin had been found, the secrets of her past unearthed.

Worse than that, she missed Billy in the garden, noticed his absence as she glanced across to an empty flower bed, a neglected fence. The grass grew taller, needing cutting. When she ventured inside she strained to hear him through the walls: a clunk, some footsteps, a low voice.

She missed his face, his easy smile, the exasperated roll of his eyes when he explained something she didn't understand: what FaceTiming meant, that a TikTok was not the same as a Tic Tac. She missed his solemn expression when she taught him something he didn't know how to do, making meringues, his face when she showed him all the fruit in the freezer, all picked from her trees. She missed his stories, like the time he and Liam got stuck up a tree chasing a squirrel in the park, even the sad stories where he needed to be heard, missed being the person he confided in.

Yet she couldn't seem to find a way, or a will, to fix it. Samantha had been so angry and she convinced herself she should stay away. If she talked to him she would have to explain and she knew she didn't have the words, couldn't find them, still grappling with the things he had thrown into motion once more. She hadn't been able to deal with it for decades, why would it change now?

The chalkboard was bare, no energy even to write up the jobs she should be ticking off. 'I knew I'd mess it up,' Elsie said, her voice loud in the kitchen. Why did her mother never speak back? What would she say to her?

Even the comforting ritual of teatime had been robbed, the bag that had contained the broken teapot taken by the binman. She had panicked, leaving the house in slippers, pulling her dressing gown round herself as she heard the devastating clink and smash of the black bin being emptied. She should have saved it; perhaps a professional might have had more luck, perhaps she should have kept the broken parts as keepsakes.

The next few days passed in a cloud of inactivity. A few days later, chased out of her house by hunger, she bumped into June in the High Street. She'd just wanted to get out, race back, and she flinched as the other woman bore down on her.

'That form isn't back. I thought you said he was keen, Elsie?' June said, her cropped hair an even more startling shade of red as she emerged from the hair salon.

'He is… he's…' Elsie couldn't find the words. So, Billy hadn't applied for the patch in the allotments. The thought made her heart sear with fresh pain.

'I'll have others wanting the spot, Elsie,' said June, 'I can't wait around forev…'

Elsie moved away without replying. Billy had been so excited by his plans, had drawn up designs: carrots, courgettes, even an artichoke plant.

'It takes two years, Elsie, but then it should produce a good crop,' he had told her, 'I saw it on a leaflet.'

Had she killed his love of gardening too?

A thought occurred to her and she found herself moving into the library in a daze of these worries.

'Good morning,' Scarlet said, a wide smile, her tone bright.

Elsie nodded in response.

'Do you want to borrow anything in particular?' Scarlet's voice carried across the empty library.

Elsie regretted coming in almost immediately, not prepared to chat today, just wanting to fetch what she was after and head home as dark thoughts crowded in once more. Perhaps if she put things in a letter it might help? She thought then of her desk, the purple fountain pen, a fresh piece of paper. One of the few things that transported her in time, out of this present mess. She might have lost Billy but she hadn't lost that.

'Can I help, Elsie? We've had a few new releases come in this morning, I've popped them on the shelf just there…'

Scarlet had moved around the counter and was stepping over to the shelf she had pointed to. 'Have you finished your last lot? You do read quickly,' she added as Elsie searched for the sign for Non-Fiction.

Scarlet was still standing in front of her. Elsie just wanted the book – it would help her fix things, perhaps. 'I actually thought of you because you enjoyed one of Hannah Richell's earlier novels and her latest is out, if you're interested?'

'No, no, I'm not,' Elsie said, the smallest flicker of surprise crossing Scarlet's face before hurt filled her eyes.

No more chatting about favourite authors or new releases, Scarlet slunk back behind the counter without another word, the tap of a computer keyboard to show she had given up trying to be nice. Elsie deserved it.

Another woman appeared, someone Elsie didn't recognise, a smile and some low voices as she returned a couple of books. Outside, people walked past the window of the library to the shops, pushing trolleys, prams or deep in conversation. It seemed the whole world just kept turning.

Elsie moved across to the shelves and started to run a finger along the correct section. There weren't too many books: the lakes of the UK, bird watching, an encyclopaedia of insects and a couple of gardening books – something Billy could glean some new information from. One looked wordy, its pages yellowed, the text too small, but the other was full of glossy photos, a calendar of when to do things throughout the year, a chatty informal style. Elsie felt her heart lift as she flicked through it.

Finding an appropriate book had relaxed Elsie a little more and she gave Scarlet a small smile as she handed it over. 'Thank you,' she said.

Scarlet passed the book under the scanner. 'Well, I'm glad I caught you. Another five minutes and I'd have missed you. I've got a dress fitting. Did I tell you last time we're getting married?'

Elsie's face fell. 'No, no, you didn't mention it,' she replied, her teeth gritting.

'I'm just looking for ways to save money, you know, and there's a sample sale on so I thought I might head into town and take a look. I've already bought the cutest outfit for Harry to wear, with a little bow tie attached!'

Elsie didn't want to discuss baby bow ties or weddings. Definitely not. She said nothing in response, just bit the inside of her cheek, and hoped Scarlet would hand back the book, that she could leave the library, the smell of books and dust behind, a smell she normally associated with positive things. She just wanted this friendly, softly-spoken woman to stop talking to her.

'How's that lovely boy then? He still helping you in the garden?' she asked as she passed over the book.

Elsie licked her lips, her throat dry as she swallowed, hugging the book to her chest.

'I was saying to my partner that I'd ask your advice on flowers we could put at the front of our house. It's north-facing and I wasn't sure which ones might work and then I thought, I know who would know…'

Elsie didn't want to hear it. Lucky Scarlet.

'The garden centre should have ideas,' she replied curtly.

Scarlet fell silent, shifting on her own stool, an uncomfortable pause between them. This felt more familiar: they hadn't really spoken in years, this was how things had once been. Hello, scan a book, leave.

Scarlet popped a biro back in the desk, slowly, and took a breath. 'I hope you don't mind me asking,' she said, looking up, 'but you don't quite seem yourself. Is anything wrong?'

Elsie looked down at her, mouth pressed together, noticed Scarlet cringe. 'Nothing of import. I don't speak to the boy any more.'

Scarlet couldn't help her reaction, her mouth opening, a line between her eyes, 'Oh, what happened? Can it be fixed?'

'Fixed? Don't be so presumptuous!' Elsie snapped. 'You can't just wave a magic wand and expect life to be fine.' She took a step backwards. 'I really must be getting on,' she announced. Busy, busy, always busy.

She thought of the old things she used to do to fill her day: the set times to walk into the village, jigsaws, Solitaire, television viewing, tea, cleaning, dusting. Busy.

No goodbye as Elsie stepped across to the door and out into the street, a quick glance back to see Scarlet watching her leave, a miserable look on her young features.

For a fleeting second Elsie regretted the exchange but how could Scarlet possibly understand anything with her bonny baby and her partner waiting for her as she walked down the aisle?

She left as it started to drizzle, her hair and woollen coat dotted with raindrops as she headed into her house. The oppressive silence surrounded her as she moved through to the kitchen, the table and counters a mess of crumbs, abandoned cups, plates, a saucepan with congealed porridge stubbornly stuck to it, a few flies resting and then circling, resting and then circling. Elsie lowered herself into the chair, reaching as she had done these last few days for the tin. The tin that had caused all this hideousness.

The items that should have brought her comfort didn't. The bag of boiled sweets, favourites from the dusty old sweet shop in the village, its shelves rammed with enormous glass jars with sweets of every colour and texture. Asking for a 'quarter' or a 'half' of boiled sweets, the bag bursting with those sugary treats. The playing cards, worn from endless games they had played together. The map with its reminders of picnics in bluebell woods, trips to the pictures.

All of it ruined with the other knowledge. Elsie picked up the photo of the baby, one finger moving across her features. A beautiful baby, hands raised as if about to clap, chubby cheeks. This was her blood relation, her half-sister. She felt a wave of shock that she had felt on first discovering this fact twenty-eight years ago.

She hadn't been truthful with Billy. She knew a lot more than she had told him.

Her mother had written a letter that was placed on the top of the mysterious items, a letter that Elsie had removed from the tin when she buried it out in their garden, wanting to pretend the whole thing never existed. A letter that, although it lived in the top drawer of Elsie's bedside table, was imprinted on the inside of her mind too, causing a constant circle of the same thoughts. Physical proof of the thing she most dreaded: her own bogeyman locked away.

My darling girl... it had said. It had revealed the truth and shattered everything Elsie thought she'd known.

Things that had never made a great deal of sense started to reveal their special meaning. Elsie recalled the date on the back of the photo of the baby – 2nd March – a day in spring every year when her mother would bake a Victoria sponge, place a candle on the top. They would hold hands over the cake and blow it out together. 'For someone special,' her mother always whispered and, strangely, Elsie had simply accepted it. A quirk; a pleasant ritual. For many years, it was simply lovely to have cake.

She'd thought of that ritual when she had first drawn that photo from the tin. The special someone her mother had always honoured in that way. Had she loved this baby more, Elsie wondered. Was she more special than Elsie had been? Was that why her mother had kept so much secret?

The nasty thought ate away at Elsie over the months after her mother's death as she moved through the house they had shared together. The same questions always on a loop. She lost weight; she didn't take care of herself; she dreamt of the red tin, the items mocking her, reminders that her mother had kept so much from her, her other pea in a pod indeed. Then, almost a year after her mother had died and she had discovered her secret, Elsie had found herself stood, mesmerised, in front of two stone pillars in a village a short way away, at a house marked on a handwritten map.

The woman in the window, in the grand house. Elsie had noticed with a jolt that she was roughly the same height, the same build as her. What else would be the same? What else would be different? People had often commented that her mother had looked similar. Elsie had her eyes. Elsie had her bone structure.

Two peas in a pod.

Elsie realised tears had filled her eyes as she stared at the woman in the window, the special someone, the sister she never knew she had.

Then there had been a delighted shout from nearby and the noise had prompted Elsie to think of a seaside visit, of watching from a towel next to her mother as other sisters and brothers played games, splashed in and out of the sea, built sandcastles. She could have had a sister, someone to play with, to tease her, to run over the sand with. She wouldn't have always had to sit sensibly on the towel next to her mother; she wouldn't have always felt so alone, so other.

The woman in the window had looked happy, watching as in the garden two children played, their cries the sounds Elsie had heard. They had been streaking across the lawn in each other's wake, rolling and giggling as they played, so close to Elsie she could have reached out. So, the baby in the photo had a family – her own family. Elsie's mother had been a grandmother.

That thought had winded her and she had staggered back from her spot into the shadow of the grand walls, clutching her stomach as the grief and sadness that had built up over the last year seemed to boil within her.

She placed the photo on the table now, her fist balled over it, obscuring the image. With a decisive jolt, she slammed it hard into the table, the noise loud in her small house.

Moving through to the front room she sat at her desk, pouring her pain and regret onto the sheet: picturing the kind face of the recipient, their gentle, understanding look as she wrote and wrote and wrote. In purple ink she replayed the day she had discovered the tin, the secrets inside and what it had meant. The way in which her world had tilted on its axis so that she started to question everything she'd been told.

She left the house, the rain gone, the sun dipping behind clouds, the wind lifting her hair, the letter safe in an envelope in her hand. She felt calmer now that she had shared her thoughts, knew that the person reading would understand. She headed down the road, turning the corner to the lane, the red postbox in the distance her destination.

As she stood in front of it she took a breath, noticing the corner of another envelope peeking from the black slot.

The postbox was finally full, long since decommissioned many, many years ago, her own letters piling up inside. All to the same person, all one-sided. She pushed the latest one in as far as it could go, jamming it hard, needing to pretend a moment longer that someone read them.

Chapter 24

BILLY

'God, is Polly coming *again*?'

Polly worked with Mum and came and 'babysat' for me, which actually she didn't really do. She just sat on her mobile phone on the sofa bitching to her best mate about her boyfriend, who sounds like an absolute melt. And Polly doesn't hide the fact she thinks our house is rubbish and, fine, our house *is* rubbish but I get all defensive when someone else points out the damp patch in the corner, the empty fridge, the papery loo paper that Mum definitely steals from work and the walls covered in random nails and no pictures.

'What, you want to go back to Mrs Maple?' Mum asked, snapping as she buttoned up her work shirt ready for her shift.

'No, but…'

Mum sighed, 'Believe me, Billy, I don't want Polly here either. For a start I have to pay her, but…'

'I'm old enough to look after myself,' I insisted for the thousandth time.

Mum bit her lip. I could tell she was tempted but then she shook her head, twisting her skirt round to do up the zip. 'It's not right. And I don't mind. I know how Mrs Maple spoke to you and I don't want you back there.'

'She could be alright,' I shrugged.

'Billy, she shouted at you and made you cry, and you *never* cry,' Mum said, a wound-up look on her face. 'And then I went round and was so rude to her, there's no way she'd watch you again even if I begged.' She straightened her clothes and started biting at a nail again, a new habit she seemed unable to stop.

'Mum, please, just for today, I promise you I'll be good! I'll even stop by the restaurant and I'll look both ways crossing the road and I'll behave myself…'

I could see she was tipping as she glanced at the door. 'But what if—'

'Come on, Mum, please?'

'I'll text Polly and see,' she finally said and I flew into her arms, the hug brief, her hand on my head.

She couldn't stop the quick grin and I felt better too – I used to always make Mum smile like that.

So, Polly wasn't coming and Mum left me five pounds, placing both hands on my shoulders before she left. 'You know where I am and you can come to the restaurant whenever. And if anything happens like you break a leg or something then do go next door.'

'What, with a broken leg?' I replied, with a silly frown. 'How would I drag myself round ther—'

'Don't tease,' she replied, hands falling to her side, mouth twitching.

'I won't break my leg. Go on, go to work.'

'You promise you'll just stay here?' she asked, letting me fetch her handbag.

'I promise. Go on…' I fussed over her, as if the roles were reversed and then, once the door was shut, looked around the front room.

This *did* feel weird.

It didn't take me long to get bored, having nothing to play with, no gaming, no TV or comics. It meant it was pretty much schoolwork or that book I was meant to have read in English. Elsie would have told me to read the book, would have forced me onto the sofa with the weird newt cushion, brought me pear squash on a tray and made me read a chapter. I wandered the house for a while, bouncing a tennis ball I'd picked up on the way back from school against the wall of my room, the marks it made adding to all the other scuffs on the dirty wall.

I had about six hours of this.

Reaching for the mobile I had hidden under the mattress, I tapped out a message, a smile on my face as the ping returned.

A few messages back and forward and it was agreed.

I knew where I was headed.

For the first time in days I was going to see someone who actually liked me. Slipping the house key, the mobile and the fiver into my pocket, I shut the front door, a tiny tug of concern that Mum might find out. But she wouldn't be back for hours: I could be there and back before she returned.

All my guilt was forgotten on feeling the relief of walking up to the pillars of the big house, Tilly practically dragging me to the front door.

'Oh my God, come on! Rory keeps trying to make me play with Grandad's trainset and I am sooooo bored. And it's so sunny so we should totally go to this place I know. It's awesome.'

I could barely get a word in edgeways but I felt the relief of someone loud and bright and happy leading the way, being swept up in her crazy enthusiasm.

'Alright, alright!' I laughed, feeling lighter than I had done in days. The posh outside of the house was a million miles from the bleak, lonely place I'd left behind and my worry about Mum soon melted away as I followed Tilly through the front door, the hallway smelling of lavender and furniture polish. For a moment I thought of Elsie.

'We'll grab some stuff from the kitchen first, sneak past Rory and hope he doesn't hear us. I told Gran you were coming but she had this meeting about the village fete next week because she's the chairperson on the committee…'

I thought back to the woman I had met with her string of pearls and her smart shirt and wasn't surprised to hear she was the type of person to be on a committee. She definitely made her own jam.

'Anyway, she's back later and promised me I'd get you to stay for high tea, which literally no one calls it, but it will be good because I think she'll make scones, we always have scones if there are visitors. She's been a bit funny, though, asking me questions about that blanket…'

We were in the kitchen now, an enormous farmhouse kitchen with an island in the middle and a bottle-green Aga with shiny saucepans hanging from the wall behind. There were photos everywhere: pinned to corkboards, stuck around the walls, framed. Loads of smiling photos of people clustered into the shot, cheeks pressed together, at barbecues, beaches, horse trials, fairgrounds; happy people, enjoying themselves. It made my head swim, all those people, all these busy lives, and somehow Mrs Maple, the old lady who lived entirely on her own, was connected to them.

Maybe I shouldn't have come. What was the great secret?

'I'm so pleased you found it…'

Why had Elsie been so cross? I batted away the feeling that she would be angry I was back here. What was I expected to do though? Tilly was about the first person in the county to seem pleased I was here and I couldn't give that up. I thought then of the school trip away coming up and felt my mood dip, barely hearing Tilly's chatter as I thought of another long school week ahead of me.

'OK, so I made us sandwiches but they're a bit crap.'

Looking up, I could see the countertop covered in crumbs, a plastic bag filled with stuff. Tilly was adding two golden Crunchie bars and there were already Kit Kats inside.

I followed Tilly through the house, stepping over a thick, soft pink carpet in a living room lined with bookshelves and expensive-looking oil paintings, out through fancy French doors and down onto the manicured lawn. Skirting the tennis court, the long grass tickled my calves as we ran, plunging into the cool of the small wood behind the house, the smell of the damp soil following us as we moved deeper into the trees. Tilly seemed to know where she was headed, swinging the plastic bag of food and keeping up a steady stream of talk.

'Rory doesn't like it here because I told him there were wolves and he's soooo gullible, he totally believed me.'

Hearing a crack to my right, I hoped Tilly was correct. I didn't know much about wolves and had definitely never seen one. The most dangerous animal I'd ever seen was a fox that used to skulk by the communal bins at the bottom of our apartment block in London. But this was the country and creepy woods could definitely have wolves.

'But I used to make dens and a wigwam and there's this cool place... Well, you'll see...' she said, ducking under spiky tendrils and pushing back branches that pinged back in my face.

'Hey!'

'Sorry!' she chimed, laughing.

The trees cleared and Tilly was sat along a fallen trunk, waiting for me to join her. In front of her was a large oval shape that, on first sight, I might have mistaken for bright green grass. Then I noticed the lily pads and the still surface being disturbed by a large winged insect.

'It's a lake!' I realised, eyes widening.

'Well, a pond. But I like to imagine it's like the one where the sword comes out of the centre. It looks super strange, doesn't it?'

I nodded. 'It's cool.'

'I knew you'd like it.' She slapped the trunk either side of her and grinned at me, and the way she said it made my heart soar. 'So,' she said, opening the plastic bag, 'what do you want to eat first?'

I went straight for the Kit Kats and she beamed.

We played stupid games next to the pond, endless rounds of Paper, Scissors, Stone and telling each other various stories.

'You know,' she said, standing up to walk along the trunk, arms stuck out for balance, 'I still don't get how you found this house on a map. Why was it on there?'

I shrugged, not really able to answer. 'I thought it was a treasure map maybe,' I started, feeling a bit silly now I'd said it out loud. Tilly seemed a bit too old to believe in stuff like that but she didn't laugh at me, just jumped from the trunk and sat down again. 'But I really don't know. Elsie, the lady whose mum drew it, she's a bit weird about it, like she's sort of frightened of it.' I hadn't really thought about it like that until the words came out. 'Yeah, frightened.'

Tilly laughed. 'It's not exactly scary. A tin with a photo of a baby in. Maybe Grandma is the baby or maybe the house has a special meaning or something. It's cool, nothing exciting ever happens here.'

She sat back for a while, probably wondering about the map and what it all meant. I didn't tell her what her grandma had said to me because of how Elsie had gone mental. That thought made me realise I should probably get home soon.

'Will your mum want to know where we are?' I asked, knowing Mum wouldn't love me being in a strange wood, miles from anywhere.

'She's OK, she's working in the house. She has another fair coming up, she sells prints of hunts and things.'

'Right,' I replied, not completely sure what that meant. 'What does your dad do?' I asked, wondering why I hadn't seen him.

Tilly twisted the handle of the plastic bag. 'He works in property.'

'Cool! Round here?'

'No, he lives in London now.'

I hadn't picked up the change in her voice. 'Oh… does he get back at weekends then?'

Tilly fell quiet. 'He left a few years ago,' she said, her voice different. 'That's why we came to live with Grandma. Grandad had died so it sort of fitted because she was alone. I see him for holidays and things though. He got married last year,' she added, the plastic bag twisted tightly round her fist, turning her knuckles white.

Her face was sad and I didn't know what to say. This was the first time things had been awkward between us and I started to panic she might not want to talk to me any more.

'How about your dad?' she asked, looking up at me.

'Oh, he's a builder, sort of part-time,' I said, a bit embarrassed she might say it was a rubbish job, or ask how often he was out of work. I thought of all the days when I'd get back from school and he hadn't moved from the same spot, sat on the sofa with a can of beer. I thought of what Daniel would say about it and knew it would be another thing to tease me about.

'That's cool,' Tilly said, picking at the bark on the trunk we were sat on, 'my dad can't put up a shelf.'

I felt myself grow a little taller.

She threw a piece of bark into the water in front of us and we watched as it was swallowed by the strange, bright green layer. 'So how come he doesn't live with you?'

I probably would have lied if she hadn't told me about her own dad and I didn't want to mess things up with the only friend I had made in months. But it still felt strange to say it out loud.

'Mum left him.'

Saying it for the first time made me realise, in that moment, the words were absolutely true: Mum had left him. For good. She had taken me with her, in the middle of the night, and left him.

'How come?' Tilly asked, twisting to face me, curiosity in her voice. 'Was he having an affair?'

'No,' I replied, realising I was sure that wasn't it. 'I think…' I said slowly, trying to put into words my suspicions, feeling nausea swirl in my stomach. Tilly was waiting, fiddling with this pink bead on a sort of leather necklace she was wearing.

Maybe that's what made me suddenly think of it. One evening, when I was meant to be in bed, Mum had let me stay up watching TV and she'd been working on one of her beaded things and all the pots were out on the table and Dad came back early from the pub. He didn't see me laid out on the sofa and he'd said something to Mum. He didn't like her reply and had swept the pots onto the floor so they rolled in every direction and I'd lain there really scared but then he went to their bedroom and fell asleep. I found loads of small silver beads under the coffee table the next day and just put them back in the right pot for Mum.

I never lingered on these thoughts. I felt sweat prickle in my hairline, felt my throat sandpaper dry as I swallowed. Still, Tilly was looking at me, head tipped to one side, ready to hear, and I didn't want to fob her off.

'He wasn't always very nice,' I said with a small cough, reaching for the water bottle she had brought. Was that it, the whole truth, I thought as I swigged at it.

Tilly didn't reply, her expression shifting into something I couldn't pinpoint. I coughed again and picked at the bark too. A large piece came away in my hand and I turned it over in my lap.

Unable to stop some of the bad memories I closed my eyes briefly, wanting them to vanish. The whispered row in the middle of the night and Mum crying the next day. Her face when Dad walked into the kitchen, all white and panicky. A smile which didn't show her teeth as she put some toast and marmalade in front of him. An anniversary dinner that had ended early, Mum locking him out, screaming through the door that she'd call the police. Him banging and banging and then her finally, after so much racket, letting him in. The shower going on in the bathroom… Horrible, horrible sounds I didn't want to remember.

The bark was breaking apart in my hands. I didn't want to think these things. I hadn't seen anything. Nothing concrete. What was it really? A memory of some unusual mornings, Mum quiet, a funny atmosphere I couldn't work out, knowing to keep my head down, not wanting to make him angry at me.

Mum had just left. People did it all the time. I hadn't seen anything.

Tilly was talking to me and I blinked, the bright green blurring in front of me.

'So, your mum ran away with you?' she asked, unable to hide her surprise.

'Yeah, kind of,' I said, throwing the bark into the water, ripples there and then disappearing.

'Woah!' Tilly replied, breaking the sudden tension.

'Yeah.' I laughed, wanting to pop the strange bubble I had created, my laugh not quite right.

We shared a look, I bit my lip, waited and then, at the same moment, we burst into relieved laughter.

'This got deep,' she said.

'Yeah.'

'You're OK though,' she added, throwing a piece of bark at me.

'You too.'

She shrugged, smiled and handed me a Crunchie. It felt nice, natural. If I'd ever had a sister I think I would have liked one like Tilly. Tilly and Billy, I thought with a grin.

Her grandma was home by the time we got back to the house. Tilly was right, she had made scones, and we sat round the big brown table that had dents and marks and water rings on it and felt like the table of a large family who drank and ate and debated and laughed. I traced a mark with my finger.

'It's so weird, isn't it, Grandma, that Billy found us on a map?' She nicked another scone from the big plate in the middle of the table.

'Very,' Tilly's grandma said. Then she looked at me, a strange expression on her face. 'And do you think Elsie might want to visit too?' she asked, as if she couldn't say what she was thinking.

I swallowed, knowing this was probably her way of asking whether I'd passed her message on, telling Elsie to come to the house. 'Maybe,' I said, not wanting to meet her eyes, not wanting to tell her how Elsie had reacted.

Fortunately, at that moment Tilly's mum appeared, rubbing her eyes and distracting us all with a story about some man who wanted to buy fourteen prints and how it made up for the bad fair she'd had at the weekend. 'He was on the phone for nearly an hour,' she said, moving across to the table with a mug.

Tilly's grandma moved quietly away.

I said goodbye, lying to them about Mum meeting me in the village, and walked back to the station on my own. The trouble was when I got there the board above told me the trains were cancelled. The next one was over an hour's wait. An hour. The longest a train was delayed in London was about eight minutes and *everyone* complained.

Biting my lip, I stood on the empty platform, wondering what the hell to do. I had no idea how to walk back and wasn't sure it would be shorter than if I waited for the next train. I could call Mum at work but then she'd know I was out *and* that I had a mobile and she would be furious and take it too.

I could go back to Tilly's and persuade them to drive me home but then I'd have to admit I lied to them too. Hitching a lift was impossible because I'd seen all of about two cars since getting here and they might kidnap me or something and that would be even worse than Mum being angry.

I waited on the platform, trains a loud blur as they passed, blowing back my hair, the noise all around me as they sped straight through. Finally, after sitting on my hands for an hour, goosebumps on my arms as the sun disappeared behind clouds, the slow train huffed and stopped in front of me and I got on, praying I wouldn't also bump into a ticket inspector and have to waste the five pounds.

Nervously, I half-jogged through the village, not worrying who saw me, just needing to get home in the hope I could beat Mum there. Sometimes her boss made her stay on and do an extra job and even though he never paid her for the time and she knew it was unfair, she was too frightened not to do it because he might stop giving her the shifts that she needed so badly. I hoped Dick had done just that today and I could be sat in the living room, looking sympathetic as Mum raged about him.

But she was there as I stepped inside the house. Stood in the middle of the front room, her back to me. I swallowed as I moved inside. She turned, her face pale and tear-stained.

'Oh my God, Billy!' she cried, rushing towards me and squeezing me tightly, her body smelling of sweat and pizza dough. The surprise of it made me freeze. She seemed frantic, her arms so tight, mine were clamped by my sides. Then she drew back, her face quickly moving to anger. 'Where the hell have you been?'

Licking my lips, I began the lie I'd rehearsed when sat on the empty platform, 'I needed a walk and I just…'

'You promised me you'd stay here,' she cut off, 'you promised… I thought your da— I thought…' She started crying again and I bit my lip, not knowing what to do.

'You're grounded,' she said, through sobs.

'But I only went…'

'I don't care. You promised you'd stay here.'

What if I really had just popped out for a quick walk to get some fresh air? This was a massive overreaction.

I felt my skin pulse as I straightened. 'So, I should have just stayed inside all day doing what? It's like *prison*!' I shouted.

Mum looked as if I'd slapped her, stepping backwards, her expression desperate and hurt.

'I'm fed up with being on my own,' I carried on, the guilt at lying to her making me sound angrier than I was. 'You don't even care. Have you noticed that I literally have no friends here?'

'I…' She started and then stopped, mouth closing, tears lining her eyes again.

'You've dragged me to the actual middle of nowhere,' I said, one arm flinging around to show up the room. Our plates left over from the pizza dinner we had on our laps the night before that wasn't even a TV dinner because we didn't have a TV. 'And then you're making me stay inside all day.'

'But, Billy, I...' Mum wasn't angry any more, fresh tears spilling down her cheeks. 'I just want to keep you safe.'

'Whatever,' I replied, starting for the stairs to my room, wanting to get up there away from her face that made me feel a million times worse. Why couldn't I stop shouting? 'You haven't even told me how long we're staying here for,' I said, turning at the doorway. 'And you won't let me talk to Dad on the phone, or even tell me why I can't. It's not like he can do anything on the phone. It's not fair!'

She nodded sadly, head dipping onto her chest. 'It's difficult. I don't want you to think...' She bit her lip. 'Just give me a bit more time, Billy. Please.'

Chapter 25

ELSIE

She broke her usual routine. It had been thrown out already after so many days with Billy, the clock becoming less important, the rituals that tied her day together forgotten, her chalkboard waiting for jobs she wouldn't do. She was visiting the wood where they had picnicked. The bluebells were gone now, everything less bright today. She didn't stay long; she had thought the place might make her feel better, the map representing all the places her mother had loved, places they'd shared, but the house sat in the corner of the map had soured everything.

Her mother had loved her, loved her so much, she thought as she tramped back through the fields behind the village, birds circling, the sun stubbornly hiding behind a bank of cloud. She knew that and yet that house in the corner of the map, the photo and the blanket had unravelled everything.

She remembered the first time she had opened that tin, the red box her mother had left at the bottom of her wardrobe, the card resting on the top: *For Elsie*. Frowning, she had read the words, her skin breaking into goosebumps as she'd picked up the various items, as she realised the significance of what she'd found.

The lies her mother had told her.

I love you, my darling, my precious girl. Always peas in a pod, just the two of them. Home-schooled, lessons in the village, on the meadow under the oak tree, in their garden learning about nature, lessons bent over lined textbooks at the kitchen table. Trips to the cinema, the woods, the river, the allotment, reading on the train. Just them.

But it hadn't been *just them*. She hadn't been her only girl. She had been the second of two daughters. She had been lied to.

Anger that she couldn't ask more questions, that she'd been robbed of that chance, swirled within her, made her fists clench. The woman she was mourning seemed to disappear in smoke. Who had she been? Who was her mother really? Elsie wondered as she tried to catch the wisps of her memories as they passed her. Had she loved her or had she been making up for the daughter she had loved more? Had the love and the closeness been real or was it all just smoke and mirrors?

These thoughts swirled as she returned to the village, mud from the fields still stuck to her boots, past the door of her own house, a quick glance at her neighbour's door, a flush of shame as she thought about the little boy who lived there. He was better off without her, she convinced herself as she passed.

The graveyard was empty and she hadn't brought along any flowers. Today she didn't feel like placing anything in front of the gravestone. She wished the woman buried beneath was alive, in their house, not just a presence that she spoke to in the walls. She needed to talk to her, needed to hear her explain, reassure.

She didn't want to kneel, so she stood staring down at the flattened ground, her arms folded across her chest. 'I don't want to feel like this,' she admitted, the years stripped back as if she was a teenager seeking comfort. 'I don't want to keep wondering why you kept your secret for so long. I thought…' She felt the tears build in her throat, her chest start to heave. 'I thought we trusted each other with everything.'

She cupped a hand to her neck, aware her voice was rising in the empty place, echoing off the gravestones, the church looming in front of her. 'You let me believe it was always best, just you and me, and that you liked it that way. But it was your guilt that made our world so…' – she dropped the hand – 'so small.'

A tear trickled slowly down her cheek and she brushed it away, her voice catching on the next few words. 'I know you would say I could have left. I nearly did and do you remember, remember what you said to me?'

It was hopeless. There was no one there to fight with and she knew too that she had allowed her life to take on this shape. She had avoided facing the other things she had learnt, still cowering from them even now.

She sunk to her knees, her trousers instantly damp as she stared at the gravestone, at the letters of her mother's name: Rosa Maple. A beautiful name. Her mother had been beautiful. She had been her mother. Her only friend. She didn't want to feel these things towards her. She didn't want to blame her in this way.

She left the graveyard, bereft and alone, intending to head straight home, to play her mother's favourite Ella Fitzgerald records and sit in the front room surrounded by the prints and figurines that had comforted her over the years, the things her mother had loved. She so desperately wanted to drink peppermint tea from the polka-dot teapot and try to feel close to her.

One of the shops on the high street made her pause, beckoned to her as she passed on the other side of the road, a chance perhaps to be comforted by a person, perhaps, not an object. She found herself crossing over.

Pushing open the heavy glass door to the butcher she glanced behind the counter, the young Darren in attendance. She waited, ready to see Mr Porter's endlessly perky face appear from the room behind.

'Good morning,' she said, approaching the counter, 'a lamb and rosemary pie.'

It was normally at this moment he would appear. 'Elsie,' he'd say, and follow it up with some comment about the weather, the village gossip, something her mother had once told him, asking her, for the millionth time, to call him Stanley.

Her pie was wrapped in paper and Darren gave her a frightened glance: '£3.85, please.'

She handed over the money.

'Stan's ill,' he said in a sudden burst. 'If you were wondering…'

She hadn't been expecting the announcement. 'I wasn't,' she replied, not wanting to be thought of as a nosy gossip.

Darren's expression changed, a hardness in his eyes. 'I thought you might care. We're all a bit worried.'

She felt the sting of his words, pictured Mr Porter's friendly face, his endless attempts to engage her, his easy manner. She backed away. She had come to see Stanley, she realised, to see someone who had cared about her mother too. Now what did this young man want from her? She couldn't have known. Why did she always get things wrong?

She was still thinking about the exchange as she walked past the chemist, not hearing the tinkle of the bell, the sound of footsteps behind her before she felt the grip on her arm.

'Elsie,' June said, her hair spiked down onto her forehead today like strange angry 'W's. 'The form, Elsie, I've still had nothing back.'

Elsie shrugged her off, thrown by the contact, the fresh reminder of the things she'd lost. 'I—'

'That's children these days, Elsie. They can't set their minds to anything. If it isn't a mobile, it's a—'

'Billy is perfectly able to set his mind to something,' Elsie snapped, her voice loud in the quiet street.

June's mouth puckered.

'If you could stop hassling me about it,' Elsie huffed, her anger spilling out onto this woman.

June put one hand on her chest. 'Hassling? I'm just doing my job. You were the one so keen for the form, others have to wait months for an allotment. But as a special favour to you, Elsie. Well, there's no need for rudeness,' she bristled, smoothing at the hair on her forehead.

Elsie didn't have the words, just continued to glare at June, her chest rising and falling.

'I'll get back to work then. It's just some of us don't like to have our time wasted.'

She left Elsie standing on the street, feeling more fed up. 'Pious, irritating…' she muttered for the next few steps, drawing up short as she saw Samantha leaving work, releasing her bun with one hand, hair falling down, her shoulders back as she untucked her shirt. She caught Elsie's eye as she stood at the pedestrian crossing, pausing as a car stopped and beeped her before she stepped into the road. No smile, no greeting.

Elsie gripped the handle of her bag, feeling the hole inside her widen. The few things that had helped her seemed to have disappeared, leaving her even more alone.

What was wrong with Mr Porter? She should have asked more. Was he at home? Was he in hospital? He hadn't seemed ill the last time she had been in there but he was the kind of person to downplay his problems. She should have noticed more. A flush of shame took over as she recalled Darren's words. What did people in the village think of her? When had she become this woman? Twenty-eight years ago she knew, or maybe even before then, after the other thing happened, so painful it took her breath away.

Elsie moved slowly home, the sky now tinged with grey, the sun losing its battle with the cloud. She could see children up ahead leaving the school, imagined Billy as one of them, dressed in his grey trousers, white Aertex. Would he be in one of the larger groups of children or would he be walking on his own? For a second, she stood stock-still in the street, wanting to weep at the thought.

She knew what loneliness felt like, remembered how she had craved friends her age, had created endless games with people in her head: tea parties, birthday parties, dances, classes. She had watched other children in the summer on the meadow playing games, older teenagers sat round benches, some lying in the laps of others. She had been sat with her mother, just them. Two peas in a pod.

Two peas in a pod and then a moment that changed everything, a moment where she glimpsed a different life for herself. She had *almost* escaped. She had got so close. And then the shutters came down, the dream dissolved and she stopped craving that other life, the one that, for a second, she'd been promised.

Chapter 26

BILLY

She couldn't watch me all the time. The house was frosty with our silence. And maybe I should have told her where I'd planned to go but I knew she wouldn't have liked the idea and she'd have said no and then what?

Dick called that morning when I was sat pretending to work at the kitchen table, Mum stirring a cold coffee and staring out of the window. Her eyes became frantic as she listened to the voice on the other end. 'But I've got Billy and… No, of course I want to… no, I need the job. Please, Rich, don't… OK, OK, I'll be there in half an hour…'

She lowered the phone on the table and sat dumbly, coffee forgotten. 'Rich needs me to work,' she said.

Dick was a jerk but I was too tired from our last argument: she wouldn't let me work in my room, what did she think, I was going to leap from the second-floor window? So, I didn't say anything, just grunted and went back to pretending to do long division.

Mum phoned Polly and I could hear the whole conversation. Polly couldn't come, Polly had 'broken up' (been dumped) with her boyfriend and was inconsolable and just 'needed to be alone right now'. The call hadn't lasted long.

'What am I meant to do?' Mum glanced at me. She sat in the kitchen chair, her nail bleeding where she had picked at the side. She left the room, headed upstairs. I could hear her sweeping round her bedroom, imagined her scooping up her work clothes from wherever she'd abandoned them the day before.

'Come on,' she said, suddenly standing at the kitchen door, dressed a few moments later, her hair tied back in a high bun.

'Where are we g—'

'Don't argue, Billy,' she interrupted, sighing and picking up her handbag, 'just come.'

I dragged my feet following her, fed up with another row, sick and tired of them. Mum and I hadn't really argued back in London and these days I felt like I was angry with her all the time.

I knew exactly where we were going when we walked out of our gate and took an immediate left.

'No way!' I said, stopping in the middle of Mrs Maple's path. 'No way!'

'Billy, we don't have another choice…'

'We do. I'll stay at home, I promise. You can go and I'll just read, or do my homework, or—'

'I can't trust you,' Mum replied quietly. 'Look, I don't want to but—'

'You can,' I pleaded, 'I really promise. I'm sorry I lied, but I really won't again.'

Mum paused for a fraction of a second and I thought I might have stopped her. 'It will be fine.'

'It won't be,' I snapped, a surge of anger, so close to the surface these days.

Then, taking a breath, she reached a hand out. 'I'm sorry, Billy,' she said, pressing the doorbell. 'I just want you to be safe,' she added in a soft voice, twisting back to face the door.

My fists were already clenched and I wanted to turn and run straight back up the path. I had my mobile in my pocket but no money or anything else. And it was about to rain and before I had even made a decision Mrs Maple appeared in the porch, her face set in a confused frown, a glance at her wristwatch.

No doubt we were interrupting the weird goose daisy dusting or the oven cleaning or the making stinky mint tea or whatever other time it was.

She opened the door a fraction, as if she was frightened we were about to mug her. 'Yes?' she said, her eyes down, not looking at Mum or me.

'I wouldn't ask if I wasn't desperate,' Mum replied, her voice embarrassed. I hadn't heard their argument but Mum told me she'd been really rude to her.

'He can stay,' Mrs Maple said, cutting her off, 'you need the help.'

Mum's shoulders dropped and she nodded once, not adding any more words.

'Come on then, Billy,' Mrs Maple said, beckoning me inside.

'Go on then,' Mum whispered, turning to me, a sorry look in her eyes.

But I wasn't letting her off the hook, glaring at her as she stepped round me. 'I don't...'

'I'll be inside,' Mrs Maple said, turning from the door.

I didn't exactly have a choice. I pushed into the house, refusing to say goodbye to Mum, slamming Mrs Maple's front door behind me, the noise reverberating in the small space.

Pulling my mobile out, I tapped quickly, just inside her porch, knowing one person who might be able to get me out of this rubbish life where I had to go round to nasty old ladies, and a mum who couldn't afford a TV, who made me do stuff I didn't want to do.

He'd asked again, three times in fact, in amongst other chat: his five-a-side football team had won their last game, work was dull, Liverpool should get a new manager, was I watching the game? Where were we now? I hadn't replied to his last message at all.

We live in Pangbourne, I typed to Dad. The last message from him had been days ago. Pressed send before I could think again. That would show Mum. I could do stuff she didn't like too.

I stomped into the house, not feeling any better, a dark worry tugging at my insides. I pushed it down.

Anyway, I was thinking too much of that other dad, not the one I liked to hang out with who bought me a football shirt with my name on the back from a special website he'd found online, and took me to McDonald's, and pretended to be a walrus when he stuck straws up his nose. That dad was the one I messaged, I thought, as I tried to shake my mood.

Mrs Maple was stood, shoulders rigid, at the counter. 'I was about to start work in the garden,' she said. 'Your pear squash is on the table.'

She pointed at the single glass sat waiting for me, the single custard cream on a plate. No teapot next to it. I felt a flush as I remembered its broken pieces scattered over the tiles the last time I was in the room. She had loved that ugly old teapot.

I looked at her, still too cross and hurt to say thank you. I left the stupid squash on the table and threw myself into a chair.

'There's no need to be silly,' Mrs Maple said when I didn't look at her.

That just made me more angry. She had been so mean to me, and I had done nothing. Not really. So, I had been to the house on her map. So what?

'Billy, I…' She took a step forward. 'I'm about to sow some biennials in amongst the tulips.'

'Great,' I said, knowing I was being sullen but not able to stop my pout, the feeling that I was there with no choice. Mum had just left me. I was old enough to look after myself. I didn't want to be passed around like a thing people had to watch.

'Well, are you coming?' she asked, moving to the back door.

'Got no choice,' I replied, scraping the chair back and making her cringe.

She moved quickly through to the garden. I disguised my surprise at the place. The grass desperately needed cutting, there were a hundred weeds peeking through the cracks of the patio again. But the flower beds were filled with different flowers now blooming, bursts of cheery colour all along the fence, the total opposite of my mood.

She snapped on her gardening gloves and stood looking at me. 'Where do you want to start?'

Great. Slave labour, basically.

I shrugged.

'Are you going to punish me all day?' she asked, hands on her hips.

God, it was so unfair! She hadn't even said sorry, it was her who had made it all awkward between us. We'd been getting on. I'd done one stupid thing wrong, and I don't even know why it was wrong, and she'd completely lost it on me. I suppose I should have told her but she was so weird about the stupid map and tin and I wanted to see what it was all about. Maybe I should have said something.

For a second a few memories nudged at me: the first time I'd heard Mrs Maple belly laugh in the cinema, her surprise jump into the water from the boat, the patient way she had taught me about the garden, the endless smiles as she handed me a custard cream. In a panic I felt like I might start crying. Those days had saved me from being really sad. In this new, grim village with zero friends she'd been like a mate.

Was it so much to ask for just an apology?

She was busying herself with a tray of seedlings, the trowel lying next door. I stood on the patio, silently fuming. She didn't seem any different. Had she even missed me? Did she really not care?

I saw the ladder abandoned on its side and moved across, wanting to do something where I wouldn't have to talk, wouldn't have to work next to her.

Mrs Maple had moved across to me as I propped the ladder against the wall, a pair of secateurs that had been lying on the patio table now in my hand.

'The wisteria needs cutting back,' I said in a low voice, refusing to look at her. It was true, the vines seemed to have grown a hundred more shoots since I'd last been there.

'You shouldn't go up in those,' she said, looking at my leather shoes. My trainers had got wet the day before and I was wearing my scruffy fake leather school shoes.

'It's fine,' I snapped, rolling my eyes, adjusting the ladder.

She stepped back, not saying anything more, her mouth pressed together.

Typical, I thought as I gripped the ladder with two hands, placed my foot on the first rung.

I could be at our house lying on the sofa.

Another rung, another step.

Bossed around by Mum, or Mrs Maple, or whoever shunted me back and forward. I could have messaged Tilly, maybe she would have rescued me.

Another rung.

My mobile beeped in my pocket. Maybe it was that that distracted me.

I moved to the next rung but my foot slipped, my weight shifted, and suddenly I was falling, falling backwards, arms propelling to catch myself, grabbing air.

Somewhere below me someone shouted my name, the voice shrill, loud, frightened.

And then everything went black.

Chapter 27

ELSIE

Oh my God, oh my God!

The ambulance seemed to take forever.

She hadn't known how to behave when his mum had appeared on her doorstep with him. Elsie had thought she was back to shout at her again, the boy stood behind her, arms folded, refusing to look her way. The glass in her windows shook as he'd slammed her front door behind him and then he was back in her kitchen, looking utterly furious. She felt her heart fill for this angry boy to whom she had been so hideous. It hadn't been his fault, any of it.

Had she said sorry? Had she told him how much she had missed him? Of course not. Instead she had only prodded him until he was stroppier, wallowing about her house and then stomping to her garden.

If only she had said something, been nicer, calmed him, shared the tea and biscuits with him, it might not have happened. Instead she'd let him stay in his bad mood, watched him fetch that ladder, known he was wearing those slippery-bottomed shoes and start up the rungs in them.

A beep, a tinny noise, had made her turn as she was halfway across the grass to the flower bed she'd been working on. And she had seen it all: the way his head had half-turned, his foot missing the rung, and then his body, oh, his small body, twisting backwards in the air. His arms flailed as he fell, her own mouth opened, screeching his name, before the awful sight of him hitting the patio, the crumpled stillness of him as she had shouted 'Billy' again, run across to him, felt fear rise suddenly and hideously in her throat.

The world stopped as she crouched over him, scratches on her knees and palms she wouldn't notice until later, spots of blood on her cotton trousers bright under the hospital lights as she sat in a plastic bucket seat. After leaving him to go inside, she picked up the telephone, dialled 999, babbled to the operator, this calm, efficient female voice extracting pointless information from her all the while he was out there on his own. Then racing back to him, his eyes rolling into the back of his head, a small noise. He was alive but what had he done to himself? Oh God!

Now here they were in this ambulance, Billy almost as pale as the sheet he was lying on. She held his hand, memories of another ambulance ride coursing through her as they swept through the roads to the town centre, the paramedics checking monitors and talking in undertones to each other. Did they seem worried? The male paramedic sat in a chair by the sliding door, throwing a reassuring smile at her, his designer stubble and caterpillar eyebrows too casual somehow for the seriousness of this moment.

She squeezed her eyes tight and made a fervent prayer: *Let it be different this time, please.*

His eyes were closed and Elsie found time hurtling backwards. The ambulance a little different back then, a bench running along one side where she sat, no seatbelt, fewer machines, a single monitor they had hooked him to, the paramedics both sat in the front, throwing worried looks over their shoulders as the vehicle roared through the streets.

There had been blood back then, so much blood, streaking their clothes, turning everything scarlet. She knew it was serious, his head sticky with it, obvious even in his dark brown hair, eyes half-closed, trying, trying to focus on her, mouth slack.

The low voices in the small space as the paramedics passed information back and forth, a beeping machine, another glance back – a good beep? Bad?

He was strong though and they were in love and only earlier that morning they had been walking through the village, making plans for Sunday lunch the next day. He was going to meet her at the pub, *their* pub, she was going to tell Mother she was out with friends after church. Sunday lunch. Could things really turn on a pin so suddenly? In less than twenty-four hours they were going to eat roast beef, crisp and puffy Yorkshire puddings dripping with gravy. He'd said it.

His other eye had closed there in the ambulance and she had held her breath, gripping his hand so tightly, she imagined the bones breaking in it.

'Open your eyes,' she'd cried. The paramedic gave her another look.

'We're two minutes away, keep talking to him, love.' She had known he shouldn't have looked as worried as he had.

'They've told me to keep talking, I don't know what to say. We're going to have a roast, you love a roast,' she'd babbled at his face, his eyes remaining shut. The ambulance blared, the noise surrounding her in the tinny space. His chest wasn't going up and down.

'His chest isn't moving,' she'd screeched, the ambulance pulling over as a beep rang out, relentless and shrill. He looked even thinner and smaller on the trolley. Why wasn't his chest moving?

The paramedic had got out of the passenger side, rushed round to the back doors, ignoring her as he leaned over him, eyes glancing up at the monitor. The driver waiting for instructions.

Cars sped past, whooshing sounds as everyone else went about their day. She had looked from paramedic to him to paramedic, heart thudding.

'Please,' she'd begged, 'please!' Her face wet with tears, fear gripping her.

The paramedic had started to attach a mask to his face.

Oh my God!

His chest hadn't been rising and falling.

His eyes had closed.

There had been so much blood.

Billy stirred, dragging her away from the deluge of her memories. His face flinched with pain as she drew an arm across his body to touch his wrist and he craned his neck to look at his feet.

'You're OK,' she said, through watery eyes. 'Lie there, you're on your way to the hospital.'

'Mum,' he croaked, head tilted towards her.

Of course she needed to get through to Samantha, dreaded what she would say, think. It had been on her watch; her precious boy. Elsie's hands shook as she placed them in her lap. 'Of course, Billy, we will ring your mother. She'll be worried.'

Elsie shook her head, determined now to stay in the present, to help, to make sure the same thing didn't happen again. The hospital would have a phone, someone could help her get through to the restaurant, she was sure. His mother should be here, not her. She clamped her hands together again.

'Ells,' he whispered, struggling to move his head more than a centimetre or so. She leant forward, one hand on the edge of the silver contraption he was propped up on. 'I'm sorry about your teapot,' he said.

She dabbed at her eyes. 'Don't you be silly,' she said in her no-nonsense voice, the crack on the last word, 'you're far more precious to me than a stupid teapot.' She was unable to stop the break in her voice, realising how true those words were, how stupid she had been, how stubborn. What an idiot to have ever pushed away a boy who had changed everything for her, who had reminded her of the wonderful things she still had in her life, who had made her laugh, given her hope.

Who needed her too. She reached out to stroke the dark hair from his forehead but the ambulance stopped and the man with the stubble was preparing to get Billy out.

They had wheeled him away, told her to wait in a yellow chair moulded to others on a silver pole. She had found a payphone, asked for help to track down the number of the restaurant in the village and a kind gentleman used his Google, the noises of the hospital, the squeak of trainers, rumble of trolleys, indistinct beeps and calls distracting as she thanked him, as the dial tone rang and rang.

'Come on,' she whispered, the receiver slippery in her palm. 'Come *on*.'

'Yeah,' an impatient voice came on the line, banging, shouts and more in the background. It was almost impossible to hear.

'Could you please pass on a message to Samantha?' Elsie started, 'I need to speak with her. Billy fell, that is, Billy is in the hospital in Reading. Can you tell her…' Elsie was cringing as she got the words out, almost drowned out by saucepans clashing, water running.

'Sam? Sorry, can you repeat that… SAM… phone!'

'I… it's her son, it's…'

'Hello?' An uncertain female voice, stressed and distracted, came on the line. 'This is Samantha.'

'It's El…' Elsie almost choked on the word, '…sie. It's Billy, he fell, he's awake but they've taken him to get checked out.'

The voice changed, suddenly alert, loud, frightened, 'Mrs Maple? What is that? What do you mean, fell? Where are you?'

Elsie wanted to weep. 'The hospital… Reading,' she said, her voice cracking, 'I'm here and he's with the doctors.'

The phone was dropped, just the drone of the dialling tone could be heard.

Elsie stared at the receiver and, with a shaking hand, placed it back on the hook.

Had Samantha heard? Should she ring her back?

She waited, sitting in the plastic bucket seat, unable to get comfortable, her palms and knees stinging from the uneven patio ground. She couldn't stop recalling the image of Billy lying there, his eyes closed.

Twenty minutes later Samantha, an apron still tied round her waist, practically flew through the double doors, her eyes scanning the small room, past the teenage girl with the bandage on her hand, the boy sat quietly on his father's lap, the elderly man holding one wrist gently in his hand.

'I got a taxi,' she said, rushing towards Elsie. 'Where is he? What's happened? Oh God… is he OK? Is he hurt?'

'Oh, let me pay you back,' Elsie replied, wanting to be practical, not sure how to answer the questions. *Was he OK?* Yes, he had spoken but since then she hadn't really got an update, too frightened to ask the woman behind the glass screen of Reception. She remembered that other visit to the hospital, the hushed voice of the doctor as he drew her into a room, shattering her heart. She patted her sides, realising in that moment she had left her purse at her home, too shocked to pick up her handbag, just the house key in her cardigan pocket, her cardigan that she had put on inside out.

'What happened?'

Elsie saw the elderly man looking across at them, Samantha's voice loud and urgent in the space.

'He fell,' Elsie said, 'he was on a ladder and he slipped.'

'A ladder? What was he doing up a ladder?'

'I... I...' Elsie didn't have an adequate response. What had he been doing up a ladder? And in those shoes. She remembered her warning, she should have insisted, should have forbidden him. And now this...

'He shouldn't be up ladders, he's ten years old. Where have they taken him?'

Samantha was growing more and more hysterical and Elsie felt herself shrinking in the face of it.

'They took him through those doors but I wasn't sure I should go. I'm not family, I'm...'

What was she? Why hadn't she joined him? The paramedic had looked at her as she had slunk back, made her excuses, loitered in the waiting room.

Samantha was already talking to the woman behind the screen, tapping now at her computer as she directed her to the doors.

Elsie went to follow and Samantha held up a hand. 'I think you've done enough,' she said, tears filling her eyes now the shock was wearing off. 'If anything happens to him I will...' Her face was white, her voice barely a whisper.

Elsie stepped backwards. 'I would... I don't know...' What could she say? Samantha was right.

'Just leave us alone.'

Elsie was left standing as the double doors swung back and Samantha disappeared through them. A glimpse of a long corridor, people in uniforms, benches, doors, a water cooler, and then nothing. The blank white double doors, a leaflet about the flu jab… she was alone.

She walked a while through the busy streets of Reading, directionless, jumping at the car horns as she stepped off the pavement, retreating backwards, someone tutting behind her. The bus stop sign made no sense and she didn't know this part of town; it had been years really since she had felt familiar with the area, and she realised how little she had left the village in twenty-eight years.

She wound her way over the river, staring mutely into the surface, knowing if she followed it one way it would twist and turn back to her village, back to the spot they had leapt into the water. It made her eyes fill with tears. Where was he now? What had he done?

She didn't have any money for a ticket and the guard on the gates took pity on her, letting her through as his colleague turned to deal with another customer, throwing her a small wink as she passed. The kindness set her off again; she didn't deserve it. If she wasn't so brittle, Billy wouldn't be lying in a hospital. They would be sat on her patio admiring their work, the atmosphere relaxed and easy once more. She ruined everything.

The platform was empty, the stopping service slowing as it approached, the doors opening with a hiss. She stepped inside, the smell of cheese and onion in the air, the carriage needing airing. She felt her stomach rumble, realised she hadn't eaten for hours, bile in her throat.

By the time she got home the day was almost through and she bit her lip as she walked up her garden path. It felt a lifetime ago that she had rushed down it, the paramedics wheeling Billy down the side path of her house, her heart hammering in her chest as she locked the door behind her.

Glancing across the fence she could see the windows of next door in darkness, the curtains still open. She clutched her chest, the other hand reaching for her door, her palm flat on the glass. How would she concentrate on anything else? How would she sleep tonight, not knowing what had happened to him?

She didn't eat, didn't make tea. She stood in the middle of the kitchen for an age, her frozen outline reflected back in the glass of the window opposite. 'What if he's not alright? What if...?' she asked aloud, wishing as she often did that a reply would come, words from the woman who had always been able to comfort her.

She couldn't face going outside, couldn't face seeing the ladder diagonal on the patio, the scene of her earlier nightmare. She wandered silently around the rooms of the house, wanting to phone the hospital, craning to hear any noise from next door, twitching her curtain for sight of them.

Darkness fell and she was sat on her sofa facing the bay window, dabbing at her palms, the cuts stinging, giving her a strange relief from her thoughts. A car's headlights swept past and she looked up, wanting them to stop outside her neighbour's house. But they kept on going, up and away out of the village.

What could she do to keep herself from going mad? She paced the room, her eyes lighting on the silhouette of her desk in the dark, the one thing that often gave her comfort when everything else failed. Switching on the lamp, she picked up the fountain pen, twisting it in her hand, the blotting pad dotted with purple ink.

She sat, knowing this letter would be different. This time she wouldn't be thinking about him, her love, the man she poured her heart out to every Wednesday. The man who had almost whisked her out of her lonely life and into another one entirely.

She would be thinking about someone still living: someone she loved now, in the present. Someone she couldn't bear to lose too.

*

I never thought I would be frightened again like I was that day, that terrible day. The day I still can't bear to think about.

I think instead of the day we first met. How I had stumbled into you at the village fete. I'd been idling between stalls and you'd bent to replace the coconuts, a leg stuck out behind you that I didn't see. You grabbed me just before I toppled and I gave a small yelp of surprise. You didn't say anything for a second and later you told me you'd been panicking because I was so pretty. You always said things that made me blush and feel a foot taller.

'I'm Philip.' You'd held out a hand and I'd taken it wordlessly, staring up at you, worried I'd mussed my hair.

We met in secret at first, which was hard as I hated lying to Mother. I would take a walk, I would take my bicycle, I would need something from Reading town centre. Sometimes she would offer to come with me and I would panic and make some excuse.

Perhaps if I'd had the course to take a real job, in an office or the such, it might have been easier. But the thought of all those people, of navigating a room of them, terrified me. It felt safer to undertake the work from home. An antique dealer sent me blank replica paintings of battle scenes and I would paint in the details, posting the prints back to him when they were finished. Mother loved seeing me at the table in the kitchen, commented on the intricate detail of the soldiers' jackets, the cobalt blue of the sky, the crimson red of their uniforms, and I could still join her in our haven, in the garden as it had always been.

Meeting you changed all that. I had a glimpse of another world that twinkled and hinted in the distance. Your earnest face, a wide mouth, ears that peeked out just slightly from your sandy hair. You were so kind that day at the fete, holding my arm as I tripped, concern etched on your features. I hadn't realised you were still holding my arm and when we both looked down, I felt a tingling run right up it.

Mother had commented that you'd liked me and for some reason I found I hadn't told her that we had promised to meet. I'd paid money on the coconut shy, no other customers around so we had talked. You had leant against the wooden stall, straw on the ground, and in a soft voice you told me you had moved to be nearer home as your dad was ill, you'd left Bristol, where you'd be training to be a chef. Your dad normally ran the coconut shy but he hadn't been able. Your face filled with hurt. I knew what it was like to love a parent yet still feel trapped. I stayed there as others threw the wooden balls at the coconuts, the two of us both aware of each other as you hurried the children along, giving out balls, wanting the bushel box to empty, wanting to keep talking.

Mother had come along and I had gone to say a quiet goodbye. She had seen Stanley on a stall, wanted to buy some horseradish sauce, and my whole body drooped with relief as she stepped away.

You'd asked me, quickly then, if you could take me out and I'd blurted a yes. I couldn't have you telephone the house and it was that thought that made me so bold. This was my moment. Mother would be back soon with her horseradish. I suggested the museum in the town centre. You'd never been. You said you'd find it. Next Saturday. Alright. Two o'clock. I'll be there.

I'd hugged the secret to my chest all week. I meant to tell her but Mother had always been so intense, I felt the house and the things inside it had become part of me, always there. I wanted something just for me.

The months that followed were the happiest of my life. That summer felt like an endless day of sunshine, walks along the river, lying in our copse on the bank, hidden by a curtain of willow trees, holding hands, kissing, whispering sweet nothings. Once the summer was over, I introduced you, pretended to Mother that we had only just met. She didn't remember the boy from the coconut shy.

Your dad's health improved and you asked me to move back to Bristol with you. I had to think about it. I didn't have to think about it.

I said yes.

Mother cried.

'Don't, please, don't leave me.'

She pleaded but I was firm. I needed to leave. The small world we lived in was too claustrophobic, too much. The endless card games, the tick of the clock, the cleaning rituals, the same rooms, the same figurines, the same way she breathed, the same look in her eye: such love. Sometimes I had to look away.

I tried to keep a reassuring smile on my face as I painted the picture of a future.

'You can visit!, Bristol isn't far. Of course we'll spend Christmas together, nothing will change.'

I was convincing myself too. She begged me not to go, not to leave her on her own.

You told me it was my choice.

I chose you.

But we never moved to Bristol. You collapsed in a Saturday football match I was watching, the ambulance ride a terrifying blur of memory and then the hospital, the faces of the doctor, and holding your dad as he collapsed against me. Leaving.

Home to the only other person I had ever loved. The world I had been about to discover over, I was grateful over the coming weeks and months for her cloying affection, quick to immerse myself in the pretence that it had always been just the two of us.

She let me grieve for you. I wept and wailed.

She told me to write to you, to pour my love, my memories, onto the page. Every Wednesday I sit and imagine you reading the words, my letters to you, reliving our precious moments, unveiling memories from my past, reminiscing about our times together.

I lost you and now I might lose Billy. The energetic, lonely, angry, gorgeous little boy with his cheeky humour and his green fingers. He might leave the hospital but I have lost him. And I know now that loss will hurt me just as much.

Chapter 28

BILLY

I felt woozy as I came to, unsure for a moment where I was, the room a strange blue hue, a figure bent over me in a chair next to the bed I was lying on.

'Mum?' I croaked, the word barely recognisable.

The figure shot up, Mum's hair askew, wiping at her face. 'Billy, thank God, hey…' she whispered, her eyes crinkling, red-rimmed even in this light.

I tried to move, feeling my body ache, my head spin.

She placed a hand on my arm. 'Stay still, darling, you've got concussion, they've said. They're checking up on you.'

'What… how…?' I needed a sip of water, a strange blur of images in my mind, made weirder by this room, the dark windows, the flashes on machines above me, the odd beep.

'Do you remember much?'

'I fell… I…' I wanted water. Mum seemed to work that out, twisting the top from a bottle and holding it up to me. My head screamed with pain as I leant forward to take a sip, the water dribbling down my chin.

She dabbed at me. 'I'm sorry, I'm… Oh God, I'm so relieved, Billy! I thought…' She was crying, tears smattering my arm, the thin gown I was wearing.

I'd been at Elsie's house, I'd fallen.

'I fell…' I said.

Mum nodded, one hand to her mouth as if she wanted to cram the tears back in.

'They X-rayed your wrist,' she said, 'no fracture.'

A head peeked around the door, a large black nurse in a well-ironed pale blue uniform. 'He's awake,' she said, smiling.

Mum gave her a nod.

'Your mother hasn't left your side,' the nurse said, moving across to the bed, her voice a little too loud, making me squint. 'She's been worried sick. You are a lucky boy to have a mum who loves you like that.'

I wanted to nod but everything ached and my eyes were fluttering shut.

'I'll come round again when it's time for medication,' the nurse said over me as I struggled to stay in the room. 'What are you doing, young man, leaping off buildings?'

I couldn't laugh or smile, couldn't join in, the strange blue room spinning.

'Well, you let us look after you now, and stop your mum worrying, eh?'

'Thank you,' Mum said, stroking my hand.

The nurse left and I felt so tired, glad of the pillow, my mum's hand.

It was only then that I saw it, lying on the bedspread.

Mum saw my panic. I reached for it, felt a sharp pain, and I was lying back again.

'Hey,' she said, stilling me with an arm.

She picked up the mobile and turned it over, her mouth turned down, her eyes sad. 'I found it in your jeans pocket. I didn't know… I…'

Normally she'd be angry but there was no way she could shout at me in this blue room, when I was like this, and for a second I was glad we were in the hospital.

'Where did you get it?' she asked, turning it over again. 'I haven't looked at it,' she added, her eyes solemn.

Suddenly it all felt so much worse and I wished she was angry at me. I stared at it, feeling an unease in the pit of my stomach, remembering then what I had done.

'A friend gave it to me,' I said, wanting to draw away her attention.

Mum nodded. 'I should have got you one. I… I was worried that…' She tailed away, her whole body hunched over.

'It's OK,' I whispered, 'I should have told you about it.'

'You didn't, haven't…' Mum looked up, wiping uselessly at her face again. 'You haven't contacted Dad?' she asked, her eyes rounded.

I swallowed, eyes flickering for a moment to the side before I shook my head, a pain swift and sudden. 'No,' I replied quietly.

She slumped in relief and I felt sickness, a swirl in my stomach. Should I tell her? Would anything come of it? What could really be so wrong?

'I'm sorry, Billy,' she started to cry, turning the phone over again in her hand, 'I don't blame you hiding it, I know I've kept things from you, I haven't wanted to… to ruin things for you. Haven't really known how to explain…'

I was too weak to say anything in response, Mum so sad and broken, bunched up in the chair, stroking my good arm. Memories rose up and were quickly pushed down again. Dad's face, my heart beating in my chest as I studied the change in his expression. Did I know what Mum was trying to say? He was my dad, he loved me. He could say nice things, he let me do stuff Mum didn't. He's a good man, isn't he? He misses me, doesn't he?

'I had to leave him. I… I was so frightened that he might, that he might…' she swallowed, 'start on you…' She glanced at the door to the room, lowering her voice. 'He was, I…'

She was struggling with whatever it was she was trying to say and I watched her frown, open her mouth, shut it again. My head was heavy on the pillow, woozy and full of too many thoughts.

'I was scared of him,' she said in a whisper. 'I didn't want to admit it. There was no warning, I didn't know what might set him off.' She was sat straighter, the mobile turning, turning in her hands as she talked. 'He hadn't done anything in years, had *promised* me when you were born all of that was behind him. He had been a bad drunk, knew it made him worse, and I'd believed him. And it did stop. We were happy, weren't we?' She smiled, choking on her words. 'And I convinced myself it was all different, he was a father, the change was real. But then he got into trouble on some of his jobs, I was nagging him, he'd said I was always on at him…' She paused, licking her lips.

She hadn't nagged him, a voice inside me said. I remembered those days, getting back from school and Dad sat on the sofa, in the clothes we'd left him in. I had homework and he wanted to help but explained it all wrong, not like the teacher, and he slammed two hands down on the side of the textbook and that made me jump, like I'd been burnt. And I was too scared to look at him. Little dots of his spit on the page. The teacher was an idiot. Yes, she was.

I blinked. An ache behind my eyes, building as the scene played over and over again in my head, as Mum's quiet voice continued.

'Sometimes he'd raise his voice, or he'd, he'd…' Her eyes slid from my face to a spot above my shoulder. 'He'd hold me, bruise me, but,' she said, putting on a cheerful voice as if she was back there, convincing herself, 'it was small, not often enough. Everyone's allowed a slip up or two, I thought.'

I'd seen her hold her arm and wince when she opened the fridge, going all small, her eyes looking down when he'd walked into the room. I'd seen it. But how had I not realised?

'And then, slowly, things got worse and I knew I had to save us, had to get us out of there before he… You were getting bigger, you'd challenge him too and I couldn't let him, I couldn't let him…' She broke down then, her face crumpling, a watery mess before she pulled herself together, dabbing at her eyes. 'And then, that day, you were at school, he…'

I squeezed her hand. She stopped talking. I didn't know what he'd done that last day. I'd got home from school and the coffee table was broken and the glass all smashed. Dad had gone out and Mum was acting all funny, not really looking at me as she told me to get to bed early, wincing as she washed something up at the sink. Something had happened, I knew that, but I knew not to ask any questions. Then she'd shaken me awake in the night. I'd followed her, knowing, the secret part of me knowing why we weren't telling Dad, why we were leaving in the dark.

She stared at my hand, squeezed me back. 'But we are safe, Billy.' She leant forward, resting her forehead on my arm. 'We are safe and I'm talking to solicitors and I'm getting a divorce, a restraining order too, and we won't have to see him again. He can't get to us, he doesn't know where we live.'

I couldn't speak, going over everything she was saying.

Her eyes were large and round, face pale, as she looked up at me. 'And I'm so sorry, Billy, I'm so sorry for not telling you all this before.'

She sat back, the confession over.

My eyes flicked to the phone in her hand and I thought of the message I had sent him. Swallowing, I felt dizzy again: he knew where we lived, he knew exactly where we lived.

'Mum, I'm going to—'

Leaning over the side of the bed, I vomited.

Chapter 29

ELSIE

She had barely slept, wrapping herself in a blanket on her sofa, jumping every time headlights passed in the road outside, dozing in fitful spurts.

They didn't come home.

She lingered the next day beside the telephone. Could she call the hospital? What would they tell her? Perhaps he had taken a turn in the night? She lifted the receiver, going to dial, before returning it.

She needed bread, cereal, things to eat, the kitchen practically bare these days. She daren't leave the house to get them, might miss them returning. She needed to see that he was alright, that he hadn't done any serious damage. She couldn't get the image of him lying on that silver trolley, head lolling as she clung to him, out of her head.

Blinking, she got up, boiling the kettle for the sixth time, forgetting why, walking off again and beginning the whole process once more.

'But I don't deserve him,' she said aloud, 'and you are to blame for that too.'

How she would squeeze him if she saw him now, tell him how sorry she was, make him feel safe and secure. He had just been an inquisitive little boy, he had just wanted friends and she had behaved abominably. Then she thought of Samantha's face and knew there was no way she would be allowed to see him, the damage had been done. She didn't deserve him; she didn't.

She was back in the front room, her heart lifting at the sight of a taxi on the other side of the road. A man stepped out and her shoulders dropped. He looked left and right before crossing the road, a slip of paper in his hand, something familiar in his gait.

She frowned as he walked up to her gate, closely-shaven dark hair, a muscular build: where had she seen him before? Surprising her, he turned and pushed the gate to next door, moving up the path, a set expression on his face that made her edge sideways, half-hidden behind her curtain as she watched him. He cupped his hand to the glass and then dropped back, staring up at the house. Something about the way he was looking gave her a chill and she hugged her arms to her chest. What did he want?

The man had gone, walking back through the gate and left towards the village, as Elsie crept back into the middle of the room. Something wasn't right. She needed to stay and keep watch.

The day dragged on, Elsie's movements sluggish, her stomach empty. She would be gone a matter of minutes, she decided, knowing she was close to falling asleep on her feet, the long, broken night catching up with her. She fetched her handbag and locked the door quickly, surprised by the warmth of the day, a hopeful sun in the cornflower-blue sky, a gentle breeze as she stepped onto the pavement.

She walked quickly, wanting to get back, fearful she would miss him. A few people were out in the village today, shopping bags slung over shoulders, the sign outside the library advertising Rhyme Time. As she approached two mothers, she recognised Scarlet dressed in jeans and a T-shirt, her baby facing outward in a carrier on her front. She was stroking his little feet and he was giggling as she chatted with another young mum, her baby in a pram, waving a toy giraffe. Elsie nodded as she passed, a quiet hello, flushing as Scarlet turned to acknowledge her and then clamped up on seeing who it was who had greeted her with a mumble. Shame flamed through her as she thought back to her rudeness in the library, a brand-new connection and she had fallen at the first hurdle. She walked quicker, only just avoiding the man in front of her.

She almost walked into him. He was staring at the noticeboard in the window of the Post Office, scowling as she drew up short. It was the same man she had seen outside the house. Tall with wide shoulders, his eyebrows drawn together as she fussed an apology.

Her fist squeezed tightly to the strap of her handbag as she looked into his eyes, a familiar shade of grey. 'Sorry, I wasn't looking,' she said, still aware she was staring.

He had already turned back, scanning the noticeboard. Then with a huff he stepped inside and Elsie felt her whole body relax as he disappeared through the door.

Milk, bread, cereal… she loaded what she could and moved back up the road, sweat pooling – she was impossibly overdressed for the day. As she approached home, she looked for signs that something had changed but their windows were still in darkness, the gate set at the same angle it had been before: they were still not back.

She felt an added urgency now, knowing the man in the village was significant, certainty forming like a stone in her stomach.

As if she conjured them up, a taxi drew up outside the house and she stood in the street watching as Samantha stepped out, glaring as Elsie stood, breath suspended, watching the open door of the car. And then, ever so slowly, he stepped out, his arm in a sling, purple shadows under his eyes: Billy.

She bit her lip, took a step forward. 'Billy, oh thank God, I…'

Samantha was ushering him through their gate. 'Don't,' she called, 'don't talk to my son.'

Elsie felt her eyes fill with tears, nodded. It was what she deserved. Hadn't she just wanted to see that he was alright? Her heart filled with the sight of him, slowly moving up his path, wincing as his mother hurried him. He glanced over his shoulder and Elsie couldn't help the tearful smile that filled her face, his expression unreadable as he disappeared into the house.

Then she remembered, dithering on the pavement before making up her mind. This was important. She moved up the path, ringing the doorbell. Samantha pulled the door back on its chain. A suspicious eye.

'I wanted to tell you someone…' she began.

'I don't want to hear it,' Samantha replied, going to close the door. Elsie placed her foot in the gap, surprising both of them, bracing herself for the pain. 'What are you…? I've got to get to work,' Samantha said.

'Please, I need to…'

'Billy,' Samantha had moved away from the door, calling over her shoulder, 'get back on the sofa.' The eye was back in the crack. 'I don't have time for this.'

'Let me wait with him,' Elsie pleaded.

Samantha didn't waver. 'Remove your foot.'

'Someone was here,' Elsie called as the crack closed, as the door slammed shut, as she was left outside, alone. 'Someone… was here.'

*

Without you I collapsed and Mother pieced me back together. She never once mentioned my plans to leave, the life I almost had that had been stolen from me. I let myself believe that this was how it had always been meant to be: just the two of us. Two peas in a pod. That there was no alternative.

Mother and the garden became my world. I would spend hours on my knees, barely feeling the damp, the soil between my fingers, as I nurtured the plants, tended to them as I wished I could have tended to you. Everything flourished when it was given attention and I poured my broken soul into each task, Mother watching on.

She would play cards with me, sit in silence, listen to me talk about you, hold me while I cried. At times it felt I had fallen back through the years, a dependent child once more. We needed each other, it was only us now against the world and the world seemed a threatening and dark place.

She was my comfort, her steadfast presence and her abiding love for me.

And Wednesdays. Wednesdays when I could allow myself to write the things I felt, the memories we had shared. I circled my grief, choosing instead to write down the times that seemed golden in my mind: the tandem ride, the terrace pub, the endless afternoons walking or resting by the river.

I didn't have an address any more but I needed to send the letters, to post them in the box I knew was out of service, to pretend you were receiving them, wherever you were. In my imaginings I would fool myself into thinking you were away, back in Bristol perhaps or working abroad in a steamy kitchen, shouting orders to the sous chef, shaking a sizzling frying pan. Busy. And alive.

Chapter 30

BILLY

Mrs Maple was stood on the street when we got back in the taxi, her face lighting up as I stepped onto the pavement. Memories from the ambulance ride the day before, the worry on her face, her shaky voice, made me want to stop and say hello. Mum didn't feel the same, pushing me gently up the path and into the house, and I let her, too tired and achy not to just follow instructions.

Then Mrs Maple rang the doorbell and tried to talk and Mum was like the rudest I'd ever seen her and then I really did feel a bit bad.

'I don't want to hear more apologies,' she'd said, reaching for the throw off the back of the sofa. 'She should never have let you go up a ladder. A reckless, thoughtless thing to do…'

'You're overreacting,' I replied as she started tucking the throw around my legs like a blanket as if I were an old man. 'Mum, it's June, it's like twenty degrees,' I added, secretly liking all this attention, something I realised I'd needed since we'd arrived in this village.

'I mean, what was she thinking? Oh, of course, send a ten-year-old up thirty feet to do dangerous jobs. I shouldn't have trusted her, but she seemed to understand…' Mum had finished with the throw and was now fussing with the two cushions we owned before moving to bring me more things.

'It wasn't her fault, you know,' I said, feeling guilty about the way Mum was speaking. She had always been the one defending Elsie and I had been the one to slip. I remembered the ambulance, the sound of the siren, the terrified look on Elsie's face as she'd sat there. She cared about me and I knew it was real, that in her own strange way she loved me.

'I wouldn't leave if I didn't have to.' Mum crouched down in front of me and placed two hands on the sides of my face. 'You know that, don't you?'

'I know.'

'And you promise me you will stay here, not move a muscle? And now you have that mobile you can phone me at work if you need anything. Alright? I'll come straight back.'

She ran up the stairs, her feet light on the carpet, grabbing what she needed for work and calling out various instructions. 'You can listen to the radio, or read a magazine... I bought a book of Sudoku from the hospital shop too... and grapes, but I'll bring back dinner from work so there's no need to eat anything until then if you don't want...' She appeared again, breathless and dressed. 'Have you got everything you need?'

'Mum, I'm OK, you can go,' I said, realising she was torn. Was this how she always felt when she had to work and look after me?

Scraping her hair back into a bun and kissing me on the head, Mum left for work. 'Love you, Bean,' she called behind her and she hadn't called me that in forever.

The doorbell rang. I'd promised her I wouldn't get off the sofa and for a second, I considered leaving it. It wasn't like it would be a friend, it would be the postman with junk or something.

A voice through the letterbox: 'Billy, can you let me in?'

I knew Mum wouldn't like it but I found myself moving from the sofa, picturing Elsie's strained face in that ambulance.

'I'm worried about you,' she called through the letterbox.

I paused just by the front door, inches from where she was standing, chewing on my lip. Then I reached up and opened it, stepping back in surprise as she piled into the room.

'Thank you, Billy, thank you,' she said, barely looking at me before she was reaching to close the curtains to our living room, even though it was being bright outside.

'Mrs Maple,' I said, the name sounding a bit strange as I said it, 'El... what are you doing?'

'There's a man,' she announced, moving to the side of the curtain and pulling it back an inch to peer outside into the street.

'Well, there are lots of men,' I replied, wondering if she had gone a bit mad.

'I think he's your dad,' she said, the curtain falling back into place as she turned to face me.

'My da...'

I swallowed.

Dad.

Oh my God!

'I messaged him,' I whispered, panic filling my voice. 'Mum's going to...' I started to fret, tugging on my hair with my good hand.

'You're OK, I did wonder...'

'I told him where we lived,' I admitted.

'Do you want to see him, Billy?' She stood there, her pale blue eyes trained on me as I shook my head left to right. I definitely did not. I don't know what I'd been thinking when I messaged him. With a cold certainty I knew why Mum had left that night and taken me with her. It was a mistake. A terrible mistake.

She eased the curtain back again and then quickly let it go. 'He's coming back,' she said, a frightened look passing her face, 'Quick!' She moved urgently across the room before pausing to look back at me, not knowing what to do by the front door. 'I've got an idea. Quiet now! Are you alright to walk, not dizzy?'

She stepped back towards me and offered me her arm and the small gesture made me smile.

'I'm alright, Ells. I can walk.'

She beamed at me then, no more Mrs Maple, and I realised how much I had missed her. She was a bit nuts but she was my friend.

'We can get out of your back door and there's a gate at the back of the fence into the alley behind the house.' She was talking to herself as I watched her fumble with the key to the back door.

I lingered. A tiny last part of me wanted to return to the living room and open up that front door and see if all my fears were somehow made up, see if he'd changed and if he'd missed us. Memories of happier times flooded my head: Dad laughing next to me on the sofa with some cheese and onion Kettle Chips, building a den in the living room, taking me to see my first football match, watching some from his shoulders.

Then the feeling I had got when Elsie asked me if I wanted to see him, like someone was sat on my chest, crept in. The way he'd got drunk at that match and dragged me along in the car park and another man asked if I was alright.

There was hammering on the front door. I imagined Dad's fist on the wood, closed my eyes. Other memories, the ones I had wanted to convince myself weren't real, overlapped. The play fight that had ended when he'd really hurt me, something about his expression as he'd twisted my arm, the meaty fingers of his hand as he gripped me a little too tightly, shouting swear words at me for messing with his stuff, spittle on my face. Or when he would look over his shoulder for me when he was speaking to Mum in that low whisper.

And he was here, now.

Outside the door.

What had I done?

Mum was going to be so angry.

Elsie looked over her shoulder at me as she cracked open the back door. 'Come on,' she whispered, beckoning me with a finger.

I paused. Mum had made me promise not to leave the house. Would she be cross again? Surely this was different?

'What about Mum?'

'We'll phone her from my house,' Elsie replied, a worried look now as the knocking stopped.

'Sam! Billy!' The voice was loud, urgent and so familiar. I froze, staring at Elsie with wide eyes.

'It's OK,' she said, reaching for me. I was glad she was there.

We moved quickly into the garden, the latch on the gate stuck with rust. What if he moved down the path of the house?

How does he know we live here? I only told him the village. Maybe he would leave soon. He had to, didn't he?

The latch finally unstuck and Elsie nudged me through the gate first, biting her lip. It was only then I saw she was wearing her house slippers: she must have left in a hurry.

A few moments later we were in her garden, inching past the greenhouse with its cracked ceiling and past the space where we had found the tin.

'Come on, let's get inside,' she said, her voice barely louder than a whisper, nervous as she encouraged me inside, clutching my arm.

The panic made my head spin. Blinking, I followed her into the house and when we were in her kitchen, safe, she turned the lights on.

'Right,' she fussed immediately, 'you sit down there, my dear, and what can I bring you? Water? Paracetamol? A custard cream?'

'Water would be great,' I said, cradling my elbow and sitting in the wooden chair she had pulled out for me.

What had we done? I had just run away from my dad.

Elsie bit her lip as she brought the glass over to me. 'Are you alright? Was that... OK?'

I nodded sadly. 'Yeah, yeah, we had to.'

'So that was your dad?' she asked, head tilted to one side.

I nodded quickly.

'How did he know where to come? I thought your mother had left without saying.' She flushed then, perhaps worried she was betraying Mum's trust. What else had Mum told Mrs Maple? Why had she known to come over and get me out of there?

'I told him,' I admitted in a quiet voice. 'I was lonely and angry with Mum and I...'

Elsie sat down slowly opposite me, a kind expression on her face. 'Oh, Billy, he's your dad, of course you want things to work out.'

'But I knew,' I continued, 'I knew he was hurting Mum, that he got... got angry and did things.' I felt my cheeks wet and realised I was crying. Elsie reached out for a hand, forgetting I was in a sling, before patting the table.

'Well, you stay here and we will work out what to do. First, I think we better—'

'Mum!' I said urgently. 'It won't take him long to find out where she works, he might already know...' I was on my feet, a sharp ache in my head and the room tilted.

'Woah!' Elsie forced me back into the chair. 'Don't hurt yourself again, I'll get the telephone and we'll phone h—'

We both froze as a sharp knock interrupted what she was saying. Elsie's eyes widened as she looked at me.

'It's him,' I mouthed.

She nodded grimly and then her expression changed. 'I've got an idea,' she said, standing and putting her finger to her lip.

'No, don't...' I felt my palms dampen as I watched her get up.

'Do you trust me?' she asked, squaring her shoulders, a determined glint in her eye.

I nodded slowly.

'Well, you stay here then and don't make a sound. Promise?'

I gave her a silent nod and satisfied, she turned towards the door. 'Right,' she said, in a voice that sounded like it might have been giving her strength. She walked purposefully out of the room and I heard her slide the lock across the front door.

'Can I help you?' she asked in a soft voice.

I didn't need to strain to hear my dad's reply: 'I was wondering if you could tell me who lives next door?' He sounded on his best behaviour, the polite voice he used on the phone to his boss when he called in sick but was really playing stuff on his laptop on the sofa and drinking beer while I went to school.

'Oh,' Elsie paused, 'I don't really speak to my neighbours, keep myself to myself, you know. In the old days people would borrow sugar and the odd egg, always dropping in on the other, knowing everyone's business, but it's very different now, young man, as I'm sure you know. No time, everyone on their phones. I've got a hundred grandchildren and they barely say a word. Just the other day, I…'

She continued for a few minutes, my eyes round in my head as I heard her build lie on top of lie, my dad's replies shorter and shorter and more and more bored as he tried to get off her doorstep.

'If I see them, I'll be sure to tell them someone was looking for them.'

'Nah,' Dad said, a hint of panic. 'Nah, you're alright, don't do that. It's nice to surprise 'em, isn't it?'

'Oh, how lovely!' Elsie replied, clapping her hands together. 'Oh, I won't say a thing, how splendid! What a thoughtful thing to do. It reminds me of when—'

'Well, you're alright, sorry to bother you,' Dad said. 'You get on then.'

A few moments later, hearing the door shut and some footsteps, Elsie was stood back in the kitchen, the same concerned look on her face as she glanced at me.

'What,' I said, staring at her slack-jawed, 'was that?'

Elsie batted a hand at me. 'I played the nice old lady card, works a treat. I do it on tradespeople so they'll fix things for me.'

'Ells,' I replied, a smile for the first time that day, 'you sly dog!'

She laughed, and I joined in and then, suddenly, right out of the blue, she reached down and gave me a gentle hug.

'I'm so sorry,' she said, her voice fast and loud. 'I'm so sorry, Billy, for everything. I don't deserve you.'

She smelt of peppermint and the garden and, with my good arm, I squeezed her back.

Chapter 31

ELSIE

The man was straining in his T-shirt and coat, thick muscles, meaty hands. Something in his eyes was cold, determined, his smile wide and false. Elsie held the door with both hands, her palms damp as she felt Billy's presence behind her in the house. Jabbering away, she could see the man lose interest, a flash of irritation before the smile was back, stretched over wonky teeth. More babbling and he had a hand up, stepping away, realising he would get nothing from the dumb but kindly woman next door.

She slumped, relieved, against the door, brushing at her cotton shirt before moving back through to Billy.

He looked wide-eyed and confused, the last few moments a strange whirlwind. He had a leaf in his hair from pushing between gardens and she wanted to reach and pluck it out. For a moment she felt nervous: was he still angry? Would he revert to the scowls and sullen silence of the time before? With relief, when his words came they were surprised and impressed and she found herself needing to hug him tight, glad she had been able to help, the unsettling memory of that man, his dad, making her want to protect him.

The panic set in quickly. 'Will he go to the restaurant, do you think?'

It wasn't a big village and they were fine in this house but Samantha needed to be warned. Elsie was moving through to the front room already, the local directory bulky, the print tiny as she looked about for her reading glasses.

'Billy, we need to phone your mum,' she said, trying to keep her voice light.

Billy's face was serious as he plucked at his sleeve. 'I told him where we were,' he admitted again. 'I just thought… I was angry and…' His eyes were filling.

'It's natural, Billy, he's your dad,' Elsie replied, needing his help, trying not to sound panicked. 'Now is not the moment for recriminations.'

She wasn't sure from his expression that he knew what that meant so she added in a gentle voice, 'You read out this number for me, will you?'

Billy moved across to sit on the sofa, looking at where she was pointing before seeming to revive. 'Hold on, I know her mobile number. It'll be quicker and she won't want Dick, won't want her boss hearing…'

He called out the digits and she tapped them in.

At the other end of the line she could hear the clash of a busy kitchen, shouts, a man's voice…

'Hello?'

'Samantha, is that you?'

'Sam, get off your mobile, I haven't got time for drama! Table five need their mains and you need to wipe down seven ready for another sitting,' she heard a man's voice say.

Samantha was distracted as she replied, 'Yes, hello, who is this?'

Elsie realised she might be angry if she realised who was phoning, might hang up. She stuck the phone out at arm's length, waving it frantically at Billy. 'Billy, it's your mum, you need to tell her he's here.'

Billy looked horrified at the thought, the phone in between them, the tinny questions from Samantha on the end of the line.

'Who is this? I'm hanging u—'

'Mum,' Billy said, taking the phone in a wobbly hand. 'Dad's here, he was outside. I'm at Mrs Maple's – he doesn't know I'm here.'

Elsie watched Billy's face, serious and scared as he spoke to his mum. 'I'll stay here. I'll wait for you, I promise… No, he doesn't know… I promise… Mum, it's OK.'

He handed the phone back to Elsie, his face strained. 'She's going to come here.'

'Good!' Elsie placed the phone back on the receiver, thinking back to the only other time she had phoned Samantha's workplace, that terrible moment telling Samantha her son had fallen. Now at least she glanced across to her sofa where he had sat back down, face pale: he was safe. They couldn't leave and go into the village to meet Samantha, Elsie had to protect him.

They sat in the living room, curtains drawn across, a lamp casting orange light around the room.

'Shall I get you some food? A drink? How about tea and a custard cream?'

'I'm alright,' Billy said, cradling his bad arm.

'Are you alright? In pain?'

He gave her a small smile. 'Nah, it's OK.'

Elsie bit her lip and nodded, sitting next to him on the sofa, fiddling with a loose thread on a cushion, not the time to play Ella Fitzgerald. Headlights moved past the window, the sun setting, darkness outside.

Billy ventured upstairs to the bathroom, taking slow, careful steps, still shaken from everything. Elsie wondered what his dad had done in the past, why Billy looked so frightened at the thought of seeing him. Samantha had been right to leave, to take him away from there.

Elsie was lost in this thought, not focusing on someone calling her name in a panicked whisper. She came to, realised Billy was saying something from the upstairs. She frowned and pushed herself off the sofa. Then she heard the fear in his voice, the urgency.

He called again and repeated the words. Elsie froze.

Chapter 32

BILLY

It felt weird being here, weird but nice. Elsie was talking in this soft voice like she thought I might break into tiny pieces and I knew she was wondering what was going on with my dad.

I pushed the worry deep inside me as I climbed the stairs to her bathroom, trying not to think of Dad. The sound of his hand hammering on the door, the steel in his voice, the way my heart beat faster and faster as I knew he was here, in the village, right outside as I realised what I'd done.

The bathroom was so green, a sort of light green toilet, sink and bath, and around the toilet was this fluffy darker green mat in the shape of a ring and there were, of course, figurines on the windowsill and along the edge of the bath and a lot of them were green.

My arm ached as I fiddled with my trousers, awkwardly twisting my clothes, strange noises from the street below turning my head. Then something I did recognise, a voice, a shrill voice, a frightened voice: Mum's voice. My head snapped up, my heart racing. I had heard her sound like that before. I couldn't open the window of the bathroom, a pain firing through my arm as I fiddled with the strange twisty lock. I wanted to smash it open. Come on! Oh my God, I had told him. I had told him where to come. Giving up, I moved to the doorway fast, my palm slipping on the handle of the door, calling down the stairs.

'Elsie, Elsie, it's Mum... Mum's outside. He's with her.'

Returning to the window, I swept aside a figurine, hearing the voice outside raised, unable to make out what she was saying.

Should I run out of the house into the street? Should I stay? I fiddled with the small frosted rectangular window, another figurine, a small china frog on a lily pad, slipping into the sink, the small tink as it smashed, the frog looking up at me with one sad eye.

Elsie was climbing the stairs when I finally released the catch and I opened the window and tried to look through the narrow gap in the direction of the voice.

'Billy, Billy, are you alright? What are you doing up there...?'

I was kneeling on the windowsill, couldn't see where Mum was.

'Don't... Please...'

Straining to see, I felt my heart leaping in my chest. Mum sounded frightened, angry.

'You'll fall again. Here, let me hold onto you.' I felt Elsie's hands on my ankles, a strange comfort in the feeling.

Suddenly I could see them. He was there, one hand on her arm, which was twisted at a funny angle, holding her close to him as he marched her past the gate. I could make out the top of his head, a small spot where he was losing his hair I hadn't noticed before, Mum still wearing her work clothes, a tea towel over her shoulder as if she had simply walked straight out of the restaurant in the middle of an order.

'I want to see my boy,' Dad was saying.

'He's not there. Please don't... you're hurting me... please, John.'

They had moved out of view but I could still hear them outside our front door, Mum fiddling with keys as he kept talking. 'You made me look like a joke, what do you think I've had to say to people when they've asked? Hurry up, the whole bloody place will be round to see what's going on…'

'I'm sorry, I…'

'I bet you've been telling the boy all sorts of things. Where are the keys, for God's sake?'

Dad sounded angrier, I barely heard Elsie's whisperings behind me.

'Don't, John! I have them, I don't want you to…'

A thump on wood, a short cry, my mum started to sob, the door slamming closed. Then the muted sound of his angry voice, whimperings, noises that made me want to clamp two hands to the side of my head like I had done back in London some nights. I knew what noises came after the shouting and so I turned, practically falling into the sink.

'We need to call the police,' I said, fear in my voice, Elsie getting me down.

She nodded, pale under the harsh bathroom light before moving into action: 'You're right.'

I took the stairs two at a time and picked up the strange old-fashioned telephone with the large buttons, jabbed the three buttons, whispering quickly as a woman on the end of the phone asked me lots of questions.

'Please… please, just come. He'll hurt her. Please… He's hurt her before.'

Once the operator told me they'd get there quickly I put the phone back down. Elsie stood watching me, her head tilted to the side, a sad expression on her face.

'Brave boy,' she said.

I wasn't brave though, I thought, as I looked towards the wall with the picture of a boat over the mantelpiece. It had gone so quiet next door. Maybe they were just talking? Maybe he had left? But I knew then that Dad got angry. I had plunged my head into so many pillows over the years, wanting to convince myself he wasn't the bad man who made my mother cry and bruise.

And I had brought the bad man here.

The police seemed to take forever, blue lights flashing on the back of the curtains, the sliver of glass as I pushed the curtain to one side and peered out.

Elsie let me outside and I ran out of her house and into the street, approaching the two policemen, pointing frantically at the house.

'He's in there, with my mum! He's angry, please, please, do something.'

There were two of them, one man with a beard and a pot belly, talking in a too-calm voice, the other a woman with blond hair barely taller than me. How were these two going to stop my dad?

They told me to go back into the house and I watched the bearded policeman approach the door and ring the bell. No answer. I felt my whole body tense. *Come on, Mum!* He knocked.

'Police! Can you open the door?'

No one did.

Come on, Mum!

He knocked one more time and the door opened. Then there was my dad's voice, silky-smooth.

'Can I help?'

'We've had a call to investigate a domestic disturbance, sir. Could we come inside, please, and speak to people within the property?'

I was waiting for my dad's oily reply, the teasing, dismissive tone, but it didn't come.

He started to close the door but the policeman stopped him and suddenly Mum was calling out and there were noises in the front room. I was straining in the doorway of Elsie's house as she held me tight.

'Hold on, Billy, it's not safe.'

Then my dad was being led outside to the police car as I shrank back against Elsie, Mum crying as the policewoman went inside.

I followed, needing to see her, worried what I'd find now I'd brought the bad man here. Dad spotted me, his face hard, his eyes small, as he saw me rushing to our front door. 'Hiding! What, you don't want to see me either?' Loud, angry words that made the scales fall from my eyes, the shake in my hand as I reached for our door. 'You run to her, you're no son of mine,' he spat. I closed my eyes, the same sick feeling inside: the fear I had always had when he got angry.

Mum was sitting in the middle of the floor of our living room, her hair half out of the neat bun she had left for work with, the top button of her white shirt dangling off, the tea towel nowhere to be seen. The policewoman was crouched over her, talking quietly.

Mum looked up, cringing, as I looked at her, immediately sitting straighter, adjusting her shirt. 'Billy, I...'

Flashes of past moments flooded me. Her moving her clothing, wincing as she stood, explaining away the shouting, her pained expression, plastering a smile on her face. I hadn't realised I was crying until I was in her arms, dampening the white shirt, repeating the word 'Sorry'. She was smoothing my hair, shushing me as she did when I had nightmares, the policewoman moving away.

Mrs Maple was in the doorway, awkward, fiddling with the hem of her shirt, half-in and half-out of the house. I helped Mum up and she gave Elsie a weak smile. 'Thank you,' she said, making Elsie blush – two pink spots in the middle of her cheeks. 'If you hadn't…' she tailed away and I knew then what she might have said.

What would Dad have done?

The bearded policeman was back. 'We'll get him down to the station, come and take a more detailed statement in the morning.'

The policewoman handed Elsie a card. 'We'll be in touch,' she said and Elsie nodded and thanked them, closing the door as they left.

Mum started to cry quietly as the blue lights moved away, the street dark once more. Elsie rubbed her back, taking charge. It was strange to see her like that, all soft and caring, like a grandma, but something about Mum being in trouble made her seem different.

'Come on,' Elsie said, helping Mum to her feet. 'I've got some things we can have in the kitchen, let's go and put the kettle on.'

And as she drew Mum out of the house, steering her with a gentle hand, I was glad we had moved next door to Mrs Maple.

Chapter 33

ELSIE

Samantha was perched on the edge of Elsie's queen-sized bed, Elsie wavering in the doorway as she looked at them both.

Billy was asleep, open-mouthed, on top of the duvet as his mother stroked his hair, staring down at him. Elsie moved around the room, drawing the curtains, folding clothes away in the light from the corridor, knowing Samantha might need her there, the reassurance of another adult.

They'd stayed up late in the kitchen once Elsie had got them back to her house, hands wrapped round mugs, biscuits and sandwiches barely touched, until Billy's head was drooping onto the table and Samantha had half-carried him up the stairs.

'Just a little rest, while we wash up,' Samantha had said to Elsie, clearly wanting to postpone going home.

Samantha left the room now, pausing in the corridor, outside the closed door of the other bedroom opposite.

'Why don't you stay too?' Elsie suggested, taking a breath and pushing open the door to the other bedroom.

'Oh, I couldn't, I... Wow!' Samantha said stepping inside, her voice changing as she looked around. 'Is this your room? It's...'

What was it, Elsie wondered, as she watched Samantha move further into the room, her eyes scanning every corner and surface. Elsie cleaned it every week but everything had remained undisturbed for twenty-eight years: her mother's bed made, the pink and grey quilt folded neatly at the foot of the bed, the bedside table, chintz lamp, lace cover and small collection of books in a pile, her old alarm clock frozen at the wrong time. The glass of the dressing table polished, perfume bottles glinting into the glass of the mirror. Elsie felt her muscles clench as Samantha sat on the dusty rose-pink stool and reached out a hand for one of the bottles of scent, lifting it to her nose, her eyes closing momentarily.

'God, I miss perfume,' Samantha said, lowering it and giving a small embarrassed smile at Elsie. 'Sorry, I'd forgotten how nice it is to smell good, rather than of onions.'

'You don't smell of onions,' Elsie replied in a soft voice.

Samantha was staring at the bottles, lifting different perfumes, reading the labels. 'When we left London,' she started to say, 'I didn't pack much. I had this expensive night cream – thirty-eight pounds a pot – it smelt of cucumber and jasmine and was the creamiest texture. I used to pile it on…' She trailed away, her hands resting on the glass surface. 'It's funny, what you miss.'

Elsie moved and stood behind her, their eyes meeting in the dressing table mirror. Samantha looked so young and sad. 'My mother loved lotions and potions, floral scents. I always thought she wanted to bring her beloved garden indoors…' Idly, Elsie lifted the bottle, spritzing it onto a wrist to smell, something she hadn't done in decades. The smell sent her spinning back through the years, a heady mix of sweet roses that reminded her of soft cashmere hugs, hair tickling her cheek. Her eyes immediately filled with tears and she turned, lowering herself onto the mattress.

They sat like that in a contemplative silence, aware of Billy sleeping next door, the quiet of the village outside, a crescent moon just visible from the window, stars pinpricks in a navy sky. Elsie got up and drew the curtains across, taking a breath and trying to keep her voice light. 'I'll fetch you something to sleep in,' she said.

'Oh, I couldn't…'

Elsie looked at her. 'Of course you can. You don't have to go back there tonight, if you don't want.'

Samantha scratched at her neck, pulled on her shirt collar. 'I don't want us to impose. You were so wonderful today, to realise he… well, I owe you a great deal.'

'You're not imposing. It would be my pleasure.'

'But I was so, so rude to you,' Samantha said, tucking a stray strand of hair behind her ears.

'You weren't rude, you were protecting your son,' Elsie said firmly, moving across to the mahogany chest of drawers, 'And if you were rude, I would have deserved it,' she added, turning to give Samantha a small smile.

Sliding open the second drawer down, she stared at the neatly folded and pressed items inside, sachets of lavender potpourri tucked between the layers, making her head swim once more. 'I care about Billy, and you,' she added, glad she wasn't making eye contact, surprised to hear the small break in her voice as she rifled through the pile of cotton before pulling out a nightdress her mother had barely worn.

Fetching a towel, a spare toothbrush she had yet to open, she placed the small pile in Samantha's arms. 'There you are, something to make things a little more comfortable tonight. Billy's asleep now so there's no point moving him. You get yourself ready and sleep in here.'

'Oh, I couldn't, this is your bedroom.'

Elsie didn't tell her it was not. Someone else would be spending the night in her mother's room for the very first time since her mother had died. The thought made her blink in surprise. The offer to stay in her mother's room had come before she could really think it through. And yet she didn't take it back.

'Where would you sleep?' Samantha asked, getting up from the stool.

'I'm not much of a sleeper,' Elsie lied, 'I have a place downstairs.'

The lie seemed convincing as Samantha hugged the small pile of items to her chest, the day's events catching up with her as she stifled a yawn.

'You go in and change,' Elsie said, 'and I'll make up the bed.'

Samantha moved into the small bathroom as Elsie changed the sheets, the strangest sensation of preparing the bed for someone other than her own mother, glad to be helping someone who dearly needed it. Samantha returned looking like a teenager, her face scrubbed, her bare feet poking out of the long white cotton nightdress, her arms crossed self-consciously in front of her, wincing as she moved. It was clear she was hurt.

'Do you want anything for the pain?' Elsie asked in a brisk voice, not wanting to betray her shock. What things had happened before, she wondered. What had this poor woman been through?

'I feel a bit silly not wanting to go back...' she said quickly, not quite able to meet Elsie's eye.

'That's not silly,' Elsie replied, reaching to pat her on the arm.

The bed was made and Elsie was just moving to leave when Samantha called out in a small voice, 'Do you mind, would you... would you stay and talk a while longer?'

Elsie nodded and removed her shoes, sitting on the small bed, back resting against the headboard. She thought about how often she'd wished she had someone here, helping the loneliness ebb away. Samantha joined her and they sat like that for a while, not really saying a great deal.

'How about I read something?' Elsie suggested, remembering then the days she had sat next to this bed and read to her mother, soothing her with the balm comfort of words.

She reached for a battered copy of *The Wind in the Willows*, smiling as she thought back to her day on the river with Billy. She would give him this copy to keep.

She began to read, her voice growing in strength as she did so, Samantha's gentle breathing the only other sound. She read in a slow, steady voice until her own eyes started to flicker and Samantha had shifted down the bed until her head was resting on the pillow, her eyes closed tight.

Elsie looked at her, her loose hair fanned around her face, her head lolling to the side. She could make out the bloom of fresh bruises on her neck. She continued to read until she was sure Samantha had fallen asleep beside her and then, ever so quietly, she slipped off her side of the bed and padded downstairs to wait for them both to wake up.

*

Then Mother died and I had found the tin. And my entire existence came crashing down around my ears.

She had lied to me: all this time she had lied.

I had a sister. She had another daughter. She had loved a man who wasn't my father. A married man. My head spun with the information, the image I had of her shattered into a thousand pieces. What else had been a lie? What else had she concealed? Did she think about this other daughter? Did she love her as much as me?

The days were a blur of grief and anger, the house my prison with its flowered walls, staring figurines, every room a memory of her. I couldn't enter her bedroom, couldn't be reminded of the woman I had loved so deeply who had hurt me so badly.

The grief over you threatened to overwhelm me. I needed to talk to you about the betrayal and I poured those words into the long letters to you. You would understand – you had always listened to me, always spoken in that hesitant way, so fair, so kind. Now it seemed I couldn't bear the crushing weight of my feelings, the anger at what I had lost. I had almost had such a different life and now I was reduced to letters to you once a week when I dreamed of lazy walks, moving in, an engagement, a wedding… children.

I sank into a black place.

My world was reduced to tiny rituals. Wake early, watch from the window as the children set off for school. Leave for a trip into the village when the school run is over, the street empty of people wanting to talk, tea, biscuits, cards, cleaning, a jigsaw, television, tea, a walk to fetch supplies, the garden, tea. If I kept busy, if I filled the day, if I never really stopped and kept ticking my chalkboard list, I could get through it.

And that was how it was for years. Until a little boy from London had appeared in the village in the early hours of the morning and forced me to live my life.

Chapter 34

BILLY

I woke up in Elsie's bedroom really late. Everything hurt, so I just lay there a little bit. Her curtains were thicker than the ones in our house and normally Mum had to shout for me to go to school.

Elsie was in the kitchen toasting hot cross buns, still wearing the clothes she had been in the night before. Her normally neat grey hair was sticking up at the back and I frowned, wondering if she had slept at all.

'You eat this,' she said, scraping butter onto the hot surface so that it immediately melted into the centre. I suddenly felt starving, reaching for the plate, the table neatly laid for three people, three bowls, glasses and a jug of milk and some cereals in the centre. A small bunch of narcissi were sat in a vase, freshly picked from the garden, the scent filling the air as I bit into the hot dough.

'Your mum's upstairs,' Elsie said, joining me at the table, 'she needs the rest so I thought I'd leave her.'

I nodded and swallowed.

'It was fine. She's in your room,' Elsie said, her back to me again, wiping the crumbs from the kitchen counter.

I swallowed. 'Why do you do that?'

Elsie seemed distracted, turning back to me as she asked, 'Do what?'

'Talk like that? You just said something out loud. But not to me.'

'Did I?'

I nodded, taking another bite of the hot cross bun. 'This is really good,' I said through a mouthful. I didn't want her to think I thought her talking thing was weird – well, it was weird but not bad weird.

Elsie looked at me for a long time and I felt worried she'd get upset and she'd made me breakfast and saved me last night. Her eyes were watery as she paused. 'It's a habit, I suppose. I've always done it. Since my mother died...' Her voice was really quiet and I felt the dough stick in my throat a bit. 'I didn't used to,' she continued, 'but sometimes I would get through a whole day without a word to anyone so I just started talking to her as if she was still here.'

I stared at the table, not really knowing what I could say. I knew what it was like to be lonely and suddenly I found myself getting up and moving across to her, reaching for her hand. Her eyes went all round when I took it. Her hand was soft, like she used hand cream like Mum used to use in London when she made jewellery, not washed up in a kitchen.

'Bet she's listening somewhere,' I said.

That sentence made her squeeze my hand and it was all getting really emotional and I hoped she wouldn't start crying or anything.

'I've been really lucky, Billy,' she said, removing her hand and carrying on wiping the counter. I couldn't see any more crumbs.

'Why's that?' I asked, scooting back into my chair.

She didn't look at me, just circled the cloth. 'To have you move next door to me. You're like my second chance.'

And then I was really worried that I'd be the one to start crying.

'Hey!'

I think we were both relieved to see Mum in the doorway, both fussing over her as she stepped inside.

The bearded policeman came back a bit after that. Mum had only just finished a half of a hot cross bun, wincing as she tugged on a cardigan, as she lifted her arm to tie back her hair. I wanted to hug her but I didn't want it to hurt. We were a strange pair, me in a sling, her with her bruised neck.

She made a statement for the police. She had wanted to make it alone but I had asked to hear it – I needed to hear it.

'Please, Mum,' I'd said. And then I'd told my own story. 'There'd been one time…'

Liam would back me up, Liam had seen it too. Liam had got his stepdad to let me stay for a few nights last summer when it had been really bad but Mum didn't want social services to know.

Listening to her tell them everything made my tummy feel sore. It was so much worse, so ugly. Mum glanced across at me as she told them things, things I had sometimes suspected, other things she had hidden from me.

'I'm sorry I didn't tell you,' she said halfway through, her hands shaking as she brought a cup of tea to her lips. Elsie moved quietly and slowly around the kitchen behind her, making the tea, topping up the pot, filling up the plate with biscuits.

The policeman told us Dad would be given a restraining order and wouldn't be allowed to come to the house again, or even near it. Mum had cried and nodded and Elsie had soothed her, circling her back again. I was glad Elsie was doing that because I didn't really know what to do. The bearded policeman was nice and asked me what I was going to be when I grew up. I told him a landscape gardener. Elsie beamed over Mum's head at that but I think the policeman was a bit gutted I hadn't said 'policeman'. He kept trying to make me try on his hat.

We left Elsie's house after that. Her and Mum had a big long hug in the porch and Mum cried again.

Then we got home and I couldn't believe it but Mum made me go to school.

'I don't want you to get behind,' she'd said, handing me my white shirt and grey trousers.

'Mum, seriously I won't.'

She wouldn't hear of it, forcing me into the bathroom for a shower and to get dressed. 'We're leaving in ten minutes.' A glimpse of old Mum was already back.

'There was an email about that trip,' she said as we walked down the road to school.

After the night before I had forgotten about the trip but as soon as Mum mentioned it, the panic came back: 'They were saying they've got rucksacks and spare walking boots, so that's good. We'll get you some thick socks and you'll need to take your cagoule.'

'What about my arm though?' I said, hoping I could still get out of it. School was one thing but surely, she couldn't expect me to go on a trip?

'I asked and they said you won't have to carry your rucksack so you can do the walk, and the teachers could give you a lift in the minibus if it's too hard.'

'But all the kids will think it's weird I don't have it.'

'No, they won't. They'll think the boy with his arm in a sling shouldn't be carrying a massive rucksack.'

'But…'

Why couldn't I think of another excuse? Not that excuses ever really worked with Mum. Even in London she was hardcore. I fell silent as we got nearer the school gate. Swallowing, I kept my head down, knew that maybe Daniel would make it worse now. It was a small place, someone would have seen the police car, or he'd see where I was hurt and make a show of it. These thoughts made my stomach leap as if fishes were flipping in it.

Daniel watched me as I walked late into the lesson. Mum must have said something to the school because Mrs Carter didn't ask me any questions about why I was late. I sat, cheeks burning, wondering if everyone had seen the blue lights the night before, had realised they were outside my house. Daniel would be loving it if he knew my dad had been arrested. I tried to concentrate on the writing on the board but it seemed impossible.

We were doing art, needed to paint part of a picture that would form an enormous class collage. I was paired up with Max at the table two rows up from Daniel and Javid.

'I'm really bad at drawing,' he'd said, giving me a nervous smile.

It had surprised me because Max was always next to Daniel, ready to laugh at whatever Daniel threw at me.

'Last week you did that windmill. I saw it, it was good, so you do the drawing bit and tell me what to paint.'

'Alright.' I shrugged, liking this tiny opportunity to get on and do something.

Without Daniel, Max was quieter and followed my instructions and was super careful with the paintbrush, trying to stay within the lines I'd drawn. 'It looks just like the picture,' he said, an amazed face and then a quick glance over his shoulder to see if Daniel was watching.

He seemed jittery and it made me feel a bit more confident. Maybe he was sort of frightened of Daniel too and not actually his mate?

'You do the bit of that fence and just keep it straight,' I told him, watching him nod and bend over, tongue out as he worked.

When the lesson ended we stepped back. Max couldn't stop the wide grin. 'That's so cool, I have literally never done anything good in art,' he said, his voice different, almost like he was being friendly. I shook my head, sure I was imagining it.

Mrs Carter was at her desk in the corner, typing something into the computer as we moved around the classroom returning our overalls, pots of paint and water. Daniel and Javid were bent over their table talking in low voices, the clink of glass and glug of liquid, a small sound that made me turn my head. With the lesson over I bristled, sensing Daniel moving across to our table, the smell of stale clothes wafting as he passed me. He lingered, giving a strange look at Max, a lift of the eyebrows that seemed to make Max look alarmed. I frowned as I heard the bell for the end of the lesson.

It was only when I moved out of the classroom for lunchbreak, lifting my rucksack onto my back, that I felt the dampness through my shirt, smelt something strong: paint.

Turning, I heard sniggers in the corridor. Mrs Carter was already a way off. Javid and Daniel pointed and laughed, Max stood quietly to their side, a quick arm punch from Daniel as his cheeks reddened. Something was dripping onto the floor beneath me and I looked down in horror to see what looked like spots of blood between my legs. For a moment I wondered if I was bleeding, then I realised it was coming from my bag: watery paint.

Shrugging off my rucksack I noticed the zip was only half-closed and looked inside to see a split paint bottle leaking all over my things

– my textbooks, my notepad, the fabric of the inside streaked with the stuff. All ruined.

I heard my mobile vibrate in my pocket. Removed the phone. A WhatsApp notification. *Daniel invites you to Year 6 chat.* There was a new message in the group. *Hi Billy. Luckily Becky had your number! Saw this and thought of you ☺.* It was the first frame of the video. Of him. A pink thigh. On the phone. Sent to the whole class. At the moment it was just a blurry still but what if Daniel sent the whole clip? How much would they all see?

Becky was walking towards me. 'Billy…'

I couldn't stop and talk to her, my thoughts going too fast, my body hot with embarrassment. Her friend called her back and I watched her bite her lip and move away. Then I saw him – Daniel, about to walk past. I didn't think as I launched myself at him. I wanted to push him to the ground and smash his stupid, smug face in. The mobile was gripped in my fist and I didn't even think about what I was doing. Just wanted to hurt him. I reached my good arm back, closed my fist and swung forward. But my feet were scrabbling. I had slipped on the red stuff and the punch missed Daniel by inches, sending me crashing to the floor.

He looked surprised as I lay there, my arm killing me. I felt more stupid than ever before and just picked up my rucksack, knowing the red stuff was still leaking out of the bottom as I moved into the boys' bathroom, a trail of red dots on the floor behind me. The cubicles were empty and I placed the bag in the sink, staring at my sad face in the mirror above it.

God, I hated him, I hated school, I hated feeling so helpless. I was shaking from when I had almost hit him. I didn't want to hit people. I knew someone else who hit and I didn't want to be him. Was I turning into him?

That thought stopped me raging. Suddenly everything didn't make me mad but made me depressed: a never-ending stream of things I was never ready for and no end in sight. I thought of Dad in the street shouting at Mum, twisting her arm and forcing her into our house. The times he had got in from work in one of his moods, the way we would creep around him, not wanting to set him off. The marks in the skirting board where he'd kicked them, the broken plates, the sound of a closed fist on the wooden table where I worked.

Dad was a Daniel, I realised. He had probably put gross things in bags of kids he didn't like, called out nasty things, had little mates to make him feel bigger. And I had tried to hit him – so was I like Daniel too, was I like Dad? That thought made me want to cry, big, horrible sobs, right there in the boys' bathroom that smelt of wee.

I raised the phone, stared at the small triangle in the middle of the screen, the blurred shot a horrible reminder that he had the video ready to play.

Chapter 35

ELSIE

'Billy, does your mum know you're here?' Elsie gasped as she opened her door to find Billy dressed in his school uniform, his face grey, mouth turned down, miserable.

He paused, sizing up whether to lie, before shaking his head slowly, tears in his eyes as she ushered him inside.

'Come in, come in.'

She hadn't seen him like this before, assuming that all the events of the previous night had caught up with him. It was only natural. Perhaps it had been too soon to go back to school.

'Do you want a biscuit?'

Another slow shake of the head.

'Have a seat,' she said, pulling out a kitchen chair with a scrape on the tiles.

He sunk into the seat, his head sagging, hands in his lap.

'What's that?' Elsie asked, noticing red marks on his hands and white Aertex shirt.

Billy shrugged, 'Nothing. Science stuff.'

He didn't seem to want to talk and Elsie fussed around the kitchen as much as she could, glancing out to the garden, trying to talk to him about the scarifying she needed to do, explaining the posh word for raking, then worrying he might try to help. His arm was still in the sling and she didn't want him to do more damage, it was her job to look after him now, so instead she suggested a game of cards.

They were halfway through a lacklustre game of rummy when his mobile beeped. School must have ended by now, the sound of children walking past the house, high-spirited and noisy, forcing her to look up. Billy glanced towards the open window, shrinking back a little in his chair. What had happened?

His mobile beeped again, over and over, and he kept glancing at the screen, his body sagging further every time.

After the twentieth or so beep, with Billy practically slipping onto the floor, Elsie placed her cards face down on the table and trained her eyes on him.

'What's going on, Billy?'

He squirmed in his seat, eyes darting from her face to the table, to the oven, to the window and back again.

'Nothing.'

'If it's nothing, show me your phone,' Elsie said in her most stern voice, holding out a hand for the mobile.

Billy looked up at her, worry streaking his features.

'Come on,' Elsie said in a softer voice, her expression shifting to concern.

He paused, clearly torn, biting his lower lip as he gripped the phone. 'You have to PROMISE me you won't say anything.'

'Not even to your mum?'

'Not even to Mum.'

Elsie didn't like the idea of keeping secrets. She thought of her own life, of the secrets she had kept inside, the secrets her mother hid.

'She'd want to know, Billy,' she said gently. 'Is it something to do with your dad? School?'

Billy's chin dropped onto his chest, another two beeps filling the silence.

'Billy?'

When he started to speak his voice was barely a whisper. 'It's Daniel again… that boy at school who doesn't like me…'

Elsie wanted to leap in, wanted to comfort, but she sat watching him as he talked.

'It's sort of…' Billy fiddled with the bottom of the tablecloth. 'Well, it's sort of got worse. He's sort of saying he might send round this thing to the other kids…'

Elsie's eyes narrowed. 'What thing?'

'A video,' Billy said, so quietly Elsie had to strain to hear him. He wouldn't look up at her.

'What is the video of?' she asked him, leaning right forward.

'It's, well, it's…' He was fidgeting again in the chair. 'It's a bit embarrassing, taken in the changing rooms at school, you know…'

She didn't know but she could guess.

'I was changing for PE, the phone must have been on the floor under the bench. I'm, well, I always…' he couldn't look up, 'I always change my pants and stuff, after sport…'

Elsie sat back in disgust. 'How unpleasant,' she said, a surge of anger coursing through her. 'And have you told a teacher? That isn't right, Billy. That is not on!'

'No,' Billy replied, looking up, panic filling his face. 'No, and I won't. I don't want to dob him in, everyone'll hate me more and you can't say anything.'

He knew he should tell her he tried to hit Daniel too, that if he told someone now, Daniel might say he went to hit him and then he'd be kicked out of school. Another problem for his mum to deal with.

'But…'

'No,' Billy said fiercely, 'please, Elsie.'

Elsie wanted to argue but she knew what it was like to want to handle something your own way. 'I think you should tell someone, someone at the school, or your mum.'

Billy looked at her, the same sad expression in his eyes. 'I know,' he admitted.

'Well,' Elsie said, wanting him to look more cheerful, 'I'm glad you've told me. We can try to figure something out.' She got up, patting him on the arm as she did so, pleased to see the grateful expression on his face.

Another beep and they both stared at the mobile.

'Don't look at it,' she called out, turning to fill the kettle. Perhaps she could convince him over tea and biscuits.

'It's OK, it's a text,' Billy replied, a tiny smile on his face for the first time.

'All OK?' Elsie asked, gently probing, wanting to march straight to that school and demand to see the head teacher, find out who this awful boy was and demand he be expelled. Imagine bullying wonderful Billy, who had enough on his plate without nasty videos being filmed. Honestly!

'It's Tilly,' he said quickly, turning the phone around so that Elsie could see the many messages sent back and forth, a blur of letters, of tiny symbols in different colours. She understood none of it. 'Wants me to go round there now.'

'Oh,' Elsie replied, drawn up short, thoughts of filling the kettle forgotten. Tilly was the grandchild of the woman, the woman she didn't allow herself to think about.

'It's OK, I won't go,' he said in a low voice, clearly seeing Elsie's reaction to his words.

'I don't want to stop you,' Elsie replied, guilt rising within her. Tilly seemed to be the one person Billy had connected with in this new place, the one person who didn't make him miserable and now he wasn't going to his new friend because of her. 'I'll...' Elsie took a breath, squared her shoulders. 'I'll come with you, if you like. I'd like to meet her.' She knew she needed to be brave, to show this young boy that he should be brave too.

Billy couldn't stop himself from looking surprised.

'The only deal is,' Elsie added, 'we have to ask your mum.'

'She'll be angry I left school early,' Billy replied, his face appalled. 'She'll want to know why. And you'll tell her...'

Elsie cut him off. 'I don't think she'll be angry,' she said, placing one hand on his shoulder. 'Not if we explain. And it's only an hour or so, hardly bunking off.' She tried to rouse him with a smile.

He didn't return it but he gave her a small nod and that was enough. They walked together down the high street, Elsie clutching the red tin to her chest, glancing into the window of the butcher. No sight of Mr Porter, who might give her some more courage. Where was he? Was he in the back or was he still ill? She chewed on her lip, distracted for a moment. He had always been so nice to her and she felt a sudden pain in her chest that something might really be wrong.

They passed the chemist and the worry faded as she saw June in the window, deliberately averting her eyes when they met. Oh dear, at some point she must apologise to her. Maybe she'd buy her another coloured weight – or something she could take on one of her fast walks – and sort the allotment out for Billy. She had been rude to her.

They stopped at the restaurant, Samantha looking up, eyebrows shooting into her hairline as she took in the pair of them.

'Is everything alright?' Samantha asked, rushing across, balling the tea towel she was holding in her hand.

'It's alright. Billy here just has something to ask you.'

After she heard everything Samantha agreed he could go, suggesting that she would call school and explain, and Billy's shoulders relaxed. Elsie's heart beat faster at the thought that soon they would be headed to the house on the map, to the people who lived there, the place she had avoided for so long.

Elsie didn't notice the man approaching until he was stood right in front of them, a table of customers craning their necks as he started to speak. 'Table three, Sam, they can't wait all day.' The man's voice was sharp and clipped, his face sallow, thinning blond hair, a cheap red tie and a polyester shirt, sweat patches under the arms. 'Sam!'

'Sorry, this is my s—'

The man took in Billy's school uniform. 'Son? You at the school?

'He's in Year 6,' Samantha said, a hint of pride in her voice, her love for Billy patent every time she spoke about him.

'My boy's in Year 6,' Rich grunted, 'Daniel.'

'Oh, I didn't know,' Samantha replied, not seeing Billy's face change.

Elsie saw it though, saw his expression widen, his mouth part: Daniel. Daniel who had caused all this pain. Her expression soured as she took in this man, this father of the boy making Billy's life hell.

'You might want to check in with your boy once in a while, you know,' Elsie said, Billy watching on in horror.

Samantha's brows tugged together as she turned to Elsie and then Billy. 'What are... Billy?'

Billy was staring at his feet.

'What do you mean by that?' Rich asked, swiping his silly foppish blond quiff out of his eyes.

Elsie tilted her chin towards him. 'I would ask Daniel,' she replied, mouth pressed together tightly.

Rich glared at her, clearly wanting to ask more, a customer nearby raising a hand. 'Sam, table three,' he ordered, waving her to them before turning back to Elsie. Samantha moved reluctantly away, a baffled expression on her face.

'Come on, Billy,' Elsie said, turning on her heel.

Billy barely seemed able to speak as he followed meekly behind her.

He didn't say a great deal on the train to Goring and Elsie tried not to watch him worriedly, consumed by her own thoughts making her stomach leap and flip. He started tapping replies to Tilly on his mobile, his face unlined, shoulders relaxing the further they moved away from the village.

As Goring chugged into view – the cheery red rooftops of the cottages in the village, the squares of gardens, ponds, ornaments in some – and the train stopped with a sigh, Elsie took a breath, hugging the red tin close to her, and stepped out onto the platform.

'It's this way,' Billy said, leading her out of the station.

She knew exactly which way it was: she had visited the house all those years ago and had never forgotten. It was only in that moment she started to think about exactly where she was headed and what that might mean for her.

She licked her lips, the sun high in the sky above them, a jaunty blue at odds with her mood. Nerves crept up on her as they got closer, her palms slippery as she stood looking up at the stone pillars of the house. It seemed even bigger and grander than all those years ago, the beautiful grey stone a shade darker, the climbers clinging to the house even more lush perhaps than in her memory.

'Are you coming?' Billy asked as he started up the gravel driveway, his smile wide as he turned to her.

Elsie nodded silently, one step crunching on the surface. Would she be there? Would she finally meet her?

Tilly greeted them at the front door: a whirlwind of wispy long hair, dishevelled school uniform, a high-pitched voice, bursting with energy.

'Oh good! I've literally just got back from school and Mum was going to make me do homework…'

She immediately dragged Billy inside the house, where another child, Rory, was quietly building something with lots of grey plastic parts on the floor of the most enormous hallway lined with mahogany panels, portraits and a large gilt mirror reflecting Elsie's frightened expression.

'That's Rory, he's building something to do with space because he's a total geek—'

The small boy looked up at Tilly's words. 'I'm not a geek, Mum's told you not to call me a geek.'

'I like space,' Billy said to him and Elsie's heart bloomed with the small kindness as Rory gave him a shy smile.

'Tilly,' a voice called from a room towards the back of the house, 'have you made a start?'

Elsie froze, back ramrod straight, as she listened to footsteps moving closer. The hallway didn't feel cavernous, it felt as if the deep wood was closing in on her as the sound grew louder, and a woman appeared in a doorway to the right. She was young, too young, and Elsie released the breath she had been holding.

'Oh, hello,' the woman said, surprised by the new arrivals.

'Mum, this is Billy, I told you he was coming. I can do my homework lat—'

'Yes, yes, I know,' the woman replied, a strange expression on her face as she stared at Elsie frozen to the spot. 'Sorry, do I... have we met?'

Elsie should have stepped forward, should have said something, but she seemed to be stuck in a strange daze. Her nose, the way it turned up slightly, the freckles spattered on her nose... It was all so peculiar. And then there was another voice and Elsie felt her whole body lurch.

'Was that the door?'

A woman, an older woman, appeared on the first-floor landing just above, staring down at their small group. Elsie watched, mesmerised, as the woman moved down the stairs, one hand on the banister. She was dressed in a three-quarter length lilac dress and low heels, her silvery-grey hair newly washed and blow-dried. She stopped halfway down, and a sound, the tiniest gasp, caught in her throat. It seemed everyone had realised something peculiar was happening. The hallway silent, all eyes watching as the woman descended the last few stairs. She couldn't keep her eyes from Elsie's face, standing at the bottom, her mouth a rounded 'O'.

Finally, Elsie found her voice, the words strangled as they emerged, 'Hello Mary, I think you might be my sister.'

*

I told you, didn't I, that I went there? A year it took, a year of staring at that photo of the baby, the blanket soft in my hands. A year of picking up the paddle brush, turning it over, studying the beautiful china pattern on its surface. Thinking of the times over the years that Mother had brushed my hair with a different brush. Crushed all over again that she had never said a word.

I lost weight, food tasted of ash in my mouth and I wasn't sleeping; dark circles under my eyes, a headache every time I moved, throbbing, always there. I wondered about her, every day I imagined her waking. Where? Did she have someone in her life? Did she know who she was?

I finally went, the pull of the map too great, those marks ingrained on my brain despite the tin being under the ground, hidden.

What would I say? I had no idea and I tried to imagine you by my side, a hand on the small of my back, a reassuring wink as I approached the house.

It was enormous, I could have fitted three of our houses inside. That thought shocked me first. The sweeping driveway, the manicured lawns of trimmed green. It was a stunning house, light grey stone, roses climbing the outside wall, the glass of the many windows glinting in the sunshine. I moved like a cat burglar around the side of the house, too intimidated to go inside.

I was startled by her face in the window. Perhaps I still would have found the courage to approach but then I saw them all, on the back lawn, that swept down towards a ha-ha, a tennis court, woods beyond. A young boy, a girl, squealing and running – their chubby legs moving quickly as a man chased them on the grass, his happy face open, delighting in his children's mirth.

A family. She had a husband who played with the children, a healthy golden-haired boy and girl. One of each. She had everything that I had dreamt of, everything I had hoped for and everything that had shattered that day in the hospital. Everything that had been robbed from me.

A pain like I had never known, worse than your death, worse than Mother leaving too. This was a woman who didn't need a strange half-sister, a lonely spinster with no friends, nothing to offer. She had everything she needed, she was happy. She didn't want someone to step in and ruin everything for her. To dredge up the past.

I backed away, hadn't realised I was crying until I reached the main road, my body heaving, my last hope gone. My golden sister with her perfect house and family. And I had nothing and no one.

I vowed never to return.

Chapter 36

BILLY

Woah! This was like on a TV show when the presenter reveals the person's real family and we were watching it for real. And now I totally get why Tilly's grandma looked so familiar. She had the same eyes as Elsie, the same almond shape, the same shade of blue. How had I not seen that before?

Tilly's grandma Mary stood still, poker-straight, one hand on that wooden ball at the bottom of their banister, another flying to the silver chain at her neck. Rory was still holding up something grey and plastic, staring from one old woman to another, and even Tilly had gone quiet.

Elsie looked awkward, the tin she had carried from her home livid red in her arms. Tilly's grandma stared at it. 'Is that…?'

Elsie nodded. 'It was Mother's, it's got your photo in it, your blanket.'

Mary stepped forward and I watched as she stood in front of Elsie for a moment and then, with tears filling her eyes, stepped forward and hugged her.

'You came,' she said into her hair. 'You found me.'

She fussed over Elsie, steering her into the kitchen and plumping cushions for her to sit on, full of questions, things she had clearly been storing up to ask.

I wanted to stay and listen to them, remembering finding the tin, the things inside, the map and all the adventures that came out of it, but evidently Tilly had had enough of the real-life soap opera in front of us. 'Come on,' she said, yanking me away from the kitchen, 'I made a den under the billiard table.'

She stole some Jaffa Cakes before we left the room and then dragged me down a wood-panelled corridor to a part of the house I had never been into. I wasn't sure what a billiard table was but I followed her into a room I'd not seen before: a large set of lights in green casing hung over an enormous table covered with green felt, the walls were painted a deep red, black-and-white photos of people on horses leaping over hedges lined the walls. Under the table Tilly had dragged about twenty cushions and a few throws, the middle littered with a random selection of toys and sweets: a torch, a tube of Smarties chocolates, a mobile, a magazine with a girl with pink plastic beads in her hair on the front cover, a banana.

'Check out this torch,' she said, crawling to get underneath the table. She flicked on the light and on the underside of the table an image of the earth appeared: vivid blues and greens. She flicked the next slide over the light and Saturn appeared with its coloured rings.

'Cool,' I replied, as she handed it to me and I clicked through all the images of space. There was the one of Saturn with all its rings, and one of Mars glowing bright red. You could see craters on it and everything.

'Rory got bored and refused to play with me because I kept calling him Uranus,' Tilly giggled.

'You're an idiot,' I said, laughing. It felt good sat in all the cushions, eating the orange and pink Smarties that Tilly passed me.

We talked and talked, about going into space. Tilly said she'd be too scared the rocket would get lost and they'd just go round and round the earth forever until they died but I thought it would be quite cool and anyway, we'd all probably be living on Mars in the future. We talked about whether there would ever be a water park we could go to because the one that was really cool with loads of flumes was more than half an hour away and whether Elsie and Tilly's grandma would tell us what all the secrets were about.

My phone was still beeping and pinging with replies in the class WhatsApp group. Messages about the trip the following week, some stupid viral video about a cat dressed up as Batman and other pings all making me tense. Would they say mean things about the video Daniel had shared? I switched off my mobile, Tilly watching me as I pressed the button.

'You're popular,' she said, nudging me.

Something about her cheery smile made me feel really sad again and I panicked and could feel my chest tighten and my throat thicken from holding back tears.

Tilly noticed, scooting onto her knees and peering at me. 'Are you alright?'

I told her everything. Daniel and his stupid mates, the red stuff in my bag, the endless teasing about my accent, Dad, Mum, the police, my crap clothes and finally, in a half-whisper, about the video Daniel had showed me earlier that day, his threat that he might send it round the class.

Tilly was silent throughout, eyes serious, never leaving my face.

At the end, once I had said everything, there was a pause and I was too embarrassed by the silence. What if she thought I was being a baby? What if she was going to stop being my friend?

'That's,' she finally said, almost hitting her head on the bottom of the table, 'that's horrible. Oh my God, that is so mean!'

It made me feel a million times better just hearing those words. 'I'll work it out,' I shrugged.

'Let's get some food,' Tilly replied, which I was learning was one of her ways of making me feel better too.

We could hear them in the corridor outside the kitchen even above the quiet classical music that was playing. Elsie's laugh was soft as I stepped into the room. When she looked across at me I was amazed to see her open face, no worry on it, a sort of glow as she smiled across at me.

'Billy,' she said warmly, a confidence I wasn't used to as she summoned me over to her, 'I was telling Mary about the garden. She has an artichoke plant, you know, we must pop out and see it. Billy here,' she placed a hand on my shoulder, 'he understands gardening, he's got a real talent.'

I bit my lip and felt heat in my cheeks, secretly pleased to hear her say something so nice about me. Elsie beamed at me before they both returned to poring over letters, gardening books and postcards.

'Tell me more about our mother, what did she love to listen to?' Mary asked.

Elsie turned back to her sister and spoke. 'She had LPs of Ella Fitzgerald. She used to dance in the living room to "Bewitched, Bothered, and Bewildered".'

'Oh,' Mary brought her hands together. 'I used to listen to her songs on cassette. I must get Tilly to upload some to my mobile, she seems to understand how to pipe things through to the speakers.'

They chatted as we ate cold chicken, potatoes and salad, the evening sky streaked with pale pinks and purples, birds chattering in the trees outside. I stared at the shadows lengthening on the lawn as it sloped away from the house, the sun sinking below the tree line. My problems at school seemed to fade with the light, with the laughter around me, Tilly making Rory wail as she stole the last strawberry in his bowl.

Suddenly, over his shout, the slow notes of some kind of jazzy music grew in volume in the kitchen, Tilly playing around with a mobile. Elsie and Mary's heads snapped up from their conversation and they both started to smile as the throaty voice of what must have been Ella Fitzgerald grew louder in the room. Then suddenly they were standing pushing back their chairs, Tilly was dragging me by the hand and we were all dancing around the big island in the kitchen to this song I had never heard before but was sort of beautiful and I didn't even feel embarrassed like I should because everything just seemed right.

When it had ended Elsie gave me a quick squeeze in close, before her eyes roved to the kitchen clock. 'Oh!' she said with a start, 'we best get you back.'

Tilly was back at the table pinging a pea at Rory and stuck her tongue out at me.

'Can't Billy stay for a sleepover?'

'Not on a school night,' Mary said, 'but another time certainly,' she added warmly, turning to Elsie too, 'You both must come and stay, and your mother of course, Billy. I know Faith will want to meet her.'

'I would love that,' Elsie replied, looking at the island where the contents of the tin were laid out. 'And you must keep the tin now… It's yours,' she said, making Mary smile.

They were walked to the front door in a warm huddle of goodbyes, Mary reaching down to ruffle my hair before turning to Elsie. She gripped both her hands. 'All this time you lived just a few miles away,' she marvelled, her eyes watery with unshed tears. 'I am so glad you decided to come, that we have found each other.'

I watched Elsie blush as her sister held her hands, unable to believe this was the woman who only a few months ago had nobody in her life. As they held each other I felt a glow in my stomach that the tin I had dug up had led us both to this house.

We walked back up the gravel pathway together waving our goodbyes, knowing we would be back there soon. Barely talking, we returned to the station, the warm feeling not leaving either of us as we sat opposite each other at a table in the carriage, our heads resting back, reliving the past few hours.

It was only as we were pulling into Pangbourne that I remembered I had switched my phone off when I was in the den and when I turned it back on, I had seven missed calls from Mum: seven calls and one text message.

Ring me back, it said, and I felt a stone stick in my stomach.

Chapter 37

ELSIE

Mary had wanted to visit it and Elsie had offered to join her.

They met just under the archway of the lychgate, the smell of roses strong as she waited, nervously fiddling with the button on her cardigan.

Mary approached, looking older than Elsie had seen her before, a slight stoop in her shoulders as she clutched a bunch of pale pink tulips, her footsteps shorter, a worried glance before she met Elsie's eyes, her face softening. She kissed her on the cheek, a wave of expensive perfume tickling her nose, and smiled as she greeted her, a slight shake in her voice as she said, 'Lead the way!'

Elsie pushed open the gate and walked the familiar route, around the side of the church, the grass sliced with shadows, headstones worn, some crooked in the far corners, some marbled, polished and more recently laid. The grass neatly clipped, the place deserted.

She steered her up the narrow path of flattened grass to the spot she had stood at hundreds of times before, kneeling to talk to her mother, tending to the grave, in the rain, in the sun, season after season for twenty-eight years. Always bringing flowers from their garden. The only visitor.

And now her sister: Mary. Her mother's other daughter, the woman she had thought of endlessly over the years, who she had thought had it all.

Their reunion had been emotional, back in that house, staring at each other in the hallway.

Mary had stepped forward. 'You found me,' she had said.

Everyone else had melted away as Mary had steered her into a beautiful drawing room, surfaces gleaming and smelling of polish, silver frames containing photos from the ages. Elsie had drawn up with a start as she saw a photo of a young Mary: something in her expression so like their mother.

The conversation had been stilted at first, both perched on the end of a large cream sofa, a pink lampshade on a table next door. Mary offered her tea but didn't show any sign of fetching it, just staring at her.

'I'm sorry it's taken me all this time,' Elsie began in a rush, realising now she was looking at this woman that she had been so stupid, so stubborn. 'I was so angry,' she admitted in the smallest voice, sinking deeper into the cream sofa, too ashamed to look up at her older half-sister.

When she did meet her eyes they were warm, not reproachful, filled with tears as Mary reached across a hand. 'I understand, it must have been so hard. You only had each other.'

The rest had spilled out then. The guilt, the anger, the confusion. 'She had always made me feel it was just me and her and I had hated the intensity at times, wanting to break out. Then I would feel terrible for wanting to leave her.'

Mary had been nodding throughout, encouraging her to go on, aware perhaps Elsie needed to talk.

'After she died, I realised she had kept so much from me. I couldn't handle the idea that she hadn't shared such a massive part of herself. It was complicated, it was...' She handed Mary the letter she had discovered originally in the tin. 'Read it,' she said as Mary placed it in her lap. 'She wanted me to find you, she was just too afraid to tell me herself.'

Mary nodded again, too moved to speak.

'She didn't want to give you up,' Elsie said, wanting to ease the pain for her. 'Her parents made her. She had fallen pregnant by accident, your father was married…'

'I know,' Mary admitted, filling in her own gaps. 'I overhead my parents talking one time, a scandal…'

There was silence and Elsie glanced around the room, the shafts of sunlight through enormous windows, a striped window seat, a book spine up, abandoned, another flash of silver of the photos. 'What wonderful photos,' she commented, seeing one of a large family group, an old wedding photo.

'That was Dennis, my husband. He died a couple of years ago sadly: liver cancer.'

'I'm sorry,' Elsie said, a stab of pain for Mary's loss.

'He was wonderful,' Mary smiled. 'I was very lucky to have him. Were you ever married?'

Elsie swallowed. 'I never married, no. I was…' Elsie twisted her hands in her lap, picturing Philip, his own head thrown back, the straight white teeth, the feel of his arms around her. 'I was engaged. He was… he was lovely,' she added in a small voice, 'but he died young and we never did…'

'I'm so sorry,' Mary said. 'How hard for you.'

'It was hard. And it made me harder. Made me shrink away from life.' And Elsie found herself sharing more, found it easy, as if she had always had a sister, as if she had always shared intimate thoughts with her. 'I think I used the death of our mother as an excuse to remove myself from it all, to try not to get hurt again. But of course it doesn't work like that.'

'It doesn't,' Mary agreed sadly.

They had talked for ages, at some points weeping, others laughing. Discovering similarities: 'I say that!', 'I remember that place.'

Elsie talked about their mother and it was wonderful to concentrate on all the pleasant memories, her idiosyncrasies, all the things that had made her so beloved. The lisp she had been embarrassed by, the passion for flowers she had passed to Elsie, her midnight jam-making sessions when she couldn't sleep, her skill at embroidery, the tiny snort she sometimes did when she was really laughing. Elsie's voice grew in strength as she added more details, realising she hadn't focused on this side of her mother for a while, too wrapped up in her hurt.

Mary had asked question after question and the afternoon had been strange and magical and Elsie hadn't wanted to leave. But they knew they had more time together – and Mary had been adamant she wanted to come to the graveyard.

Elsie stepped back as Mary knelt in front of the grave, reaching to trace her finger over the letters on the headstone – 'ROSA MAPLES: BELOVED MOTHER' – and resting her bunch of white roses at the bottom, the stems tied with a purple satin bow. She stayed there a while, head bowed, and Elsie felt tears creep along the edges of her eyes as she watched her sister's shoulders tremble with the moment.

Elsie joined her on the ground, her knees damp from the rainfall the night before, shoulder soon damp with her sister's tears, as Mary buried her head in Elsie's shoulder.

'She never forgot you,' Elsie told her, feeling like the older sister in that moment. 'Every year she would make the cake for you, light the candle. She loved you,' she said, certainty in her voice, realising this was the first time that thought hadn't been accompanied by pain.

Elsie started to cry softly as she still tried to make sense of the complicated feelings about the mother she had loved so hard, who she had resented at times for keeping her so close. An intense childhood, no real friends, home-schooled, wrapped in cotton wool and kept safe. The daughter who wouldn't be taken away. And Elsie had almost escaped the life she both loved and resented and then Philip had died and she had stayed home, heartbroken and alone, her mother's sole companion until she died. The tin had shocked her. The tin had shown her that it wasn't just love that made her mother love her, smother her, in that way, but other feelings too: guilt and fear.

'She would be so pleased,' Mary said, one arm around her little sister, 'so pleased you found me. Hadn't that been why she had given you that tin?'

Elsie nodded, pulling a tissue from her sleeve. 'But I wasted all those years. I came to see you, filled with curiosity, and as I stood staring at you in that house, your husband chasing those children on the lawn, your smile as you'd looked on, I didn't think you would want your life disturbed, and,' Elsie took a breath, 'and I suppose I'd been jealous too. Such a rich life.'

Mary shook her head slowly. 'I always wondered. I knew I'd been adopted, and I'd always wondered what happened to my birth parents, always wondered if I'd had any siblings. I was so envious of friends who had them, who used to squabble and berate them, I'd think, you lucky sods...'

'But I was broken then. You seemed to have your Philip – your husband and children, and I was so jealous, expecting someone who needed me and instead finding someone happy and enjoying the life I had hoped for myself. The life that was stolen from me.'

'I did need you,' Mary said quietly. 'And I am so grateful that we have each other now, and can make up for all that time.'

Elsie couldn't help the smile that lit her up as her sister spoke, realising for the first time how lucky she was to be given this second chance to be a sister.

'You never found out more about your father?' Elsie asked.

'No, I never did. There was a man, Harold, he sent me a card, he emigrated to Australia… I was only very young… it contained a cheque for fifty pounds, which at the time seemed a small fortune. And later, I wondered, when I overheard my parents, if he'd been the one…'

Elsie frowned, a distant memory tugging at her. 'Harold,' she repeated, recalling something her mother had told her once in a soft, sad voice. A trip to Oxford, punting on a summer's day. A drive to the countryside, her hair blowing in the wind. A love she had felt for somebody. Elsie had thought she was talking about her own father.

'There was a man,' Elsie said slowly, 'I think she had loved someone deeply.' How had she never realised that her mother had been harbouring a broken heart? They lived in each other's pockets, side by side, but there was so much distance between them, so much she didn't know.

'Did you find out more?' she asked, looking at her older sister, realising together they had the answers.

'My parents told me when I was eleven that I'd been adopted when I was a baby. That my real mother had been very young and was not in a position to keep a baby. And they were so loving and I was so happy that I accepted it, in the way that children do. I wondered, of course, and I can't believe she lived so close, all this time, that we never met.'

'She would have wanted to, but she wasn't a selfish person. If she believed you were happy, she wouldn't have wanted to have changed that.'

Mary was quiet as Elsie spoke and then without thinking, Elsie dropped her hand by her side and found Mary's, their fingers entwined as they stared at the grave, as they both forgave the woman who lay beneath.

Chapter 38

BILLY

Mum had been ringing because we had been summoned into the school the next morning, first thing. I had a sleepless night worrying about all the things they might say. Was I in big trouble? Had they heard about Dad? Would they arrest me like him? Had Daniel told them I'd tried to hit him? Was I going to be suspended? Expelled? If I had to leave the school, where would Mum and me go? I'd just started to like it here and we'd have to move to a new place for a new school because Mum didn't have a car. I couldn't rest, eyes flying open every time I wondered what they might say the next day.

I hadn't told Mum everything earlier. She hadn't bothered to change out of her work clothes, her feet resting in a plastic tub of soapy water as she grilled me.

'What's happened? What did Mrs Maple mean in the restaurant? What's this Daniel got to do with it?'

I tried to play it dumb at first but I could see I'd have to tell her something. 'Daniel doesn't like me,' I'd begun, Mum leaning forward and sloshing bubbles on the carpet. 'And he put something in my bag and he also took a sort of video of me.'

Mum went mental immediately, which suited me because she stopped asking questions and I didn't have to tell her about the part where I'd tried to hit Daniel in the face. I didn't feel too bad about it, not really: he deserved to be punched and I wish I hadn't missed but still, I was quite pleased Mum didn't know.

We were early for the meeting and I thought it would be just us but outside the Headmistress's office was Rich, Mum's manager from work, and Daniel sitting right there. Mum and Rich said hello to each other a bit awkwardly and I sat on the edge of one of the shiny wooden chairs that had scratches in the surface: people's initials and someone saying Mr Williams was a willy, which reminded me that I called Daniel's dad a dick because he was called Richard and that thought gave me the confidence to sneak a peek at Daniel.

He was sat on another chair a few feet away, not looking at me, but he didn't have his usual scowl on and his eyes were all tiny, his face covered in red blotches, like he was allergic to something. There'd been a kid in my class in London who got like that every time he ate kiwi fruit. Daniel sniffed and I realised the blotches weren't because of kiwi fruit but because he'd been crying. *Daniel had been crying.* That thought almost distracted me from Mrs Kendrick, who opened the door to her office and asked us all to step inside, her face serious.

'I'll dive right in, if that's alright with you both. It has come to my attention,' she said, perched on the edge of her desk, a pot of biros and a plant pot inches away, 'that there exists a video, a video that was created originally by you, Daniel.'

Daniel didn't deny anything, sat nodding miserably in the bucket chair as Mrs Kendrick asked him to hand over his phone.

His dad produced the mobile from his pocket. 'Daniel showed it to me last night,' he said, glaring at his son. 'He has assured me he is very sorry but obviously realises he needs to accept whatever punishment you think he deserves.' He handed over the mobile, my eyes following every move.

I bit my lip as Mrs Kendrick took the phone, my whole body stiff that she might actually watch the video. Instead she handed it over to Daniel.

'Daniel, can I rely on you to delete this from your mobile immediately and let me know immediately if it has been posted on any social media sites as that will change things?'

'It's not Miss,' Daniel said, his voice cracking as he took the phone. With shaking hands, he tapped in his password and started to press buttons, the video deleted from existence. 'Done it,' he whispered, his voice wobbling as he stuffed the mobile in his pocket.

'I don't need to tell you we take these matters very seriously,' Mrs Kendrick continued, 'and it would be remiss of me if Daniel did not receive an appropriate punishment. Daniel, do you have anything to say?'

I waited for him to start speaking up, to tell her that he hadn't sent it round everyone, that I had tried to hit him, that I had gone mental and should be punished too. Daniel stayed completely silent, then, after a moment, he looked up, straight at me. 'I'm really sorry,' he said, wiping his eyes with the back of his hand. 'I'm really sorry – I shouldn't have sent it.'

I was so shocked I didn't reply, just sat in my chair gripping the sides. Mum was huffing behind me.

'There will be a short suspension at the start of next week and I think Daniel should be excluded from the end-of-term trip.'

I found myself opening my mouth, I found myself talking: 'It's alright by me if he comes.'

Mrs Kendrick looked over at me in my chair and Rich and Daniel turned to stare at me.

'If he's deleted it, it's OK by me, if that makes a difference,' I said, looking up at Mrs Kendrick.

Daniel was looking at me, his mouth open like a goldfish.

'Boys, if you could step outside, please, I just want a quick word with your parents.'

I slid off my chair, wanting to get out of the room, all my worries from the night before melting away. No suspension! No need to move! I glanced across at Daniel, worried for a moment that the second we stepped outside the blotchy tearful Daniel would dissolve and old, evil Daniel would return.

'I didn't tell on you,' I said quickly, worried everything that had been said inside the office was a lie.

Daniel looked at me, his mouth downturned as he closed the door behind him. 'Nah, a couple of people messaged me, telling me to delete it and Dad made me hand over my phone anyway, something about an old lady who knew something.'

I couldn't keep from smiling as I thought of Elsie back in the restaurant defending my honour. I shrugged, swallowing down the smile. 'Well, thanks for not telling them I almost hit you.'

Daniel's eyes widened. 'Yeah, but you didn't.'

'I know, but,' I shrugged again, 'you could have made it look bad for me.'

Daniel sniffed, fiddling with the sleeve of his shirt. 'Well, thanks for, you know, saying that stuff about the trip.'

'S'OK.'

'I don't mind being in a group with you, you know,' Daniel said, 'not if you don't. And Max likes you, he didn't want me to put that stuff in your bag in art and he was one of the ones who messaged me…'

I thought of Max, who had shown a small glimpse of kindness in that lesson and realised I hadn't imagined it. That thought made me feel better too.

'Anyway, I'm…' Daniel took a breath and held out his hand, 'I'm really sorry.'

I took his hand a bit awkwardly – I had never really shaken hands with anyone my age, only adults. His grip was firm as he looked me in the eye.

'Alright,' I said, feeling a small flame of hope bloom.

His dad appeared in the doorway just in time to see us release hands.

'You know,' Daniel added as his dad moved out of the office with Mum, 'I know you like football. If you ever want to play, over the summer, I only live behind the allotments not too far, if you wanted…'

'Thanks,' I said, the flame growing brighter. 'Yeah, maybe.'

Mum couldn't help a surprised look at us. Rich had a more serious expression on his face.

'I'm glad Daniel has apologised,' he said, his voice stern, Daniel cringing at the words. Then he turned to Mum, adding, 'And I'm sorry for the shifts, for being stressed. Clearly I wasn't keeping my eye on the ball at home.' He couldn't resist a glare at his son before turning back to Mum, 'Let's sit down next week and sort out the shifts going forward, make sure you're happier.'

Mum's eyes widened further. 'That would be great, thanks, Rich.'

He gave her a grateful beam before turning to his son, mouth moving into a thin line. 'Come on, Daniel. Home!'

I *almost* felt sorry for him.

*

I think this is goodbye.

Meeting you, spending those months together, were the happiest times of my life. I know you would have been a wonderful friend and partner and I still grieve for the things we never got to do. It was cruel to lose you so young, to miss so much of what you would have done. You were a caring, generous person and I know you would have taken care of me, of us.

But I see now that I need to let you go, I need to stop reliving the thousand memories from our past and look forward, into a future. You are still with me, I take you everywhere in my head and heart. You are the voice that tells me I can do it, you are the hand on my arm to steady me when I stumble. You were the most beloved man and I hope you are happy now that I have found another way to take that step into the unknown.

I love you, Philip – you were the best thing and I was so lucky to have known you.

Chapter 39

ELSIE

He was moving slowly down the flower bed, the watering can in his hand, careful to ensure the water avoided the leaves like she'd told him, wetting only the base of the plant. He was such a good boy, she thought, delighted to see him taking such care.

He had appeared that afternoon carrying something in both arms, placing it down gently on the dresser. 'For later,' he'd said cryptically. He'd downed his pear squash, full of stories from the previous day at school, the first time she'd ever really heard him share any good news. 'Javid is going to bring his iPad on the trip so we can watch movies in the tent and Max said that I can swim in his pool this summer. They live in this massive house apparently…'

'That's wonderful,' Elsie said, relishing the feeling of having his company again. Over her shoulder, she suddenly noticed the chalkboard. She hadn't written on it in weeks, some old list half-completed still written on the black. She found she didn't care and turned back to keep listening to Billy.

'…and Mr Williams told me I'm getting better at tennis and should join the summer club he runs on the courts next to the playground so I think I might—' He drew up short when he turned to see what was resting on her table. 'Hey, that's my name…' Then he stared round at her. 'Is this…?'

She nodded and smiled, reaching across to hand him the letter confirming his allotment. He took it wordlessly, just turning it over. 'For me?'

'For you! The whole thing. I don't want you digging up my garden to plant carrots and artichokes so I thought this was the answer. We can get down there this weekend and plant something. You could sow some spring cabbages, they'd be good at this time of year.'

'Cool!' he said, running to the back door and grabbing his flowery apron. 'I'm going to check on the box balls, I'm worried a caterpillar is at them.' He disappeared through the back door. He'd forgotten to even eat his custard cream biscuits, he was in such a hurry.

'He loves it, he loves the place like we did,' Elsie said to the walls, feeling her mother's presence in the house. She smiled, realising the pain was truly lessening, that she wanted to say something she should have said a long time ago. 'I'm sorry,' she said, biting her lip, 'I'm sorry I've been blaming you. I know I need to live my own life. That you loved me.'

And after those simple words she felt better, a small glow in her chest as she pulled on her own overalls and stepped outside to join Billy in a place that meant more to her than she could possibly ever express. A place she had shared with her mother, learning every detail, pouring her love into it, and now passing it down to someone else who was showing as much enthusiasm for nature and gardening as she had. She smoothed at the earth, her pale pink nails like the inside of a shell.

She had been to visit Scarlet that morning, had returned a book she was only two-thirds of the way through as an excuse to see her at the counter. At first Scarlet had been stiff with her, one word of hello as Elsie had handed the book over. Elsie had regretted moving inside, wondering quite what she had expected. The old her would have pretended not to care, wouldn't have tried to make amends.

That thought propelled her forward. 'I needed to tell you how sorry I am, for being so rude, so cold,' she began. A man on an ancient desktop computer glanced in their direction but Elsie didn't want to make an excuse to be silent.

Scarlet had started to scan a small pile of books sat on the counter.

'I can see you're busy…' Elsie smiled, trying to melt the frosty younger woman.

Scarlet gave her the smallest shrug, a wary look in her eyes.

'It was unfair of me to take out my frustration on you,' Elsie continued.

Scarlet placed a hand on the top of the pile, her expression softening as Elsie bit her lip.

'I just want you to know how much I appreciate how kind you've always been to me over the months and years I've been coming here. I haven't deserved it and I'm going to make sure I treat you a lot better from now on in.'

Scarlet had stopped the pretence of stacking any more books and was now just sat on her stool, staring up as Elsie finished, reaching into her handbag.

'I wanted to give you a couple of things to say sorry,' she said, handing over a soft toy for Harry and a card with a voucher inside. 'The fluffy dolphin is for Harry, the card and voucher are for you, for a massage or something relaxing, I wasn't sure…'

Scarlet accepted the card and toy. 'I—'

'Please don't thank me, I just wanted to show you how sincerely sorry I am.'

Scarlet's standoffish welcome had dissolved, the atmosphere light and made lighter by the departure of the elderly man on the computer. It was just the two of them in the library as Scarlet told Elsie about Harry taking his first steps, convinced he was also starting to speak: 'I was *sure* he said Bubble.'

Elsie told her about Billy, about his upcoming trip, about his discovery of the map and everything it had unearthed.

'That sounds fascinating,' Scarlet said, her eyebrows lifting as she asked more questions.

'I have a sister, a half-sister.' Elsie's heart swelled at the thought. She was seeing her later that day for coffee. They planned to meet regularly, swapping books, news, old family stories. Elsie felt excitement build in her chest as she thought of the future as part of a bigger family, her lonely existence a lifetime away.

And then, a wonderful thing. She had been walking home and she had passed the butchers. She had been expecting to see Darren in his peaked white hat but there, behind the counter, larger than life, was a man with a wrinkled face and kind eyes. He was throwing his head back, laughing at something a customer was saying. Elsie found herself moving as if in a trance to the door of the butcher.

'Mr Porter,' she had said from the doorway. The man looked over at her, his bushy eyebrows raised in surprise as she found her feet moving right inside, right around the counter itself, before her arms reached out and pulled him into an embrace. 'Stanley,' she said, 'you're well.'

Stanley, who had never been short of things to say, simply stood there dumbfounded, arms clamped to his side as she squeezed him tight. She hadn't realised how frightened she had been. She took a step backwards, feeling heat creep into her cheeks even in the chilly cold of the air-conditioned room.

'Elsie Maple,' he said with an enormous smile, 'and I never thought you cared.'

Her face had been serious for a moment. 'It is wonderful to see you here, Mr Po— Stanley,' she corrected herself. 'You have always been such a tonic and I was so scared here when Darren told me you've been ill.'

'Benign, Elsie. I was lucky, they found something but you can't get rid of me yet.'

She moved around the counter. 'That is so good to hear, I am so pleased.' She caught sight of Darren and the other customer, an elderly gentleman in trainers, simply staring at her. 'Well,' Elsie said, suddenly very aware of all her limbs, backing out of the door, 'it was just a real, real treat to see you looking so well. I'll see you soon, Stanley,' she said, burning with heat now.

Mr Porter had started to chuckle. 'I'll look forward to it, Elsie, I really will,' he had said, giving her a wonderful smile.

Elsie was still smiling as she sat back staring at the area under the tree she had been working on. How different it looked now: a line of perennials, new bulbs planted beneath the soil ready to grow next spring, the soil rich. The patch she had ignored, neglected for so many years, looked as loved as the rest of the garden. She had bought a beautiful rose bush for the spot where the red tin had been uncovered. Was it really only a few months ago that Billy had swept in overnight and upturned her whole world?

'Let's head in for tea,' she called, standing up, her lower back aching as she rubbed at it.

Billy raised his head from the patio where he'd been weeding and grinned at her. 'Good idea.'

He scampered ahead and by the time she arrived back in the kitchen he was holding out the bag he had turned up with, an eager expression on his face.

'What's that?' She smiled, stepping forward.

'I saw it, in that shop next to the butcher… a present…' He tailed away, his face flushing as she raised both eyebrows. She knew he barely had any money, in fact all his money had come from the jobs he had done for her. 'I don't need a present,' she said, accepting the bag as he thrust it towards her.

It was heavy, she thought, as she set it down on the table. Billy stood watching her as she lifted the item out of the bag. It was big and round and wrapped inexpertly in some Christmas wrapping paper. She tore at it carefully, touched by the effort he had obviously gone to.

Inside was a teapot, cream with navy blue polka dots. 'Oh,' she said, as she set aside the paper, one hand on her chest, 'oh, how lovely, Billy!'

He looked like he might melt with embarrassment as she stepped across and gave him a warm hug. 'Well, I did break yours first,' he coughed, clearly trying to retain some cool.

'It's so thoughtful of you,' she replied. 'Let me get the kettle on then and I'll make us some peppermint tea in it… You get the custard creams.'

Chapter 40

BILLY

The air smelt of sausages, the barbecue on the terrace a massive silver one that looked like a spaceship and Faith, Tilly's mum, stood waving a pair of tongs in one hand and a glass of pink wine in the other as she talked to Mum.

Turns out Faith knows someone looking for someone to run a handmade jewellery stall at the fair and she and Mum have been talking for the last hour about pendants and chains and beads. I thought back to times in London when Mum had sold her stuff, her joy stood behind the stalls of the London markets, hair tied in a knot, bright lipstick on as she chatted with customers. Then coming back home, sliding the things into the box under her bed so she wouldn't leave out a mess. Dad had hated a mess.

I wasn't sure how we'd ended up in this enormous garden in this posh house with these really nice people. Rory had invited a friend over and we were playing tennis on the court, making up our own game, where you hit the ball and then have to run round to the other side in a never-ending circle to keep the rally going. It was hopeless because sometimes Tilly would just fall down in a heap of giggles, or start chasing me with her racket, or Rory would get distracted by a helicopter or a red kite or a cloud in the shape of something funny and totally miss the ball. But I hadn't laughed like that in forever.

Also, Liam's mum had agreed that Liam could get the train down to see me so tomorrow, Mum and I were meeting him at the station and he was coming for three whole days. I think he didn't have a new best friend 'cos he'd asked if I wanted to go and stay at his grandma's in her house by the lake that summer. And Tilly had invited us for a sleepover on one of the nights and Mum and Elsie were going to come because the house has, like, a million bedrooms. Well, eight, but still…

Also, Max had messaged me since the trip to ask whether I wanted to go to his house and play Fortnite with him and it was really weird but nice of him even though I knew Mum might not like it 'cos the weapons are so realistic, so I replied and said that I hoped it would be OK.

The school trip went really well in the end. We'd had to hand in our phones to Mr Williams on the first morning and use these orienteering maps that were massive but Javid had brought along his dad's sat nav which he'd rolled up in a T-shirt so our little group of four didn't get lost. And Daniel nearly got chased by a cow and we'd all legged it. Max almost dropped his rucksack, he was so scared.

We set up a tent which took like an hour because there were so many pegs and none of us understood the instructions on the label. Then we were starving and we lit this little fire thing and had these weird boil-in-a-bag meals that were actually really nice. I had chicken casserole and a custard kind of thing. We told bad ghost stories in the dark with the torches under our chins and then we crept round the girls' tent pretending to be werewolves until Mr Williams told us to go to bed. Becky told me they'd been cry-laughing inside the tent. She invited me to her birthday party over the summer holiday, which is cool.

The sound of Mum laughing again made me look through the wire of the tennis courts and I could make her out standing next to the barbecue. She was wearing bright orange lipstick today which made her teeth look even whiter and she had one of her funny coloured headbands on and she'd had her hair cut. She was giggling with Tilly's mum as they prodded and poked at the gas barbecue.

Mum had told me the solicitor was finalising the divorce. She said I can choose to see Dad if I want but there would need to be someone else with me as a chaperone person at a contact centre. I'm not sure I want to see him yet. Since that night with the police I've had a few dreams about the things I never really wanted to think about and I might wait until I'm a bit older and see what I think then. Mum seemed a bit relieved.

'Hey Billy!' Tilly called from behind me. 'Rory's got a new game but we need to go and grab three more tennis balls.'

I grinned at her and gave her a thumbs up. I had never met anyone with more energy than Tilly. I felt like I had this mad sister now and it was nice because I could tell her all these things and she listened and never told me I was stupid or anything.

Mum gave us a five-minute call for the food and Rory had found a whole bucket of old tennis balls and was pelting them at Tilly as she shrieked and hid behind the net: 'Rory, I'll tell Mum!'

'Rory!' his mum called.

I couldn't help laughing.

Elsie and Mary barely glanced up. Elsie was sat in a deckchair on the lawn holding an orange drink which had lots of fruit in, swatting away a wasp as she listened to Tilly's grandma. They seemed to always have stories to swap, sometimes about the olden days and Elsie had got me to get loads of boxes down from the attic and she had shown me loads of photos and diaries of their mother.

Mary was really nice and she knew loads about vegetables and had given me some cuttings for the allotment. I'd told her I was going to grow tomatoes but she'd said maybe I needed to do cabbages because they'd be ready for winter. I wanted to check in the book Elsie gave me from the library 'cos it had loads of helpful stuff in it. Elsie had given me my own copy of *The Wind in the Willows* too and she'd read me a chapter whenever I went over now. At first, I pretended to be really into it just to please her but actually I did really like it, especially when she did all the different voices.

Looking at Elsie next to Mary I'd never think she was the lady I was dumped on when we first arrived in the village. She'd got me to help her clear out her mum's bedroom in the house and she'd bought me a bed for the times when Mum worked late. She had said I was allowed to paint the walls any colour and I had asked if we could do a mural of space and she said yes, which is so cool. She looked so relaxed and I thought then of that map in the tin I'd found in her garden and how none of this would have happened if I hadn't dug it up. That thought made me feel warm and I left the tennis court and walked up the garden towards the group.

We ate sausages and burgers that were charred and piping hot in the middle and then had bowls of strawberries with cream and sugar. Most of the others had got up to go to the kitchen, helping to clear away, and I was sitting with Elsie as she watched me finish my burger.

A thought struck me then, something that I had wanted to tell Elsie for a long time.

Her eyes were closed and the sun was warming her face as I turned to her, my voice low and serious.

'Ells, can I tell you something?'

She opened one eye, sitting up when she saw me staring at her, something clearly on my mind.

'Of course,' she replied, shifting in her chair to face me, her expression serious. 'Go ahead,' she said, all her attention on me.

'The thing is,' I began, 'I needed to tell you... I've been wanting to tell you since we first met...'

'What is it, Billy?'

Elsie waited, holding her breath, watching me as I leaned in really close, my words almost a whisper.

'I really hate custard creams.'

*

Dear Mother,

I've never written to you. Isn't that strange? When you were alive there was never any need and when you were gone I never knew what to say.

I am sorry.

No one knows me better than you. No one has ever loved me more than you. I know that, I have always known that.

I don't blame you. I used my anger towards you and your secret as an excuse not to face the world, not to face my fears. And look how much I almost lost.

Meeting Billy has made me want to live in the present again. I don't want to stay stuck in the past, I want to make new memories. I have moved into your bedroom now, I wear some of your favourite clothes: bright colours, things you would have loved to see me in.

Your daughter Mary is beautiful, wise and kind. You would have loved her and I am sorry that you never met each other. It is my greatest joy to share all my memories of you with her. She is endlessly fascinated, asking me details that send me spinning back through time and thinking fondly of our life together: two peas in a pod, we were.

I love you, Mother. I hope you know that. I hope you are glad that Mary and I have found each other and that your family lives on in your beautiful grandchildren and in the stories we tell them.

I think of you often; you are so much a part of me, and now I have others around me too who make me whole.

Your Elsie

A Letter from
Ruby Hummingbird

I want to say a huge thank you for choosing to read *The Garden of Lost Memories*. If you did enjoy it, and want to keep up to date with all my latest releases, just sign up at the following link. Your email address will never be shared and you can unsubscribe at any time.

www.bookouture.com/ruby-hummingbird

I really wanted to write a moving story about two unlikely friends and the importance of choosing our own family. This book was such a challenge at the beginning because Elsie started out as such a misery! I really hope you understood why she was as prickly as she was and hopefully, you were really rooting for her by the end of the novel. As for Billy… bless him, I already miss writing his chapters. He was a joy to write and I really hope you loved him as much as I did.

If you did enjoy *The Garden of Lost Memories* it would be amazing if you could leave a review online. However brief, they all help readers to discover my books. I also love hearing from my readers – you can get in touch on my Facebook page or through Twitter and Goodreads.

Come and tell me what you loved and also recommend other books to me – I'm always on the hunt for my next read.

Thank you so much for choosing to read my book,
Ruby Hummingbird

@RubyHummingbirdAuthor

@HummingbirdRuby

@RubyHummingbirdAuthor

Acknowledgements

This book was a challenge and I really wanted to do the story justice. An enormous debt of gratitude to my editor Christina, who thrashed out the plot with me and continued to ask questions throughout the process. Working with you has been a pleasure from start to finish. You have an enormous energy, an exceptional editorial eye and great chat! I always look forward to catching up with you and hope these books find readers.

To the hard-working team at Bookouture – thank you all. Thank you to Natasha Hodgson for the great copy-edit. Kim is a tour de force and there are countless others who work tirelessly to ensure every book is given a chance of success. Thank you to the Little, Brown Rights team: Andy, Kate, Hena and Helena, who continue to try to get editors around the world interested in my books.

To Clare, my lovely agent, and the rest of the Darley Anderson team. You are a fantastic agency and I am lucky to have you on my side. Thank you for all you do for me.

Thank you to my parents for being so encouraging about my first book – I hope you love this one too! Thank you to my husband for putting up with the endless disappearances for edits and more. To my kids – I love you loads.

Lastly, I want to say a particular thanks to the numerous book bloggers who left glowing reviews of my first book – *The Wish List* – on their own blogs, NetGalley, Goodreads and Amazon. It was amazing to read such lovely thoughts and feel that Albie had touched you all too. Your support definitely made an enormous difference and the book would not have done so well without you all. I really hope you love Elsie and Billy just as much and I can't wait to hear what you think.